TRUTH

SEER

Books by Kay L Moody

Truth Seer

Healer

Lie Maker
Coming July 1, 2019!

IF SHE CAN'T FACE HER OWN LIES,
THEY'LL NEVER SURVIVE.

TRUTH SEER

KAY L MOODY

MARTEN PRESS

Truth Seer
Truth Seer Trilogy Book 1
By Kay L Moody

Published by Marten Press
3731 W 10400 S, Ste 102
South Jordan, UT 84009

www.MartenPress.com

Cover by Shawnda Craig
Edited by Deborah Spencer and Emily Chambers

ISBN: 978-1-7324588-0-2

To Nancy
You were the first to inspire me to write.

ONE

IMARA KALU WATCHED AS HER SISTER, NAKI, tasted the air and predicted the weather for tomorrow. Weather taster. It was a common hila, but few had perfected it like Naki. Naki's chest puffed out, and her head tilted back, which made her sapphire blue graduation robes prominent. A gold chain hung around her neck, which meant she was hila wasomi now. Elite. Attached to the end of the gold chain was a medal with the word *Valedictorian* glowing in gold.

Imara pulled her attention from Naki and tapped the delicate golden ring on her finger. A hologram display popped up with her name, the time, her location, and four of her most common apps. Imara tapped the ring again after noting the time, and the display disappeared. Eight more minutes before her life would change forever.

Imara frowned at the crowd of people in front of her. Why did parties always have to be such a disappointment? As if to punctuate her question, two people walked past, and Imara heard their idle conversation.

The girl placed ruby red nails over her equally ruby red lips in mock surprise. "You really helped build the bridge here in Alexandria?"

"Yep," the guy said with a smile.

Lie.

The girl moved her red nails down to a thick, silver necklace. She spun the chain around her finger. "The Egyptian Council should give you a medal. But how did you know the steel beams were too heavy?"

The guy grinned and said, "I'm a weight feeler."

Truth.

The guy continued, "I felt the beams out of curiosity as I was walking by one day, and I could tell the bridge would fail."

Lie.

"I'm hila wasomi, you know. I just graduated today."

Lie.

Imara stood at the edge of the room, trying to ignore their conversation. She twitched at his latest lie and finally decided to say something. Ready to put the guy in his place, Imara turned to face the couple. The guy jerked toward Imara with a sneer. Instead of acknowledging her presence, he grabbed the girl with red nails and said, "Let's go dance."

The girl smiled, and Imara could see this was what the girl wanted all along. Imara huffed to herself. She watched red orange whips of selfishness dance behind both the guy and the girl.

Parties were the worst.

People lied all over the place to impress attractive strangers. The whips of selfishness and prickles of greed in the room were so thick, the colors almost obscured the people.

Imara tapped her gold ring again and sighed. Four more minutes. Frustrated, Imara shot a glance back at Naki. Naki twisted her long black braids and chatted away. Naki was the one who made Imara come to the graduation party. Their parents left as soon as the graduation was over, but Naki insisted Imara go to the party. Imara would have rather spent her Friday night packing for the next day.

Imara brushed a wrinkle from her colorful party dress. The abstract splotches of magenta, crimson, canary yellow, and powder blue rippled as her hand touched the smooth fabric. She knew the wrinkle wouldn't release, but Imara brushed the fabric with a heavier hand.

It's not like Naki needed someone to talk to at the party. A small crowd of people surrounded Naki, hanging on her every word. Imara noted with a touch of pride that at least Naki wasn't lying. Of course, Naki's intentions weren't completely selfless. She always craved attention. But at least when she got it, she only used it to tell great stories.

Imara sighed heavily and looked out at the crowd. Selfishness. Greed. Lies. Her eyes flitted over the colors, and the crease in her forehead grew deeper. Manipulation. Imara flinched when she saw it followed by a quick nose crinkle. Why were people so bad at places like this?

Imara looked out again, daring herself to see something positive. Red orange whips, burnt orange prickles, raven black rashes, short flashes of violet light. Disappointing as it was, Imara had never seen anything different at a party. She didn't expect to now. But then a new color caught Imara's eye.

Turquoise blue smoky swirls. Hope.

The rich turquoise blue swirls were cheerful and bright and danced like no one was watching. Bewitched, Imara let her eyes land on the young man to whom they belonged. He was right around her age with surprisingly symmetrical features. The hope swirls dancing off his skin almost perfectly matched the neat shirt and tie he wore. The guy scratched the

9

back of his tall Egyptian neck. His smile grew as he spoke to a young woman wearing a dusty mauve dress. As his smile grew, so did the smoky swirls.

Imara ran her thumb across the fabric of her dress. She tried to recall if she had ever seen someone with such genuine hope and delight. He moved his hand away from his neck and raised it up to his head. With half a smile, he ran his long fingers through the healthy portion of dark locks on top of his head. Imara pinched the fabric of her dress, completely mesmerized by this stranger. It helped that he was wildly attractive, but the turquoise smoky swirls of hope commanded her attention. Pure goodness like this usually only existed in children.

A smile grew on Imara's lips as she reached up to tug the short hair on the back of her neck. Her gaze lingered when, suddenly, he turned and looked her right in the eyes. Imara twisted her body to the wall with a sharp intake of breath. Her face burned as she blushed. She clamped her hands over her ears. Her rich brown skin was too dark to reveal her blushing, but Imara knew her ears still managed to turn red when she was embarrassed. Naki teased her for it all the time. But how could the guy see red ears from all the way across the room? Covering her ears probably looked a lot stupider than if she had done nothing.

Just then, a ringing sounded in Imara's ear. She nearly jumped out of her shoes when she heard it. Imara sucked in a breath and tried to release it through a long, calming exhale. The ringing sounded again, and Imara glanced at her ring. She left the large room and entered an empty hallway. How could she let herself get flustered like that right before this! She'd been waiting for this phone call all day. Professionalism was imperative.

Imara took one last breath then tapped the ring on her finger. She clicked the phone call app on the hologram, and a woman's face appeared on the hologram screen. Imara pushed the hologram screen away from the ring so the screen was directly in front of her. Then she used her fingers to enlarge the screen.

"Hello," Imara said with a smile.

"Imara Kalu?" the woman asked. Her eyes stared down at her desk, but she glanced up to see Imara nod. The woman's afro bobbed as she nodded. She said, "I'm with the Kenyan police force, and I'll conduct your final interview this evening."

Imara nodded and said, "Safiya Otieno, right? The chief gave me your name."

Safiya nodded, the black curls atop her head bouncing again. "Your resumé is impressive, Imara. You have more experience than most college graduates we see. The chief was impressed by the interrogation you did last month. We tried to get information from Imamu for weeks, and you did it in one night."

Imara beamed. This interview was going better than she expected. But then a slithering rope of emerald green betrayed Safiya's compliments. Apprehension. Imara froze the smile on her face as she braced herself for bad news.

"Now, you know we can't use your word as evidence in court?"

"Yes, of course," Imara said. "I know the law. And the chief explained the technicalities. I can only use my hila to steer the interrogation in hopes of getting a confession. My word alone isn't enough."

Safiya nodded while a thicker emerald green rope of apprehension slithered out from her skin. "There has been some concern that you aren't hila wasomi yet."

Imara cut in, desperate to defend herself. "Yes, but my hila graduation is in three years. And I've gone to Nazari Academy of Hila every summer since I was thirteen. Their summer training program for hilas is the best in the world. And their standard for hila wasomi is higher than any other training program. They never let people graduate early, no matter how skilled they are."

"I see," Safiya said, unimpressed.

"I could get a letter of recommendation from the head of my department. Her name is Carlotta Santini, and she's a world-renowned truth seer. She's taught me every summer since I started hila school. She says I'm the best student she's ever had. I'm sure she would be happy to tell you more about my qualifications."

From the corner of her eye, Imara noticed a teenage girl with silky black hair and black lipstick, which stood out against her creamy white skin. She stood over a young boy at the end of the hallway. The teenage girl rested her elbow on a hover cart and wore a sharp smile. The boy stood with his shoulders square and his feet planted. From a distance, it looked like they were just talking. But Imara could see more than the average person. Blood red flames of anger burned out from the girl's skin while forest green corkscrews of jealousy twisted through the flames. Charcoal balls of panic bounced off the boy's olive skin.

Imara glanced back at her hologram and tried to pay close attention. But worry nagged at her insides as she stared at Safiya. Emotions this strong, even in kids, could lead to trouble. Imara stepped closer in case she needed to intervene.

Safiya scrolled through the hologram screen on her desk. "Yes," Safiya said. "I believe one of our officers spoke to Professor Santini. You can have her send a letter of recommendation, but I don't think it will make a difference at this point."

Imara frowned and searched for a quick defense. Before she thought of anything, the boy down the hall let out a small yelp. Imara's eyes darted toward him. The teenage girl turned toward the boy, unaware of Imara's presence. The girl's blood red flames of anger grew. Imara shuffled toward them on the balls of her feet. She was close enough now to see a round patch pinned to the boy's slate blue dress shirt. The patch was black with an elaborate lime green *T* stitched onto it. It was a symbol for the taggers. Imara couldn't decide if it was bravery or idiocy that made the boy wear the tagger patch openly. Even in an open-minded city like Alexandria, taggers were considered crazed extremists.

The teenage girl pushed her black hair behind both of her ears while she leaned forward, spitting out words Imara couldn't hear.

"Imara?"

Imara forced her eyes back to the hologram and said, "I'm so sorry. Could you repeat the question?"

Jagged indigo waves of annoyance rolled out from Safiya's skin, but they were minimal. Safiya said, "We rarely hire consultants; we prefer permanent, long-term employees. We want to know if you are committed to Kenya, especially since you go to hila school in Egypt."

"I'm from Kenya. And I went to college in Kenya." Imara spoke without thinking and wished she had spent more time creating a solid argument.

"Yes, but you live in Egypt now, isn't that right?"

13

Imara nodded and clenched her jaw to force it into a smile. "Yes, but only for hila school, which is over now for the summer. I'm moving back to Kenya tomorrow. I usually live in Kenya even for hila school. I didn't this summer because there were night seminars, and I didn't want to commute."

"I see," Safiya said, not completely unimpressed, but not as convinced as Imara had hoped.

Imara stole a small glance back at the girl and boy and took a few steps closer to them. Now she could finally hear their conversation.

"You didn't deserve that scholarship," the black-haired girl said. She leaned forward over the boy as she spoke. "You stole it from me. I know what you did."

Imara was surprised their conversation had nothing to do with the tagger patch on the boy's chest. At least not yet.

The boy shivered, which made the black patch flutter against his dress shirt. "I didn't do it," he said. "I promise. It wasn't me."

The girl frowned, and her black lipstick thinned against her pursed lips. In a loud whisper she said, "Liar! I'm a sound seer. I can see the unstable vibrations in your voice."

"I'm just nervous," the boy stuttered.

"You're a fanatic. Why would I trust you? You taggers think you're better than the rest of us, but you're not. You do bad things too."

There was the mention of the tagger patch Imara expected.

The girl snarled at the boy. Her face relaxed, and a sinister smile passed over her lips.

"Tell me why you want this job," Safiya asked.

Imara clenched her jaw. She fought the urge to do a thought-clearing shake of the head. She looked back at the hologram and tried to ignore the girl and boy in the hall. "I've always wanted to use my hila to help people. With my hila, I can protect the people of Kenya by putting criminals behind bars. Ones that otherwise might not get caught."

Safiya smiled and looked at the screen on her desk. Imara used her distraction to glance back at the teenage girl. Burnt orange prickles of greed joined the forest green corkscrews of jealousy coming off her skin.

"There's only one way to make this right," the girl said. She pointed her chin toward a waterfall that spilled into a decorative pond. The tiny crystals imbued in the water were invisible to the naked eye, but they made the water glitter with characteristic golden sparkles.

The tagger boy shuddered at the sight of the waterfall. "Please don't," he said with a whimper.

The girl pulled the hover cart in front of her, and Imara stood with indecision. If she wasn't professional, her dream job was out the window. But she couldn't stand by and do nothing.

"How have you used your hila to protect people in the past?" Safiya asked.

Imara forced her eyes back on the hologram. The second she did, the hover cart moved away from the teenage girl with a jolt. It would crash into the boy before he could react.

Without a thought, Imara lunged forward and used her body to shield the boy. Metal and wheels blasted into her side as the hover cart hit her with full force. Imara fell to the ground in a heap, and a sharp pain stung in her hip.

TWO

IMARA PUSHED HERSELF TO A STANDING
position and clutched her hip. She checked on the boy first.
He stared at her with his mouth gaping open. "Thanks," he
said.

Imara smiled and looked to the girl. She now had wine-
colored fear spikes growing off her skin. She pushed her silky,
black hair behind one ear and raised a foot about to run.
Imara took hold of the girl's shoulder with a gentle squeeze
and pointed to the ground with her other hand. The girl
dropped her head and sat against the wall.

Finally, Imara turned back to face the hologram screen,
afraid of what she would see.

Safiya held one finger over her mouth in thought. She
took a moment to stare curiously at Imara while Imara
rubbed her foot against the back of her leg. After several long
seconds, Safiya said, "Did you just jump in front of a hover
cart to protect that boy?"

Imara got ready to nod.

"In the middle of our interview?" Safiya finished.

Imara swallowed and dropped her eyes to the ground as
she nodded.

To Imara's surprise, Safiya laughed. "That's exactly the kind of dedication we need."

Imara looked up, and a smile crept onto her face. "Really?" she said.

Safiya nodded with a kind smile. "Yes, Imara, we'd be happy to hire you. I am officially extending an offer. I'll send the paperwork over in the morning, and if you get everything finished in time, you can start on Monday."

"Thank you so much!" Imara said. "I can't wait to help with interrogations. This has been my dream since I was twelve. I'll finish the paperwork as soon as I get it. Thank you so much."

Safiya smiled. "I look forward to working with you. See you Monday."

Imara's face stayed calm while she ended the phone call, but the moment Safiya's face disappeared, Imara's eyes squinted with joy. She punched her fist in the air and felt her cheeks stretch wide from a smile.

Imara tapped her gold ring, and the hologram disappeared. She did one last, big smile, but then bit her lip as she turned to the boy. He tilted his head to the side and stared at her through narrowed eyes. His surprise passed quickly, and soon he smiled. "You saved me from the eraserfall," he said.

Imara glanced at the waterfall with golden sparkles and shot one eyebrow up while her mouth twisted into a knot. She did her best to not sound condescending. "There's a protective shield over the eraserfall."

The boy's hair tousled as he shook his head from side to side. He pointed to the teenage girl. "She stole the key from

Mr. Nazari. She took away the shield and was going to push me into the eraserfall."

Imara tried to hide her amusement. "You need more than a key to take away the shield. You need two administrators and a police officer. Look." Imara reached out for the waterfall. Just before she touched the water, her hand stopped with a jerk. A red shield covering the eraserfall was visible for half a second.

"Oh," the boy said. He looked down, and his olive cheeks grew pink.

Imara turned back to the teenage girl. The girl scratched one ear with her black fingernails. She shifted her weight to one side as far away from Imara as possible without scooting over. She kept her eyes on the ground, refusing to make eye contact with Imara. "Please don't tell my dad," she whispered.

"What's your name?" Imara asked.

"Keiko," she said with a frown.

"You told him you stole a key?" Imara's gentle voice was a sharp contrast to Keiko's greed and fear. "Is that the kind of person you want to be?" she asked. "A thief?"

Keiko shook her head, but didn't offer any words in response. Keiko kept her eyes glued to the ground. Even after waiting a few moments, Imara didn't see the color she wanted. She'd have to try again.

"Tell me about the scholarship," Imara said.

Imara directed the question toward the boy, but it was Keiko who answered. "Someone corrupted the file for my scholarship essay. I would have won, but this tagger fanatic destroyed my essay."

The boy jostled his head back and forth. "It wasn't me."

"I saw you with the scrambler!" Keiko yelled back.

"I was bringing it to Headmaster Bello. I didn't even know it was a scrambler."

"Liar!" Keiko said.

Imara cut through their argument with a dulcet voice. "He's not lying."

"You don't know that," Keiko said with a sneer.

Keiko opened her mouth to speak more. Before any words escaped, Imara turned to the boy and said, "Why don't you go find your parents?"

The boy nodded and ran without a second glance down the hall back toward the party. Imara watched him and saw someone by the doorway. Whoever it was went back in to the party before Imara could recognize anything. Imara squinted with her head cocked to the side, but then turned back to Keiko.

"He's lying," Keiko said. Blood red flames of anger burned around her, growing with each syllable. "I would have won the scholarship if not for him. He deserves to be punished."

Imara stood back. She watched Keiko's forest green corkscrews of jealousy twist and grow around the anger flames. The colors hung heavy and thick when Imara finally spoke. She kept her voice gentle and barely above a whisper. "He thought you were going to push him into the eraserfall."

Keiko swallowed, and her shoulders slumped.

"Did you see how terrified he was?" Imara asked. "Can you imagine if you had been in his place?"

Keiko looked down at the ground, but clenched her jaw.

Imara turned her head down to catch Keiko's eye. "To erase a hila is to kill a part of someone's identity. It's meant for people who use their hila to destroy or take away lives. The worst of the worst. An eraserfall is an execution."

Keiko's eyes shot up, and words tumbled out of her mouth. "I know all that. Obviously I knew the shield was still there. He was completely safe. I just wanted to scare him, not hurt him."

Imara tilted her head to one side and gave Keiko a significant look. Imara said, "Not hurt him? You pushed the hover cart at him. That would have hurt him if it wasn't for me."

Keiko's head fell, and Imara finally saw the color she was waiting for. Mustard yellow drips of guilt slid off Keiko's skin. Keiko slumped her shoulders closer to the ground and picked at the black polish on her finger-nails.

Imara rubbed her hip, which still stung. She said, "The hover cart hurt me, and I'm older than that boy. He would have been hurt a lot worse."

"I deserved the scholarship," Keiko said while flurries of sepia desperation overpowered the mustard yellow drips of guilt.

"Is that the kind of person you are, then?" Imara asked. "You get revenge through fear and pain? Revenge won't get you the scholarship. Was it worth it? Would you be happier if he were in pain?"

The mustard drips of guilt returned, thicker now. Keiko blinked to hide the tears forming in her eyes. "No. I would feel worse." Keiko sniffed. "I'm sorry you got hurt."

Imara reached out and helped Keiko to her feet. "I'm fine," Imara said. "Next time you think you've been sabotaged, try telling the headmaster or Mr. Nazari. There's no reason you need to take justice into your own hands."

Keiko nodded and wiped her nose with the back of her hand. She looked at Imara expecting more chastisement, but Imara simply said, "Where did you get this hover cart?"

Keiko pointed to a door that led to the kitchen.

Imara nodded and waved Keiko away. "Go back to the party," Imara said. "No more revenge."

Keiko nodded with a smile and turned so fast her black skirt spun out around her.

Imara shook her head as she grabbed the hover cart. Why did she even bother with the girl? Keiko looked to be about sixteen and already had the worst jealousy Imara had ever seen. Keiko did eventually show guilt, but strong emotions like Keiko's weren't easily overpowered.

Imara rolled the hover cart through the door. The moment Imara entered the kitchen, a blast of heat from hot stoves assaulted her. Workers bustled from one end of the kitchen to the other, which only increased the temperature more. Imara wiped her hairline with her fingertips and sighed from the heat. If she stayed in here much longer, she'd have to adjust the thermostat for her underclothes.

"This hover cart was out in the hall," Imara called out. "Can I leave it here?"

Pots and pans clanged, and knives clattered. The head chef shouted orders to the cooks and waiters. No one seemed to hear Imara's question.

Imara surveyed the room and decided to direct her question toward a specific person rather than the entire kitchen. She chose the waiter standing closest to her. His back was to her as he arranged glasses of water on a shiny, silver tray. His large, rough hands looked tan and brusque. It was strange to see them handle the slender, delicate glasses.

"Excuse me," Imara said to the waiter.

The waiter started at the sound of her voice and stepped back in surprise. His foot twisted when it made contact with the ground. He swayed backward and reached for the counter to stop himself from falling. Instead of the counter, his right hand slapped against the shiny, silver tray and sent it soaring through the air. Imara watched with horror as the tray came crashing down on top of her.

The glasses fell and broke on the ground almost in a rhythm. A sharp scream escaped Imara's mouth. Her previously gentle voice was all but gone as she spewed out accusations. "How could you be so clumsy? I can't. I can't do this."

The waiter grabbed a towel for Imara, apologizing profusely as he went. But it wasn't the liquid spilled over her dress that made her lose control. It was the tray.

THREE

IMARA GRIPPED THE SILVER TRAY IN HER hand and tried to look away, but her eyes transfixed on her reflection. Imara looked at her dark brown skin, so blemish free it was enviable. She looked at her slender neck and the soft black curls tumbling over her forehead. Then her black eyes with golden flecks that almost looked like stars. She looked, but she didn't see. All she saw was writhing, splattering, and festering. The waiter approached her and Imara threw the tray at him.

"Get that thing away from me!" she shouted.

Imara snatched the towel from the waiter's hand and dashed out of the kitchen before anyone could stop her. Once in the hallway, she stopped and leaned against a wall to catch her breath. Her chest fell with heavy breaths and she clenched her fists to stop them from shaking. Imara cringed with guilt when she saw the waiter's terrified face in her mind. She gulped and squeezed her shaking fists. It was too late now. What was done, was done. When her hands finally relaxed, Imara dabbed her colorful dress with the towel.

The skirt of her dress was still damp, but at least the liquid was clear. Imara tapped her ring and scrolled through the apps on the hologram until she found the one for her temperature-controlled underclothes. She turned the temperature up to help dry the rest of the liquid.

Imara looked at the towel in her hand and squished her mouth into a knot. She glanced back at the door of the kitchen. Imara squeezed the towel and took a step toward the kitchen. But before her other foot came forward, Imara dropped the towel and turned toward the party. They'd find the towel anyway. She didn't need to bring it back to them.

Imara's hands quivered as she walked toward the party. She would find Naki and tell her she was going to bed. Imara had a busy day tomorrow with moving home and filling out paperwork. She'd already had more than enough excitement for the night and didn't want another ounce of it.

Imara was only a few steps away from the party when her steps faltered again. Her heart pattered in her chest, and a shudder went through her body as she remembered the ugly sight that faced her in the mirror. Imara forced the thought away and took a deep breath. She brushed her party dress for no reason other than to keep her hands busy.

At last she was ready. Imara stepped through the doorway and hugged the wall, away from the hustle. She wanted to go home more than anything. She grabbed a piece of toasted bread topped with hummus from a passing waiter. Imara chomped down on the spiced hummus and toast, begging her nerves to relax.

Imara scanned the crowds for Naki. Imara found her surrounded by a smaller, but intent crowd of people. Before Imara moved, a smoky turquoise blue swirl caught Imara's attention. Her heart pounded when she saw the stranger she had admired earlier. He was almost close enough to touch. Even with his back to her, Imara appreciated how his tailored dress shirt brought out his best features. He looked good in turquoise blue. Imara flicked her head to the side and scolded herself. She was staring again, except this time he was staring too.

Staring at Naki.

Imara's smile fell faster than it had appeared.

Of course he was staring at Naki. Everyone loved Naki. She commanded attention everywhere she went. She was charismatic, funny, beautiful. Imara let out a silent sigh. *Oh well.* Apparently the young man wasn't destined to be her true love as she had jokingly imagined. Of course she knew that. But it was disappointing to have her hopes dashed so immediately.

No. It was a good thing. She didn't need some stupid romance. Not right now. And not with someone from Egypt. She'd just have to find a reason to be grateful for his interest in Naki. On a whim, she decided to say something, to fully admit to herself that nothing was there.

"That's my sister," Imara said.

His shoulders twitched when he turned to Imara. A flush of heat came and left his cheeks so fast Imara almost missed it. But it didn't matter. She saw his embarrassment in a flash of violet light. He wore a cocky smile to mask the emotion. "The valedictorian?" he asked.

Imara nodded, but didn't offer any other information.

"Is she your older or younger sister?" he asked.

"Older."

He squinted one eye and said, "How old are you?"

"Twenty-one."

He ran his fingers through his thick, dark locks and made a smug face. "Ah, well, I'm Twenty-four."

Imara saw right through his attempted bravado. Her hila helped. A mischievous smile played on her lips. "Then you're the same age as my sister. Did you just graduate?"

He shook his head. "Nah, I'm mashimo. I don't have a hila."

Imara's eyebrows raised high on her forehead. "Mashimo? That's rare. Almost everyone has a hila now."

He shrugged and turned his body away from the party and toward Imara. When he leaned toward her, Imara's pulse quickened. Why was he looking at her like that? With a smile he said, "I'm an enigma, what can I say?"

Imara swallowed and smoothed out her skirt. His advance meant nothing. Hadn't he just been staring at Naki? She turned her head to the side to look aloof. "If you don't have a hila, then why are you here?"

He wore another grin, and Imara had to admit, it looked good on him. She brushed a curl from her forehead trying to hide the thought. His smile grew, and Imara pursed her lips. He could see right through her, she knew it.

"My dad owns this school," he said. "I live in Cairo, but I always come to the graduation party." He turned back to steal another glance at Naki. He did it fast, hoping Imara wouldn't notice. She did.

Imara pushed another curl off her forehead. She tried to maintain her aloof expression, but it was difficult with this juicy tidbit of information. "You're Abraxas Nazari?" she asked.

He waved his hand around. "Everyone calls me Abe. Abraxas is so stuffy."

The turquoise hope swirls around Abe spun faster, and an involuntary smile forced itself on Imara's face.

Abe took a step toward her and said, "What is it?"

Imara scrunched the smile down. She shook her head, trying to play it cool. She said, "Your father is very proud of you."

Abe did a half smile, and his brown eyes glowed bright with a joke. "How do you know that?" He leaned closer and said in a voice only she could hear, "Are you a troublemaker? It can't be good if you have to talk to the owner of the school."

Imara waved off the remark, but a short chuckle escaped her. "Everyone knows your father. He talks about you a lot."

Abe's grin turned flirtatious. It made his eyes stand out. They were a deep russet brown and strikingly beautiful. He said, "Well, I wish my father would have mentioned you. I might visit the school more often if I knew someone as beautiful as you was here."

Imara's cool laugh caught Abe off guard. She said, "You obviously don't know my hila."

His eyes grew wide in anticipation. "Why, what is it?"

"I can see the truth," Imara said.

Abe shrugged. "Then why did you laugh? I do think you're beautiful."

Imara pursed her lips. "You think my sister is beautiful too." Abe's grin fell, and his ears turned pink, but Imara wasn't finished yet. "You're trying to decide between the two of us." She turned her head and shook the curls off her forehead, trying to salvage her aloof expression. "You'll choose her," she finished.

It only took Abe a moment to regain his cool. Instead of surprised, he looked genuinely curious. "You can see that?" he asked.

Imara shrugged it off, but felt the corners of her eyes droop. "No, but everyone chooses Naki. People don't like to be around someone who can see their lies. Everyone has truths they would rather hide."

"I wasn't deciding between the two of you." Abe's flat response wasn't at all what Imara expected.

Imara shrugged again. "It doesn't matter if you were. Isn't that what parties are for? Talking to beautiful strangers? You can have her. I was about to leave anyway."

Abe's head turned up a notch. "Why?" he asked.

"I have things to do."

"But, um. But we're already talking. Shouldn't we at least finish our conversation?"

Imara rolled her eyes. "I was about to tell my sister I'm leaving. Come on, I'll introduce you to her. Then you can tell her how beautiful you think she is."

Abe did a pointed glance back at Naki and shrugged. "She is pretty, but—"

Abe turned to fully face Imara and scratched his neck while he found the perfect words. A small smile formed on the corner of his lips, and he glanced down at the ground. He said, "I liked how you jumped in front of that hover cart to save that boy."

Imara's eyes widened. Her cheeks burned, and she resisted the urge to cover her ears, which were surely red as roses now.

"Do you always throw yourself into things to protect people?" Abe asked.

Imara swallowed, and his smile grew. He leaned in closer and said, "That hover cart must have hurt."

Imara smiled and bit her lip, unable to keep the emotion from her face. "You were spying on me," she said with mock accusation.

"No," Abe retorted.

"Yes, you were," Imara said and squished up her mouth as if that proved the point.

Abe sighed. "Ok, fine I was. But you were the one staring at me from across the room. How could I not be intrigued?"

Imara blushed yet again, and she hoped Abe would think red ears were endearing or something because she had a feeling it wouldn't stop any time soon.

"Why were you staring?" Abe asked.

Imara looked away. How could she answer that?

"You saw something," Abe said, proud of his discovery. "With your hila. Am I right?"

Imara nodded.

"What did you see?" Abe asked.

Imara's mouth clamped shut. She never expected such an intimate question from a complete stranger.

Abe frowned when he saw her reaction. "I'm sorry. Is that inappropriate for me to ask?"

"Uh," Imara paused and blinked twice. "No, it's just, people don't usually ask me what I see." She looked down. "They're too afraid of what I'll say."

Imara smiled, but stared down at the marble floor. "And when I call someone out on a lie, they usually try to justify it or make it seem less significant. Very few people own it like you just did."

Abe fought back a grin and rubbed his chin with his thumb. He said, "I told you, I'm an enigma." Suddenly his hand shot out away from his body. Imara watched in wonder as he snatched a baba ganoush topped pita triangle from a waiter's tray, all the while keeping perfect eye contact with Imara. He popped the triangle into his mouth and smiled while he chewed. He was only trying to impress her, but it surprised Imara how well it worked.

Abe licked the tip of his pointer finger and said, "So, what did you see?"

There were thousands of things she could have said, but simplicity would probably be best. "Hope," she said.

"Hope?" Abe said, impressed. "You can see feelings?"

Imara nodded. "Emotions, motivations, lies." Imara looked down and said with a touch of guilt, "I can see a lot."

"No way," Abe said, even more impressed. She didn't expect a reaction like that. Most people were intimidated by her hila. He seemed to think it was the coolest thing in the world. "What does it look like?" he asked.

His admiration encouraged her. Without fear she said, "You've heard of aurora borealis?"

"Yeah, the northern lights?"

Imara nodded. "That's sort of what it looks like."

Abe smiled. Not cocky like before, but full of wonderment. "Fresh," he said. "Does it come out of their eyes? Or heart?"

Imara laughed. "No, it comes off the skin, or through their clothes. There are different colors for different feelings. And different shapes too. Some emotions are wispy, some are sharp, some are like water droplets. If the feeling is directed toward a certain person or thing, the colors point in their direction. What were you talking about when I was staring?" Maybe it was rude to ask, but curiosity got the best of her. She had to know what made him to feel such strong hope.

"My job," he said.

"What do you do?"

"I'm an entrepreneur."

"Like your father," Imara said.

Abe nodded. "Yes, but my business is just a baby right now. We're still working out a lot of kinks. I love it though."

Imara tapped her foot inside of her shoe. He was being vague on purpose. He was making her ask questions, keeping her intrigued. "What kind of business do you have?"

Abe smiled and slid his thumb across his jaw-line as tangerine pride glowed from his skin. He was waiting for this question. He seemed certain it would impress her. "Oh," he said with a shrug. "We help rescue kids who have been kidnapped by a child slave cartel."

Imara's eyes went wide. "Is that dangerous?" she asked.

Abe waved his hand. "Nah. It's not that bad."

Lie. And yet, Imara was intrigued by the lie rather than put off by it. He tried to make his work seem less impressive. Which was hard because he rescued children.

From a slave cartel.

What could be more impressive than that? Imara tried and failed to think of a more altruistic business.

Abe's face grew serious, and the importance of his work overcame his desire to impress her. He said, "They target orphans. Kids who are in care of the Egyptian Council and have no family. They take kids from care homes, pretending to be from the Egyptian Council, then delete their identity records. No one realizes the kid is missing because no one is left who cares about the kid. It's disgusting. So, we uh, we try to keep tabs on all the kids. And when one goes missing, we go after them."

It took a great deal of effort for Imara to close her dropped mouth. Finally she said, "That's incredible."

31

Abe shrugged and gave such a beautiful aloof expression, Imara was almost jealous. "What can I say? I have soft spot for orphans."

Those words were rehearsed. He played it off as though he thought of them on the spot, but Imara could tell he hadn't. Still, no matter how rehearsed, his passion for his work was every bit as evident through his body language as it was through the turquoise hope swirls dancing off him.

Abe's eyebrows lowered, and the playful look on his face fell. He said, "Look, I know it sounds like I made that up to impress you, but I didn't. It actually is true."

Imara raised an eyebrow. Why did he care so much what she thought of him? "I know," Imara said with a smirk.

Abe laughed. "Oh yeah." He shook his head. "You throw yourself in front of hover carts, and you call people out on their lies. I like you, truth seer."

Imara smiled and held his gaze. She didn't even mind the blushing this time.

"What's your name?" Abe asked.

Imara said her name, but at the same moment, a noise rose from the center of the large room. Imara's eyes followed Abe's gaze toward the noise. A small crowd stood together saying something in unison. Wine-colored fear spikes spotted with a raven black rash of anxiety grew out from every member of the crowd. Among them, Imara noticed the tagger boy from the hall. The lime green *T* on his chest fluttered as his body shook with fear. But his wasn't the only tagger patch in the group. The woman next to him had one and so did the man next to her. And two more people behind them. And... everyone. Everyone in the small group wore a black patch with a lime green *T*.

FOUR

THE GROUP OF TAGGERS SPOKE IN UNISON IN the center of the room, their voices too quiet to hear. Imara reached up to tug the hair on the back of her neck. She stared carefully at the crowd, waiting for their next move.

This wasn't the first time taggers chose Nazari Academy of Hila for one of their demonstrations. A graduation party was hardly the time for a political display, which was one of the many reasons they were considered fanatics. They didn't exactly follow rules of etiquette.

Now that the taggers had everyone's attention, their low whispers grew to loud shouts. In unison they chanted a phrase over and over again. They said, "We will not be silenced. We will not be ignored. We will bring the darkness to light."

Mr. Nazari got to the small crowd of people by the fourth repetition. He smoothed his hair and patted his jacket down. He wore a polite expression, looking completely unperturbed. It was a strange expression considering the jagged indigo waves of annoyance coming off his skin in droves. But then, Mr. Nazari hid his emotions well. Imara always noted a disconnect between his feelings and his expressions.

As professional as ever, Mr. Nazari smiled. "Thank you for being here. As you know, this party is to celebrate the graduates. This is not the time for a demonstration. I'd be happy to arrange something for you next week. We can have a press conference and everything."

It sounded like a reasonable offer, but the taggers ignored Mr. Nazari. They repeated their phrase and with each repetition got louder.

Mr. Nazari adjusted his cuff links, patted his jacket again, and took a deep breath. Outside he was the picture of calm. The colors coming off his skin told a different story. The jagged indigo waves surrounding him were joined by burnt orange prickles of greed. This tagger disruption made the other guests uncomfortable, and Mr. Nazari didn't like how it might affect his bottom line. He raised his voice. "This is neither the time nor the place for you to force your ideas on my students and guests. I will not allow my school to be violated in such a manner. If you do not leave immediately, I'll contact the police."

The taggers chanted louder, ignoring Mr. Nazari. Imara tapped her ring. She scrolled through the hologram until she found the camera app and pressed record. Several people were already recording with their rings, but it was good to have as many witness recordings as possible for things like this.

Mr. Nazari tapped his own ring and a hologram appeared before him. Just before he clicked the phone app, an alarm went off inside the school. This silenced the taggers. Metal bars clanged over the windows, and a large *click* indicated the doors to the outside had been locked. Imara and many others looked to Mr. Nazari. Why would he activate the lockdown protocol now? Unfortunately, Mr. Nazari looked as confused as anyone. He tapped the phone app on his hologram, but nothing happened.

Mr. Nazari's eyebrow twitched showing the first physical sign of annoyance. He spoke to his guests. "Where is Headmaster Bello? Has anyone seen him?"

Abe turned to Imara and said, "I have to go." He touched the patterned black ring on his finger. When his hologram opened, he selected a syncing app. He clicked her picture and said, "I've got your info. I'll try to catch you later."

Imara nodded and watched Abe join his father. Abe seemed excited to deal with this turn of events, but Imara only frowned. With the school on lockdown, how would she get home? And how would she get her paperwork from the Kenyan police force?

Imara tapped her toe and narrowed her eyes. *Taggers.* If this demonstration did anything to keep her from her dream job, she didn't know what she'd do.

Imara heard Abe's confident voice deep in the crowd. "I heard Headmaster Bello say he was going to the library."

Mr. Nazari nodded. "Will you go get him, Abraxas?"

Abe nodded and as soon as he left the room, Mr. Nazari turned to the crowd of taggers. He said, "I don't know how you got access to our lockdown codes or how you disabled communication, but I will not stand for it. I'll make sure you are punished to the fullest extent of the law."

Mr. Nazari marched to a stone podium that stood at the head of the room. He brushed his fingers against the hieroglyphics carved into the front before he stepped up to the podium. He tapped his ring and took a moment to find the microphone app. Through it he said, "I am terribly sorry for the distress you have been caused. Communications have been disabled, but as soon as Headmaster Bello is here, we will use our codes to remove the lockdown. Please try to enjoy your evening. The doors will be functional soon enough."

Mr. Nazari stepped off the podium and headed for the door next to Imara. Just as he got near, Professor Santini rushed into the room. Her dark, wavy brown hair flew behind her as she ran straight to Mr. Nazari. She wore black pants and a neat pink blouse. Her honey brown eyes were wide as she looked into the room. "What happened? Are we on lockdown?"

Mr. Nazari let out a long sigh. "I'm glad you're here, Carlotta. I thought you left already."

Professor Santini said, "I was on my way out when I heard the alarms and the doors lock. Is there a criminal loose? Do we need to use the eraserfall?"

Mr. Nazari shook his head and sighed again. "No, no. It's nothing serious. Just a group of taggers decided they will not be silenced." Mr. Nazari rubbed the bridge of his nose and breathed out until his calm expression returned. "Their antics are getting more and more desperate. You'd think they would realize they'll never make tagging mainstream. It's been twenty years."

Professor Santini's eyes glanced over to the taggers. A sad smile formed on her lips and she said, "Maybe we should let them speak. Perhaps they wouldn't resort to such antics if they had a platform to be heard."

"I suggested that. I even offered a press conference. And then they put the school on lockdown. I'm less inclined to listen now. I'm going to find Jabari. My son said he was in the

36

library. Jabari and I can use our administrator's codes to remove the lockdown. Would you try to keep things sane in here, Carlotta?"

Professor Santini nodded and looked out at the room as Mr. Nazari left through the door. Professor Santini's eyebrows raised when she noticed Imara standing near. She quickly joined her and said, "Imara, how are you? Do you need anything? You're frightened, I can see."

Imara couldn't hide her fear since Professor Santini was a fellow truth seer. Imara shrugged. "I am a little scared, but mostly annoyed. I need to get out of here."

Professor Santini's eyebrows shot up even higher. "Your interview! How did it go?"

Imara smiled, and without a word, Professor Santini knew. She always understood Imara like no one else could.

"Congratulations, Imara. When do you start?"

Imara frowned. "On Monday if I get the paperwork finished in time. But I can't receive it if communications are down. And I have so much to do before I can start, but first I need to leave."

Professor Santini gave Imara's forearm a gentle squeeze. "This will be over soon enough, Imara. You'll see."

Professor Santini looked out at the crowd of nervous guests. She asked Imara, "Can I see the recording on your ring? Did you get the lockdown?"

Imara nodded and touched her hologram screen to play back the recording. "I got the lockdown, but Mr. Nazari was talking before that and I didn't record any of it."

Professor Santini nodded and leaned forward to watch the recording. When it was over, she left Imara and addressed the crowd of taggers. In a calm and soothing voice she said,

"What do you want? If you initiated lockdown, there must be a reason, so what is it?"

Her gentle voice sounded as sweet and genuine as it always did. Imara knew from experience that it made people listen. This was the voice Imara tried to emulate when she spoke to Keiko.

The taggers stood still until one person started speaking, and soon the rest joined. Not that they said anything useful. They only repeated their phrase from before. "We will not be silenced. We will not be ignored. We will bring the darkness to light."

Professor Santini shook her head. "Very well. You may stand here as long as you don't hurt anyone."

Professor Santini spoke to a few people around the crowd of taggers, but Imara couldn't hear. Eventually Professor Santini returned to Imara. "Everyone is calling them extremists under their breaths."

"Their methods are getting more extreme," Imara said. "They put the school on lockdown."

Professor Santini nodded. "True. Perhaps the label is becoming more accurate. Do you think they deserve to be heard?"

Imara shrugged. "To be honest, I don't care. Taggers are an Egyptian problem. I love Egypt, but I want to go home."

Professor Santini chuckled, her honey eyes bright as she smiled at Imara. "You didn't have to stay for the party. Why didn't you leave with your parents?"

Imara shrugged again and turned her eyes down. "Naki asked me to stay."

Professor Santini said, "Well you know what I always say, you can't have a perfect life without family."

Imara smiled with one side of her mouth.

Professor Santini's skin glowed with tangerine pride. "I know you'd do anything for Naki."

Just then, Mr. Nazari, Headmaster Bello, and Abe entered the large room. Professor Santini joined them while Abe went out into the crowd. Imara watched as Mr. Nazari, Headmaster Bello, and Professor Santini spoke in whispers.

Mr. Nazari left the group of three and went back to the hieroglyphic podium at the head of the room. Again he used the microphone app on his ring. He carefully avoided the eyes of any taggers while he spoke. "It seems these fanatics changed the lockdown codes, which means we cannot release it. If the lockdown is still in place by morning, the police will be notified. They should be able to contact the city and override the lockdown."

Several murmurs rose up from the crowd, and Mr. Nazari fought to regain control. "I know, I know. It's not ideal, especially with communications disabled. But we have extra bedding we can bring in. And there are plenty of open beds since many of our students have already gone home for traditional school. We have enough food as well. It's inconvenient to be sure, but it's only one night."

A few party guests yelled at the taggers. "Let us out of here! We have lives and families."

The taggers response was immediate. "We will not be silenced. We will not be ignored."

Another party guest cut the taggers off before they could finish. "Why would we listen after you locked us in here? Now we're angry."

A man with a round scar on his forehead and a tagger *T* on his chest yelled out, "Our ideas have always been ignored, but not tonight. Tonight you'll finally accept what we are fighting for."

The man with the round scar suddenly ran out of the room and Headmaster Bello chased after him.

As soon as they were gone, Abe took a stance in front of the taggers. The turquoise hope around Abe swirled and expanded by the second. He said, "We already know what you're fighting for. That's why we refuse to join you."

Every tagger in the group turned on Abe and glared at him. Even the little boy Imara saved earlier.

Abe glared back at the taggers. "We're not ignoring you, we're disagreeing with you." The turquoise swirls twisted as fast as boiling water and grew further out from his body. With finality he said, "Tagging is dangerous and stupid."

Imara raised an eyebrow at these words. She admired Abe's passion, but dangerous? Maybe tagging wasn't fair, but it wasn't dangerous either. The worst thing about taggers were these silly demonstrations. The lockdown was serious too. She never imagined they would do something so extreme.

The arguing amongst party guests and taggers continued to escalate. Mr. Nazari fiddled with his cufflinks while a raven black rash of anxiety surrounded him. Above the noise, Imara heard a voice say, "We know where your tagger hideout is. You can't hide anymore."

Imara leaned against the wall behind her. She considered just going up to her room for the night. If she couldn't go home, at least she could leave the party and all of this political nonsense. As long as the city could override the lockdown in the morning, her plans didn't have to change.

The colors in the room thickened and darkened with each passing minute. The party was bad enough, but this was just sad. Fear. Anger. Selfishness. Imara rolled her eyes and turned to leave. Through the doorway, a dark figure entered the room.

Imara sucked in a breath at the sight. The darkness didn't come from emotions, but from clothing. All of it pitch black. The person wore heavy black boots so shiny, they were like mirrors. There were also black pants, a black top, and a heavy black trench coat. The turtleneck top was thick like a bullet-proof vest, making the torso look rectangular and sharp. Over the hands and up the arm were thick, black rubber gloves. The look was completed with a black helmet and dark, shaded goggles. Every inch of the body was covered.

Amidst the black, a large lime green *T* was stitched onto the chest. It perfectly matched the taggers' patches. Imara gaped at the figure. This must be the mysterious Judge the taggers had been talking about for months. They said he would come and then everyone would be forced to listen. Just like they promised, it was impossible to decipher any identifying characteristics from the Judge.

The only unique characteristic he had were the grass green threads of desire flying out from his body. Grass green meant it was non-romantic desire. Hundreds of threads left his body and curled themselves around each person in the room. Imara couldn't know for sure what the desire meant, but when it curled around every single person like that, it was almost certainly desire for power.

The Judge went straight to the hieroglyphic podium. His helmet turned as he scanned the entire crowd. Every person in the room had stopped talking. Breathing seemed a chore when the Judge required so much attention. All eyes stayed stuck on the Judge, waiting for him to act. After several long seconds, the Judge activated his ring. Instead of choosing the microphone app, he shrunk the hologram and clicked an app Imara didn't recognize. In an instant, every hologram in the room activated. Imara looked down at her ring confused, when she heard a voice that made every muscle in her body freeze.

The voice came from inside her head. If it had been any other voice, she would have thought it was a recording from her ring. Hardly disconcerting. But the voice Imara heard inside her head was… her own.

She wasn't thinking these words, so how could she hear them in her head? Imara looked back up at the Judge. He moved his hands, gesticulating in sync with the voice in her head.

The voice said, "I have been called a fanatic, an extremist, but no more. From now on, you will call me the Judge. For years, criminals have been punished but then returned to society. We allow them to make the same mistakes again and again. They are given a chance to change, but of course they never do. As taggers, all we ask is that criminals are tagged with their crimes before they are returned to society. In your hearts, you know this is right. Tags are meant for protection, not discrimination. Tags will protect society from those who would be villains. I will be the perfect judge of each crime. I will bestow proper, objective judgment. Someday you will trust me as much as you trust the Egyptian Council. No one can hide their darkness anymore. We will bring the darkness to light!"

The Judge carefully traced the *T* on his chest with a gloved finger. Then the voice began again. "My demands are simple. Let me into the prisons. I will tag murderers and molesters only. No other crimes for now. This will teach you the value of tagging. When you are ready, we will move to the next phase. You have three days to accept, or I will kill the hostages."

Imara's head shot up. Hostages? What hostages? Imara searched the room. Had she missed something? But everyone else wore the same confused expression she did.

The Judge reached into his trench coat and pulled out a small golden device. Buttons and levers and screens covered one side of the device. Another side had a digital screen. Imara stared at it with wide eyed wonder.

"You are naïve if you think you can stop me. None of you will ever forget this day." The Judge pressed a button on the golden device, and several people gasped. Imara looked deep in the crowd. A few people pointed to the names on their hologram screen, but Imara couldn't see why. Her own name looked the same as it always had.

"You have three days for my demands to be met."

Suddenly the Judge stepped down from the stone podium and walked toward the crowd. Most people stepped back on instinct. The Judge plowed forward with no indication of fear. He held the golden device above his head and said, "You cannot stop me. I will not be silenced. I will not be ignored. I WILL BRING THE DARKNESS TO LIGHT!"

Without warning, the Judge grabbed hold of several people who stood nearest to him, and in a flash, they were all gone. At the same time, everyone's rings deactivated and the bars over the windows raised. The lockdown had somehow been undone.

Imara's heart thumped, and a bead of sweat formed at her hairline. Wine-colored spikes of fear filled every corner of the room. Mouths were dropped and fists clenched. The room was still, but an energy radiated from every person. Pandemonium was mere moments away from erupting.

Imara shook her head. The taggers said they had a transporter, but no one believed it. Transporting was new technology. It was only used for garbage or other things that didn't need to be perfectly put back together after transportation. But a transporter that could transport people? It seemed unreal.

Imara swallowed when a party guest turned on one of the taggers. He grabbed him by the shoulders and started yelling. Imara didn't hear the words. Her mind too full of a thousand thoughts swirling and tumbling around. There was more shouting and now shoving. Mr. Nazari was, for once, visibly agitated trying to maintain control.

Imara couldn't decide what was more unsettling: the elaborate costume that looked like it came straight from a comic, the voice from inside her head, the kidnapping at the end, or the fighting now. None of it felt real. Real life wasn't this dramatic. But as Imara stood there, a feeling tugged at the back of her mind. Something was wrong. Something important.

Imara flitted her eyes around the room looking for something, not quite sure what. She searched. Nothing. She moved to another position. Still nothing. Her feet propelled her toward the crowd. She pushed people out of the way as she looked. It didn't matter. The feeling inside her confirmed it.

She breathed faster with each second and stopped pushing. The crowd parted and all eyes were on her as she reached the podium.

She knew. She knew what was gone. She whispered, then shouted the name. "Naki!" she screamed.

Imara felt a hand on her shoulder and a soft voice said, "She's gone."

FIVE

IMARA'S STOMACH TWISTED IN KNOTS AS SHE turned toward the hand on her shoulder. It belonged to Siluk, a fellow student. His nostrils flared and twitched on his pale face. His straight black hair was disheveled. Imara grabbed him by the shoulders. Her voice was breathless as the words came out. "Where are they? You said you know where the tagger hideout is. I heard you bragging about it earlier. Could you smell it on them?"

Siluk shook his head and frowned. "No, I didn't figure it out. Darius." Siluk glanced at the crowd of people surrounding them, and Imara realized everyone was watching her. Siluk turned from Imara and spoke to the crowd. "My friend Darius said he knew where the taggers had their secret meetings. But it was just a guess. He didn't know for sure."

Imara tightened her grip on Siluk's shoulders. "Where?" she asked.

Siluk spoke to the crowd again, trying to release himself from Imara's grip. "My friend thinks the hideout is in the Catacombs of Kom el Shoqafa. The one that flooded twenty years ago in 2101. It's closed to the public, but it gets a suspicious amount of traffic. He had other reasons too, but I don't remember them."

Imara took her hands off Siluk but glared, forcing him to make eye contact. "How big are the catacombs?" she asked in a low voice. "How long will it take the police to search them? Hours? Days?"

Siluk shrugged and looked to the ground with a grimace. "I don't know," he said. "Darius is the history buff. I don't know any of that."

"Where is Darius?" Imara asked.

Siluk looked down. "He's gone. The Judge took him, too."

৪০৪০৩৫৪

Imara squeezed her fists and tapped her toe. Her eyes widened when her ring chimed with a notification. She checked the message and clenched her jaw. Her mom asked for an update. Again. Imara couldn't blame her. She was just as frustrated at the lack of information. The police had been there for over an hour, and all they did was question people about the asterisks on their names. The suddenly appearing asterisks were the reason everyone had gasped when the Judge had pressed the button on the golden transporter device. Imara still didn't know why her name was asterisk free.

Now that she thought of it, the police had done one other thing. They locked the taggers into a room— where they were promptly transported out by the Judge a few minutes later. Stupid. Imara knew the police felt useless against the taggers, but she had lost her patience fifteen minutes ago. The police asked minimal questions about the hostages. All they seemed to care about were the stupid asterisks.

47

She was sick of waiting. Imara would have to take things into her own hands. She marched up to the most official-looking police officer she could find. She didn't care that he was busy questioning a party guest. "Excuse me," she said.

Imara took a step back when the party guest turned around. It was Abe. She hadn't even noticed, but here he was talking to the officer, probably about his name. She frowned and said to him, "You got an asterisk?"

Abe tapped his ring and showed her his hologram. Right at the top it said, *Abraxas Itafe Nazari**.

But the asterisk shouldn't have been there. It was against global law to have symbols in a name. Letters only. No one understood the technology the Judge used to add asterisks to all those names.

Abe scowled. "Apparently only the people within twenty-five feet of the Judge got one. I guess it's good to know there's a limit to how much tagging the Judge can do."

That explained why Imara didn't have an asterisk. "Have you ever seen this before?" Imara asked the police officer, allowing herself a momentary distraction.

The officer nodded. "They did this about a year ago. It was only two people then."

"But you fixed it, right?" Abe asked. "You figured out how to change the name back?"

The officer tapped his ring and fuddled through the hologram until he found a notepad app. He stared at it and stumbled through the words as he read, "The Egyptian Council has expended every effort to amend the names of the individuals targeted by the extremist group, taggers. We have engineers working tirelessly—"

"So, no?" Abe said frustrated.

The officer looked down and said a quiet "No," while he turned off his ring.

Abe shook his head. "I thought maybe they were bluffing, but taggers actually have the power to destroy people's lives. Or the Judge does anyway. He has a golden device. It tagged us and transported everyone."

The officer nodded. "Yes, we know about the device. It seems to be unique. The taggers insist the Judge has the only one. And your life is hardly destroyed. You only have an asterisk on your name now."

Abe shot an angry glare at the officer. "It's not about the asterisk. It's about the potential. Everyone I ever meet will see the name on my hologram. It's my official name, it goes on every record. This time they only added an asterisk. Next time they're going to add a tag. Murderer. Molester. Maybe those kinds of people deserve it, but the taggers won't stop there."

Imara was intrigued by his tightened fists and clenched jaw. If someone really were a murderer, then everyone around him probably deserved to know. How much more intense did Abe think taggers would get?

Imara turned to the officer, ready to tackle the real reason she had approached him. "Do you have a hostage negotiator?"

The officer sighed and tapped his ring back on to type some notes. He said, "Yes, but usually in a negotiation you have someone to negotiate with. We don't know where the Judge is. We have no idea how to contact the Judge. We don't even know how to meet the demands."

"You have to save the hostages," Imara said with force. She didn't understand why, but it seemed like the officer had already given up hope.

The officer turned his eyes down to avoid eye contact. "We will do everything we can, but we have no idea where to start looking."

Imara lowered her eyebrows, confused. "What about the catacombs of something or other." She pointed to Siluk who sat across the room. "Didn't he tell you about them? The tagger hideout is probably a good first place to check."

The officer clenched his jaw, which was barely noticeable. That didn't stop her from seeing the plum-colored worms of discomfort wriggling out from his skin. He said, "The Catacombs of Kom el Shoqafa. It's a nice idea, but we have more important leads to check out."

Imara looked at him, still confused. "You just said you had no idea where to start. Why don't you start with the catacombs?"

The officer shrugged, "The catacombs are probably the wrong place. We can't waste time or resources on a place that isn't guaranteed."

"You can't waste time or resources? Are you even going to look for the hostages at all?" Imara's voice rose with every syllable, all while the officer avoided her gaze.

"Of course we'll do everything we can, but the catacombs are not one of the options."

"Why?" Imara asked.

The officer licked his bottom lip, and his nose scrunched up, but he finally said with surety. "We already checked them out, okay? It's the wrong place."

Imara watched as the officer's skin dulled to a sickly gray.

Lie.

She hardly needed her hila to see it. He wasn't trying that hard to hide it. But he did an excellent job of hiding his fear. Nothing in his body language indicated fear, but sharp wine spikes shot out from his skin at all different angles. Imara watched, not sure what to make of them. Finally she asked, "What's in the catacombs?"

The officer laughed and shook his head. "Skeletons," he said while rolling his eyes. "They're catacombs. What do you expect?"

Imara glared at his offhand remark. "You're scared," she said. "I can see it." She did her best to bore holes into the side of his head with her eyes since he still refused to look at her.

The officer shifted, obviously uncomfortable with the accuracy of her statement. He pursed his lips. "No one is going into the catacombs. It's full of illusions and traps. It's too dangerous."

Imara's anger melted away, and desperation took over. She hoped her eyes communicated the begging in her voice. "Please," she said. "My sister is one of the hostages."

The officer looked up, surprised, and sorrow filled his eyes. He averted his gaze yet again. "I'm so sorry."

Imara clamped her mouth shut, and the dread in her stomach tightened to a knot. "You think she's going to die," Imara said.

The officer ducked his head down deeper. With a quiet voice he said, "We don't know anything yet. We think the Judge will contact us in a few days, and then maybe we can negotiate something."

Imara shook her head and clenched one hand into a fist. "That's not good enough. What if you can't come to an agreement?"

The officer showed no chance of changing his mind. Fear and anger and desperation boiled in Imara's heart. They grew and hardened until they came together and formed an idea. Imara's eyebrows lowered into a determined glare. "If you won't go into the catacombs, then I will."

The officer's eyes widened. "You can't do that."

"Is it illegal?" Imara asked.

"No," the officer said. "It's suicide. We only know one thing about the catacombs. When someone goes in, they don't come out."

Imara's determination only grew. "You said illusions."

"So?" the officer said.

"I'm a truth seer. Maybe I can see past the illusions. Or Professor Santini can. She's much better than me."

"Carlotta Santini?" the officer asked.

Imara nodded.

"No," the officer said. "Professor Santini has to stay here. With Mr. Nazari and Headmaster Bello gone, she's next in charge. We're setting up a task force in the school, and we need someone to coordinate with us."

Imara heard his words, but only seemed to process one part. She turned to Abe and said, "Your father too?"

Abe nodded with a frown, and Imara finally understood the cobalt blue drops of sadness pelting off his skin.

The officer stood and waved to another officer standing behind Imara. He turned back to her and said, "You're free to go."

"Do you need me to describe that tagger guy who had the scar on his head?" Abe asked. "You think he's the Judge, right?"

The officer shook his head. "No. Well, yes, he is definitely the Judge. But we have several recordings with clear shots of his face. We already know his identity." The officer tapped his ring to make one last note and then looked at Abe with a serious expression. "Would you please try to convince this girl to go home? I can't reiterate enough how dangerous the catacombs are."

Abe nodded until the officer walked away. Once the officer was out of earshot, he turned to Imara and said, "Do you really think you can see past the illusions?"

Imara blinked at Abe's question. She was expecting a lecture and already had a defense, especially since she had only met Abe that evening. She didn't anticipate his hopefulness. "I don't know," Imara said, deciding it was only fair to be honest. "The officer was really scared. Maybe they've gone in with a truth seer before, but maybe not. Truth seers are rare. I can see past illusions, but I still have a lot to learn."

Abe looked into her eyes with fierce determination. "If you think you can do it, then I'm with you. You know as well as I do, the police already consider the hostages dead."

Imara nodded just as her ring chimed again. She stared at it for a moment then said, "If we're going to do this, I think we need to be stealthy. I'm pretty sure the police will try to stop us, and I know my parents wouldn't want me going into the unknown like this. They'll tell me to let the police handle it. But the police aren't going to do anything."

"I can be stealthy. What do you think we need?" Abe asked.

Imara shrugged. "I don't know. Food. Change of clothes. Something to sleep on. It could take a few days. I don't know how big the catacombs are. I don't even know where they are, but we can look that up. Do you have any of your things here?"

"No," Abe said. "But I can borrow my dad's stuff. His house is close by."

Imara nodded. "Meet me back here in an hour. I'll try to have a plan by then."

As Abe walked away, Imara opened the message app on her ring and started a message to Safiya Otieno. Her fingers faltered on the keys as the reality of what she was about to do set in. She glanced at Abe. Maybe she should call this whole thing off. What if the illusions were worse than she thought? Imara got ready to call out to him, but before she could speak, Professor Santini came up, her honey eyes filled with concern.

"The chief told me you want to go into the catacombs to rescue Naki," Professor Santini said.

Imara swallowed and looked down. "The police won't go near the catacombs. If there's a chance I can save Naki, I have to try."

Professor Santini squeezed Imara's shoulder. "I wish I could go with you, but the police won't let me leave."

Imara's head tilted to the side. "You're not going to try and stop me?"

Professor Santini smirked. "Would that do any good?"

Imara looked down and let out a soft chuckle. "No."

"I didn't think so." Professor Santini's face hardened with resolve. "Trust me. I understand more than anyone that family is everything. Instead of stopping you, I think I might be able to help you." Professor Santini glanced over her shoulder at the police and tugged Imara out of the room.

Soon they bustled through the hall toward Professor Santini's office. Professor Santini glanced back and said in a hushed voice, "I asked if I could download a map to the catacombs for you, but they said it's not public record. That is complete poppycock. They just don't want you to go. There's nothing dangerous in that map and you'll need it in the catacombs."

Now at the office, Professor Santini used a key from her hologram ring to unlock the door. "Be a lookout for me, would you dear? What I'm doing isn't strictly legal."

Imara shut the door all but a crack and looked out in the hall. "What are you going to do?" she whispered.

"Oh, just hack into the Egyptian Council's records to find a copy of the map."

Imara's eyes went wide. "You're going to hack into Egyptian Council?"

"Imara, you need that map. I can't let you go into the catacombs without it, no matter what it takes."

"But Professor, you could get caught."

"If you insist on going into those catacombs, then I'll do everything I can to help. Now listen carefully. I asked the chief about the illusions. He didn't know much, but it sounds like they are projections. You know how to see past projector illusions; you'll just have to concentrate."

Imara nodded, trying to borrow some of the confidence Professor Santini had in her. Imara bit her lip. "What if there are troxler puzzles? I haven't mastered troxler puzzles yet."

Professor Santini looked up at Imara with a short chuckle. "No one would design a troxler puzzle except a truth seer. Projector illusions and camouflage illusions can be designed by anyone. And you know how to see past those. Imara, you are the best truth seer I've ever seen. You can do this. Question everything you see. It will get easier as you go since you'll get used to seeing past the illusions. Trust your hila, and you can do it."

Imara bunched the fabric of her party dress into her fist, but she nodded. Professor Santini went back to the hologram. After a few minutes, she stood up and said, "Got it. Turn on your ring to make sure it sent to you."

Imara successfully pulled up the map of the catacombs then left for her room. She changed out of her dress into moisture-wicking black leggings and a bright raspberry-colored shirt. She grabbed a backpack from the floor and threw in extra clothes for herself and Naki. Next she added two space saving-sleeping bags, two water bottles, and everything else she could think of. She left half the backpack empty for food.

Imara smoothed the hair on the back of her neck then flounced the curls on top of her head. She tugged at the strands of hair on the back of her neck while she stared at the jar of coconut oil on her desk. With a nod to herself, she threw the coconut oil into the backpack. It took up valuable space, but she'd never be able to tame her curls without it. Hopefully it would take less than a day to find the hostages anyway.

Finally, Imara sat on her bed and opened a new message on her hologram. This one was for her parents. She gave as much information as possible without actually telling them she planned to go into the catacombs.

Next, she messaged Safiya to let her know she was going to be busy rescuing Naki for the next two days. It was easier to think of the words now that she was sure of her decision. She had two days until Monday. She would simply rescue Naki, then fill out her paperwork when she got out of the catacombs.

Two days. She could do it in two days.

Imara grabbed her packed backpack and went down to the kitchen. Keiko stood just outside the door. She stared at Imara in awe. "I heard Professor Santini say you're going into the catacombs."

Imara nodded. "My sister is one of the hostages. But don't tell anyone. The police don't want me to go."

Keiko smiled. "Come with me."

Keiko pushed Imara into the now empty kitchen. Keiko brushed her silky black hair back and pulled oxy-gone containers out of the cupboards. She filled them with food from the fridge and pantry. "How much do you think you'll need?" Keiko asked.

Imara found some bread and stuffed it into a container. "At least enough for two days. But it might be good to have some extra just in case. Oh, and food for the hostages. And another person is coming too."

Keiko nodded. "I'll just get all the extra food in the fridge. Hopefully it's enough."

Somebody opened the door and Keiko jumped. She clutched her black skirt and shook her head. "Dad, you scared me," she said.

"What are you doing with her?" the man asked Keiko. Imara recognized him as the waiter with rough hands who had dropped the silver tray on her.

Keiko pointed to Imara. "This is the truth seer I told you about. She's going to rescue her sister and the other hostages."

The man looked at Imara while tiny wine-colored fear spikes grew off him. "You're a truth seer?" he asked.

Imara nodded.

"Then what do you see when you look in a mirror?"

Imara took a step back and tried to swallow the sudden lump in her throat. How could she respond to that? She cleared her throat. Her hands shook as she threw the containers of food into her backpack. "Thanks for the help," she said, and left the room without another word.

Imara took deep breaths as she walked down the hall. She eyed the doorway to the party with each step. She didn't want to go back in there in case the police tried to stop her. She peeked inside the doorway, trying to catch a glimpse of Abe. Instead, she heard his voice from behind.

"I'm right here," he said. "Are you ready to go?"

Imara turned around and frowned when she saw Abe wasn't alone.

"Oh," Abe said when he saw Imara staring. "This is the guy whose friend figured out the tagger hideout is in the catacombs. His name is Siluk."

Imara lowered her eyebrows at Siluk. With only mild hostility, she said, "Hi."

Abe smiled. "I told him he could come with us."

"What?" Imara said. She gripped the strap of her backpack and pursed her lips.

Siluk leaned forward with pleading eyes. "Darius is my best friend. You have to let me help."

Imara narrowed her eyes to tiny slits but said nothing.

"Come on," Siluk said. "I'm strong. I packed some tools. I'll be useful, I promise."

With great effort, Imara relaxed her clenched jaw. "You understand how dangerous it is?"

Siluk nodded. "Abe told me everything."

Imara rolled her eyes and said, "Fine. Do we know everyone who was taken hostage? Just Naki, Darius, and Mr. Nazari?"

"And the headmaster," Abe said. "He hasn't been seen since the lockdown lifted."

Imara nodded. "Professor Santini said the catacombs aren't guarded, but they are pretty big. I think we should go into them and camp for the night. Then tomorrow we'll explore the catacombs and try to find the hostages."

"Sounds good to me," Abe said. "But we have to assume the taggers are in the catacombs as well. Luckily, I have some experience avoiding unfriendlies, so we should be fine. I'll explain my plan on the way."

Imara never thought she'd be grateful for a child slave cartel, but Abe's experience with them would certainly be useful. Imara opened the map app on her ring. "Do either of you know if there's a bus that goes to the catacombs?"

"There's not," Professor Santini said from behind Imara.

Imara turned around to face her professor.

"Take my bubble car," Professor Santini said. "I'll send a key to your hologram ring. GPS should get you there."

Imara smiled. The weight of the task ahead felt lighter knowing she had the support of her beloved teacher. "Thank you so much, Professor. I couldn't have done this without you."

Professor Santini pulled Imara into a quick hug. Her voice cracked as she said, "You can do this, Imara. They're just projector illusions."

SIX

IMARA LOCKED PROFESSOR SANTINI'S BUBBLE car with her hologram ring after she and the others got out of it. The moon shone down on taupe-colored dirt littered with shards of clay. A modern structure of metal and glass stood out against the dirt. But its dusty windows and scuffed walls revealed it had been abandoned for a decade or so. In front of the metal structure, an ancient spiral staircase led deep underground. Imara clutched both of her backpack straps as she approached the staircase.

Siluk gulped, and wine fear spikes poked out from his skin—a raven black rash of anxiety covering them. Imara clutched her backpack straps tighter and took a deep breath.

Abe turned to Imara slowly. "You sure you can see past the illusions?"

Imara tugged the hair on the back of her neck. With each of her shallow breaths, her skin tingled with fear. It was too late to back out now. She was doing this no matter what. She just wished she didn't have two other people depending on her. Her own life she could risk, but theirs?

She squeezed her eyes shut.

They were just illusions. She could see past illusions. Imara held her breath as she looked down the spiral staircase.

A frown tugged the corners of her mouth down. Fear threatened to pull her away from the staircase and back to safety.

Abe's eyebrows lowered with a frown. "Are you reconsidering— oh, you're already going." Abe started when Imara's foot hit the stairs. He nodded and clapped Siluk on the shoulder. "Come on, Siluk. We are not going to die. We got this."

Imara scanned the sand and umber-colored walls as she went down the spiral staircase. She noticed every crack, every crevice, every clump of dust. Her ears heard every shuffle of clothing, every footstep, every breath.

Abe said, "What do you think we'll see wh—"

"*Shh!*" Imara said. "I'm trying to listen for anything dangerous."

"Oh, good call." Abe's voice again interrupted the silence. "If something is in there, hearing it first could definitely—"

"*Shhhhhhhh!*"

Abe clamped his mouth shut and mouthed the word *Sorry*.

The corners of Imara's mouth turned up in a smile.

Abe squinted ahead and whispered, "I usually talk to keep everyone—" Abe stopped as soon as Imara flexed her jaw. "It doesn't matter," he said, and this time he kept his mouth shut.

Each time Imara lowered her foot to the next step, the skin on the back of her neck bristled up. Something was wrong, but she couldn't figure out what. Maybe it was the eerie silence or the thick dust, or maybe it was something else entirely. A droplet of sweat slid down her cheek. She brushed it away with the back of her hand.

Thick and sticky saliva filled her mouth as the air grew warmer with each step. The humidity was nice for her skin, but the added heat made it almost unbearable. Naki must hate this place. As a weather taster, Naki was more sensitive to strong temperatures and heavy humidity than the average person.

That thought sprung another. She should have realized it earlier. Heat rises. The air should be getting cooler the deeper they went, but instead it got hotter. Despite the heat, Imara shivered at the thought.

"Look!" Abe said.

He traced a carving in the wall with a slender finger. The crude carving wasn't ancient like everything else around them. The sharp cuts made a *T*, obviously carved with modern tools. Abe ran his fingers across the *T* and said, "*T* for *taggers*. It's the same style as the patches they wear."

Imara smiled and looked ahead. "Good. We're on the right track."

Siluk sniffed, and Abe flinched at the sound. Abe reached for his backpack and said, "I have some tissues if you need."

Siluk sniffed again and said, "Thanks, but I'm fine."

Abe shrugged and continued forward.

Imara stepped off the last stair and looked out at the catacombs ahead. A short tunnel led to a circular structure of some sort, but it was too dark to make out. Imara activated the flashlight app on her ring. The tunnel ceiling was void of any rope lights or sticky lamps. She huffed at the realization. They'd have to rely on their rings for light.

"Try this," Abe said. He shrank his hologram screen to the size of the flashlight then used his fingers to push the screen above his head. In that position, the hologram was both out of his sightline and perfect for illuminating the path ahead.

Imara nodded and copied his technique. Siluk activated his ring, but before he touched the hologram, he said, "I don't have service down here. Do you guys?"

Imara pulled down her screen to check, but she didn't have service either. And neither did Abe.

Siluk said, "I thought you could get service up to five hundred feet underground now."

"You can," Abe said.

"Maybe the taggers blocked service somehow so no one would find their location." Imara's swollen fingers pushed the hologram back above her head. She squeezed her fingers into fists, trying to control the heat swelling. She glanced up at the hologram with wide eyes. "I just realized something. Our temperature controlled underclothes can't work without service. That's why it's so hot in here."

Siluk sniffed. "We're going to stink if we're down here for very long. I'm already sweating."

Imara rolled her eyes at him, and with a huff turned back to the catacombs. The three flashlights lit the tunnel well. Imara still couldn't tell what the circular structure at the end of the tunnel was, but she'd find out soon enough.

Imara stepped forward with tiny steps. Even with the explanation for the heat, an eerie quiet danced through the air. Goosebumps formed on her flesh. She couldn't shake the feeling that the walls were made of eyes, watching her every movement.

Siluk sniffed again, and it only seemed strange because it was so loud. There was no whir of technology or air circulating through vents. In the silence, the still and quiet seemed louder than anything.

Imara stepped a toe's length at a time, afraid to trust anything she could see. Once past the tunnel, the circular structure became clear. A stone half wall formed a circle around an opening that led deep into the ground. Four large stone pillars stood ceiling to floor, equally distanced apart around the circle. The rough stone had been carved into jagged edges.

Imara stared down the circular opening beneath the pillars. The opening led to a long shaft that went much deeper down into the catacombs. A pulley system connected the four pillars together. Attached to the ropes from the pulleys was a wooden platform with raised sides. The circular shaft plus the wooden platform almost looked like a well, except the bucket was shallow and big enough to fit two people at a time.

Siluk stared at the platform. "I think the ancient Egyptians used this shaft to lower bodies into the deeper level of the catacombs."

"Creepy," Abe said, but he wore a smile.

Imara reached for one of the pillars. She wanted to test the strength with her hands since she didn't know if she could trust her eyes. The moment her fingers touched the stone, a burst of heat blew into their faces.

Fire.

The flames weren't visible yet, but smoke billowed out from around the shaft. The fire would be on them fast if they didn't act.

"Hurry!" Abe shouted. "Get on that wooden platform. We'll go down the shaft."

Siluk stepped forward, but Imara screamed, "NO!"

They looked at her in surprise, while charcoal balls of panic bounced off their skin. Siluk took another step toward the shaft, and a raven black rash of anxiety broke out over his wine fear spikes.

"Something is wrong," Imara said.

"What?" Abe asked. But Siluk took another step toward the shaft, ignoring Imara's warning. He glanced back at the smoke, and his fear spikes grew.

He would be on that platform soon if Imara didn't do something. Imara took a deep breath and tried to think like an outsider. Like someone watching this moment, but not living it. Like a school assignment. She had to stop them, but how? She had to change her method. People never listened to screams. She knew this.

Imara closed her eyes and thought back to a difficult lesson with Professor Santini. Imara sat in a desk at the front of the classroom. The two other truth seers in the school sat on either side of her. Professor Santini droned on about the cones and rods in the eye while everyone's eyes glazed over.

Professor Santini sighed and clicked out of the book she was reading on her hologram. When she spoke, it was with a soothing and gentle voice. The voice was key. That was number one.

Professor Santini stood in the middle of the room and said, "Pretend I'm a cone, and this classroom is the iris." Teach by example. Words aren't as strong as actions. That was number two.

Finally, Professor Santini said, "What does my position indicate? What limitations do I have?" Questions. She always did the questions. That was number three.

Imara opened her eyes and spoke in the calmest, gentlest voice she could find. "Go back to the staircase," she said.

This voice stopped Siluk in his tracks. With the fire almost upon them, Abe and Siluk didn't know what to do. Instead of waiting, Imara acted. She put her body in between the shaft and the others so they couldn't climb onto the platform. Then she pushed them toward the staircase. In a soothing lilt she said, "Do you want to be trapped inside the catacombs? We can go up the staircase to avoid the fire, can't we?"

As she spoke, Abe and Siluk stopped resisting and ran of their own accord toward the stairs. They made it just before the flames reached them. They hurried up the steps to safety. Imara climbed up the first two steps but then she turned and faced the fire. She stared at it and frowned. Abe grabbed her hand to force her up the stairs. She shook her head and pulled her hand away from him.

Imara stepped closer to the fire, and Abe and Siluk screamed. Abe grabbed her hand again to pull her up the stairs, but in a gentle voice she said, "Look."

She reached out until her hand touched the flames.

"Stop!" the others yelled. They screamed, but Imara stepped down the stairs and let herself be engulfed by the flames. In their hysteria, neither Abe nor Siluk realized Imara was free from harm.

"Look," she said with the same soothing lilt. Her calm silenced them, and she continued. "It's a trick. The fire's not really here. It's just hot air."

The skin around Abe's eyes stretched tight from how wide he held them open. His wine fear spikes jutted out almost as long as his arms. With a deep breath, he reached his hand toward the flame. "How did you know?" he asked.

Imara turned back to the fire. "I can see it. It looked funny, and the more I looked, the easier it was to see the truth. Now it looks like a shadow of a fire, and the flames flick with mechanical-like movements."

Siluk swallowed and took a step down, but didn't reach his hand out. "Why wouldn't you let us go down the shaft?" he asked.

Imara shook her head trying to get her thoughts to organize themselves. She said, "I don't know exactly. There was something funny about it." The jumble of thoughts in her head scattered everywhere, not at all like a school assignment. She thought back to the shaft, but couldn't remember what gave her pause. "I'd have to look at it again. Let's go."

A short noise of protest from Abe stopped Imara from stepping forward. She glanced back and said, "It's perfectly safe."

Both Abe and Siluk stared at her with quick and unsteady breaths. "Do you want me to hold your hands?" Imara offered, though she felt a little silly saying it.

Siluk scoffed, and Abe threw his hand across the air. "Oh, no. It's fine, I can do it. I mean unless Siluk doesn't want to feel left out because he has to hold your hand."

Siluk laughed. "No way. I can—" Imara watched a shiver go down Siluk's spine, but he lifted his chin. "I can do it."

Imara chose not to respond and turned back toward the shaft. With each step, the shadow of a fire seemed to die down. Abe and Siluk confirmed that it shrank with each step they took.

At the circular shaft, Imara stared at the pulley system and rope and wooden platform. She stared but didn't know what to look for. If this was a projector illusion then maybe something was hidden in the shaft that she couldn't see. Or maybe the rope or platform were only images being projected.

But even the best projectors flickered to some degree. Most flickered at a lightning-quick interval too fast for human eyes to detect. But not too fast for the eyes of truth seer. After several seconds of deep concentration, Imara found the inconsistency. Every few seconds, frayed rope strands appeared for the briefest moment. As she stared, the illusion melted away, and only the truth remained. The frayed rope was very old and badly damaged. Flimsy.

"It's the rope," she said. Imara pulled hard on the rope. It snapped in half with very little pressure. Without the rope, the wooden platform tumbled down the shaft. When it reached the bottom, the wood splintered and broke apart, the pieces flying everywhere.

Imara heard a heavy gulp from behind her. Abe whistled and said, "Good thing you didn't let us get on that platform."

"Come on," she said. "Let's keep looking."

A small path went along the outside of the shaft. To the left was a room, to the right were two small nooks filled with tombs. Imara peered into each nook looking for a flicker. To her relief, she saw nothing. Harmless.

Imara circled back to check the room on the left side. Now that she was close enough, she noticed the room looked like it had no floor. Imara gulped and took a step back. "Let's skip this. It's just a room, and I don't think it leads anywhere."

Imara moved to the other side of the shaft, across from the tunnel where they entered. A short flight of stairs descended to a small landing. A large stone table filled most of the landing. The rest of the second level was too far for the flashlights to illuminate. Imara moved forward, searching for more flickers.

Steps away from the staircase, something tugged at Imara's muscles to stop. Abe and Siluk lifted their feet for another step. Imara grabbed their arms. Her voice shook as she said, "Don't step there."

Abe frowned at the ground, and Siluk stepped back. "Is it dangerous?" Abe asked.

Imara stared at the wall next to them. "Extremely."

At this, Abe and Siluk took another step back as charcoal balls of panic bounced off their skin. Imara squatted down and brushed her fingers across a wire held tight from one side of the wall to the other. "It's a tripwire," Imara said.

Imara ran her fingers along the wire. When her fingers could no longer reach, she followed the wire with her eyes. The wire went up to the ceiling where Imara stared for ten full seconds before she saw through the illusion at the end of it. A large, black rubber ball hung from a rope. Long, silver spikes jutted out from the rubber ball. If the tripwire released, the spike ball would drop and impale anyone nearby.

"The tripwire is attached to a spike ball." Imara chewed her lip while she stared at it then looked down at her feet. Then back up at the spike ball. "I have an idea," she said.

Imara brought Abe and Siluk to one of the empty nooks on the right side of the shaft. She went back to the tripwire and stood against one wall. If she was close enough to the wall, hopefully the spike ball couldn't reach her.

Imara took three seconds to breathe then pulled the tripwire. The ball fell with a loud *whoosh*. Imara hugged the wall and tried to scoot away in case the ball got too close. Imara's eyes widened as the ball fell. Not straight through the passage like she expected, but straight toward her. Imara pressed her body against the wall and shuffled away, but not fast enough. A spike's point slid across her thigh. A scream escaped her mouth before she could stop it.

"What happened?" Abe called out.

"Stay back!" Imara screamed.

She finally shuffled out of the spike ball's reach. It swung like a pendulum back and forth through the passage. After several swings, it lost most of its momentum. Imara took short steps away from the wall and reached above the spike ball to grab the rope that held it. She breathed out in relief and said, "You can come back now. It's safe."

As soon as Abe was in view, he said, "What happened? Did you get hurt?"

"No," Imara said. "The spike ball scratched my leggings, which were my favorite, by the way." She shook her head. "It just scared me though. It didn't cut all the way through the fabric. Is there a jagged rock or something we can use to cut this rope? I want to get the spike ball out of here."

"I have a knife," Siluk said.

"Oh." Imara raised her eyebrows in surprise. "Perfect."

Imara took the knife from Siluk since he and Abe still couldn't see the spike ball. As she sawed the rope, Abe touched her arm. "Are you sure you're okay?"

Imara nodded and kept sawing.

"Well, in that case," Abe said, "Thanks for saving our lives. Twice."

Imara glanced back at Abe just as the knife severed the rope. He wore a broad smile and Imara noticed a greenish glint in his russet brown eyes. She smiled and kept her eyes on Abe as she handed the knife back to Siluk. "I expect you to return the favor if the chance arises."

Abe laughed. "I'll do my best."

Imara carried the spike ball to one of the empty nooks and then joined Abe and Siluk at the top of the stairs. Everyone kept their eyes on the stairs as they stepped down. At the bottom, Abe looked up and clenched his jaw. When Siluk looked up, he shrieked. He covered his face with one arm. With the other, he grabbed a rock from the ground and threw it at another illusion, barely missing Imara's ear.

"I know," Abe said. "Those snakes are creepy."

Siluk bared his teeth and backed up against the staircase. "I don't do snakes," he said. "I can do bears. Give me a bear any day. Or a wolf. I can handle a wolf. Or a moose or ten foot deep snow or a rushing river. But I don't do snakes."

Imara used the calmest voice she could muster. "It's an illusion. The snakes can't hurt you. You did the fire, you did the tripwire. You can do snakes."

Siluk shook the dark hair out of his face and took in a deep breath through his nose. He peeked up at what appeared to be huge pouncing snakes. "Okay, just tell me there isn't really a snake down here."

"Not a live one," Imara said, forgetting her calm voice.

"There are dead snakes?" Siluk took a step back onto the stairs.

Imara waved her hands apologetically. "No, sorry. I didn't mean to scare you. They're statues. They're carved into the wall." She stopped and reminded herself to use the calm voice again. "But the snakes aren't real, and they can't hurt you. Just trust me."

Siluk stepped down the remaining steps and rested his arm on the oval table in the center of the landing. On either side of the landing, two small passages were filled with tombs. The tombs were cut into the stone and almost looked like honeycomb, but with square cavities instead of hexagons. The cavities were about an arm's length high and an arm's length wide and just deep enough for a body.

After ensuring the passages were empty but for tombs, Imara turned her attention to the crypt room ahead of her. The large doorway had one snake on either side of it. A stone pillar sat in front of each snake. Through the doorway, a crypt sat in front of each of the three walls: the left wall, the back wall, and the right wall. Each crypt came up to Imara's waist and had beautiful carvings above it. Imara went to the crypt on the right, searching for an illusion.

The sand-colored carvings depicted a man with a short cloth wrapped around his waist. He held a contraption with beads. Next to the man was a cow-like animal with horns. Next to the animal was a man holding large wings with his arms.

The carvings were beautiful and would have captivated her attention in normal circumstances. But right now she was more concerned with illusions. Imara turned her head down to the top of the crypt. At first it looked like thick stone, but after awhile she noticed a flicker. A large hole appeared in the middle of the crypt. Water trickled in a little stream through the hole of the crypt. Imara squinted her eyes and said, "There's water here that we can use to fill up our water bottles. The taggers must have figured out how to dam the flood waters so they could get water in this spot."

Siluk nodded. "Yeah, Darius said even this level flooded during the big flood twenty years ago. He said the taggers probably rebuilt the dams, and all three levels of the catacombs are safe now. But he knows a lot more about it than me. He studies history when he's not at hila school."

The crypt on the back wall looked just like the first one. It was waist high with beautiful carvings above it. Imara rested her hand on top of the crypt, and the stone warmed her fingers. She slid her hand across the stone and stared at it, watching for another illusion.

"What?" Abe asked after several seconds. "Do you see something?"

Imara looked again. She narrowed her eyes and stared without blinking. But finally she said, "No. There's nothing."

Imara glanced back at the crypt with water. "How long can someone live without water?"

Siluk stood in front of the third crypt, but his gulp was still loud enough to hear.

"I think about three days," Abe said.

Imara nodded. "The Judge said the hostages had three days. You don't think he meant..."

"Three days is a lot," Abe said. "We should have plenty of time."

Imara tried to ignore the pit in her stomach. Three days wasn't that long, but it would be enough. It had to be.

SEVEN

IMARA SHOOK HER SHOULDERS TO CALM herself. She could find Naki in three days. She just needed to trust her skills like Professor Santini said. Imara glanced over the crypt room. "We should probably find a place to sleep. We can go down that shaft to the third level in the morning and start exploring." Imara bit her lips. "Although, with the rope broken…"

"I have rope," Siluk said. "And I agree we should find a place to sleep, but this room isn't big enough. And I'm not sleeping out by the snakes."

Imara turned back to Abe. His hands were jammed into his pockets, and he stared at her without breaking eye contact. The intensity of his gaze caused a flutter in her stomach. She pinched the inside of her cheek with her teeth to keep from smiling. She said, "I saw a good place to the left of the shaft. I'll go set everything up and you two can get water. The hole is in the middle of the crypt. It should be easy to find even though you can't see it."

Abe nodded, still staring at Imara. Siluk frowned and turned back to the final crypt on the left side of the room. The corners of Imara's mouth turned down as she walked to his side.

"What is it?" Imara asked.

Siluk frowned, but didn't take his eyes off the crypt. "It smells bad," he said.

Imara searched the crypt for any sign of an illusion or opening or anything. The striations in the stone varied exactly like regular stone, which meant nothing obvious was wrong. But she kept staring and finally saw it. A slight flicker in the center of the stone. Imara focused on that spot and narrowed her eyes as she concentrated even more.

Imara stared until her eyes watered, and finally she saw the flicker again. This time, a black button appeared during the flicker. She concentrated on the button until it became a steady in and out image. After a few more seconds, the stone image faded, and the button was clear as day.

Imara pressed her thumb into the large, black button, and the crypt started to open like a door.

Imara shivered as she prepared herself for danger. Inside the crypt could be another trap. A spike ball. Or a laser. Or even dead bodies. The door slid at a glacial pace, and Imara stared inside, never breaking concentration. Imara prepared herself to fend off any threat.

"What is it?" Abe whispered.

"It's a..." Imara narrowed her eyes. "I think it's an outhouse."

"What?" Abe asked dumbfounded.

"It smells like crap," Siluk said.

Imara nodded and said, "Yeah, literally."

Abe laughed, and all of the tension prickling inside them released in an instant. "And here I thought it was going to be a closet of guns or swords or something. Guess we know what to do when nature calls."

"Speaking of which," Siluk said. "Do you mind if I use the facilities?"

Imara pointed inside the crypt. "Just go straight ahead. There's a chair thing. You should be able to feel it if you stick your hands out. I'll go set up the beds so you have some privacy."

Abe perked up. "I'll go with you. Because of the privacy thing." But then he winked at Imara, and a smile overtook her face.

"Lead the way," Abe said to her.

Imara and Abe went back up the short staircase. Imara stopped at the room they had passed earlier. She stared until the illusion covering the floor melted away. The room was large enough for all of them and more to sleep. Along the back wall, and two side walls, long stone structures came out from the wall.

"What do you think of this spot?" Imara asked.

Abe's eyes flitted around the room. Short, wine-colored fear spikes poked out from his skin, but they were blunted. That was a good sign.

He turned his mouth up to a grin. "It looks like an enormous, never-ending pit to me, so it must be excellent."

Imara snickered and found herself staring at the toned muscles in his arm rather than the colors coming off it. She jerked her head away to point at the stone structures. "Sorry. The ground is stone, but there are also these stone things built into the wall. They're sort of like couches."

She stepped into the room and placed a hand on the stone couch to the left. "Can you see this?" she asked.

Abe nodded. "Yes, and those other two. It looks like you're floating in the air though."

Imara smiled again. He seemed to be enormously amused, and she liked that. "We can sleep on these couches tonight. Hopefully we'll find everyone tomorrow, and we won't have to stay more than one night."

Imara stared at the ground. "I wonder…"

She unzipped her backpack and unrolled a sleeping bag as she threw it on the ground. "Can you see the sleeping bag?" she asked.

Abe's eyebrows went up. He squished his mouth up and said, "Nope. It went down the pit of doom."

Imara snickered again. "Pit of doom?"

"If you could see it, you would agree."

Imara grinned but tried to focus. "Do you think if we got something taller than the sleeping bag you'd be able to see it? You can still see me, right?"

Abe pointed. "Your feet are gone, but I can see your legs from your ankle and up."

Imara scanned the bottom edge of the room. "I wonder what's causing the illusion. If we can find the projector, we can probably turn it off."

"I'll help you look," Abe said.

Imara's eyebrows rose high on her forehead as Abe stepped into the room. His eyes avoided the ground as he walked, but his fear spikes hardly grew as he walked on the "pit of doom." He went straight for the edge of the room and kicked the stone, feeling for a projector.

That was smart. Imara hated to think it was convenient that Mr. Nazari had been taken hostage, but it certainly was helpful to have Abe here. Imara probably wouldn't be here without him.

Imara kicked the edge of wall just like Abe did, but soon they went through the entire room and found nothing. Imara picked the hair at the back of her neck. "The projector is probably hidden with another illusion. A stronger one, I bet.

78

Maybe it's attached to the ceiling." She looked up with her hand resting on her neck.

Abe stepped toward her. Something about his steps sounded different than before. They were heavier or more purposeful maybe. She glanced back at him, and he ran his fingers through his hair with a cool smile. Just as his confidence threatened to sweep her off her feet, Abe's foot caught on the sleeping bag that still lay on the ground.

His arms flailed, and his feet danced as he tried to balance himself. He turned his head, looking around as he wobbled. A gasp escaped him when he looked down at the floor. His eyes shut tight, and he stepped around for balance.

Imara jumped forward and caught hold of his arm. She steadied him immediately. When he opened his eyes, several flashes of violet embarrassment shot out from his skin.

Abe tilted his head to the side, and he snapped his fingers into a finger gun. "I forgot about that sleeping bag."

Imara smiled. All at once, her hands burned in awareness of his skin's warmth. She dropped her hands away from his arm and averted her eyes. "It's impressive you can stand on this floor at all, considering it looks like a pit of doom."

Abe shrugged, the violet flashes of light all but gone. "Oh, it's not so bad."

Imara turned and sat on one of the stone couches. "Do you want to know a secret about me?"

"Yes," he said as a smile played across his lips. He sat down next to her, and that intense gaze of his seemed to stare straight into her soul.

Imara picked the hair at the back of her neck and looked at the ground. "I'm terrified of heights. I couldn't be in this room without my hila."

Abe shook his head, brushing off her comment. "Everyone is a little bit afraid of heights."

Imara clenched her fists and tried to smile. "I didn't say I was afraid, I said I was terrified." She looked to the side. "You know that walkway at the school that's in between the two large staircases? It's like a balcony; the banister looks out over the entrance to the school."

"I know the one."

Imara looked down and took a small breath. She said in a quiet voice, "I have nightmares about leaning on that banister and falling because it's not secure. Any time I have to go across that walkway, I stand as far away from the banister as possible. It freaks me out every time."

Abe stared into Imara's eyes, seemingly deep in thought. She could see his emotions, but he couldn't see hers. This gave her an advantage, and for some reason she felt the need to even things out by telling him a secret.

"Did something happen that made you so afraid of heights?" he asked.

Imara shook her head, and as she did, Abe scooted an inch closer to her. "No," she said. "Nothing I can remember anyway."

Abe moved his hand closer to hers, and Imara's cheeks flushed. She willed her hands to stop sweating, but it did no good. She hoped a smile would help her relax. With lips turned up, she said, "You must be very brave to walk on a floor that looks like a hole. I'm impressed you did it so easily."

Abe took her hand, and Imara slammed her mouth shut to keep her heart from leaping out. He smiled and said, "You're just saying that to make me feel better for tripping."

"I'm not. You are brave."

He squeezed her hand and leaned in close, and before she knew it, he kissed her. Their lips only barely brushed against each other before he pulled away, and she wished he had lingered just a moment longer. But considering they only met a few hours earlier, a short kiss was probably the most appropriate.

She looked down and felt his chin brush against her hair. Maybe it was short, but Imara's heart pounded, and her palms were all sweaty, and she was sure her emotions would burst right through her. For one small moment, all of the danger around them seemed to vanish. All concern for hostages and fanatics and illusions were mere shadows in the back of her mind. For one moment, it was just Imara and Abe and a simple kiss.

"We should probably get back," Abe said, returning them to reality. "I need to set up the intruder alarm box so we can sleep, and I still have to teach Siluk how to use the stun guns in case we run into any taggers."

Imara nodded, unable to control her smile even a little bit. She said, "Will the intruder alarm still work without service?"

Abe zipped open his backpack and pulled out a small black box with an electronic screen on one side. "Not all the features, but the sensors can still tell the difference between footsteps and us moving around in our sleeping bags. I'll have to turn it on and off manually, but that's not a big deal. You helped us through the illusions. As long as we survive the night without getting attacked by taggers, I think we can do this."

EIGHT

THE NEXT MORNING, IMARA'S ALARM RANG,
and she sat up with a start. She tapped her ring to silence the
ringing. She turned to Abe to ask him to turn off the intruder
alarm, but he was already awake and rolling up his sleeping
bag. His teal blue shirt pulled tight across his shoulders as he
stretched his arms. He winked at Imara when she caught his
eye.

She returned his wink with a giddy grin and then looked
over at Siluk. He dived into his sleeping bag. Abe and Imara
shared a look, and Imara rolled her eyes.

Abe got up and tapped Siluk's head. "Wake up, Siluk. We
have to go find your friend. What's his name again?"

Siluk sat up with a grunt. "Darius." He grunted again and
got out of his sleeping bag. "I hate waking up," he said under
his breath.

The three of them packed their sleeping bags and went to
the crypt room to fill their water bottles. It was slow going
with all the illusions, but Siluk made it past the snakes
without too much flinching.

While Abe and Siluk were in the crypt room, Imara left
them to explore the two levels they had already discovered.
She pulled up her map from Professor Santini and wrote

notes on it about the illusions they had encountered. Over the shaft, Imara wrote *fire when you touch the shaft*. In the room with couches she wrote, *pit of doom*. And over the pillars that stood outside the crypt room, she wrote *pouncing snakes*. Imara walked through the whole area one last time. As she expected, there was no other entrance to the third level except through the shaft. That meant they had to use Siluk's rope.

Soon she gathered Abe and Siluk at the shaft. Imara kept her hands off the circular stone so she wouldn't set off the fire illusion again. Siluk pulled the remaining frayed rope from the pulley system and replaced it with a rope from his backpack. The platform may have been smashed to bits at the bottom of the shaft, but the pulley system was in perfect condition. They lowered themselves down the shaft one at a time.

Once at the bottom, Imara arranged her hologram screen so the flashlight and map were side by side. The path ahead led to an intersection. The path to the right of that branched off into small passages filled with tombs. Any of the tombs might be a good place to hide a hostage, so Imara started off in that direction.

Abe and Siluk walked on either side of Imara with their stun guns ready for taggers. Imara marched forward ready to do her job of seeing through the illusions.

Imara took careful steps and tried to look at every part of the path all at once. She glanced from one part of the path to the next until her eyes fell on a mound of dirt. It didn't look wrong so much as it *felt* wrong. Imara glared at the spot until the mound shimmered out of focus. She focused on the shimmer, and the mound faded away. Underneath the illusion was a pit with sharp rocks at the bottom. The pit was large enough for two people to fall into. It sat in the middle of the path, which made it difficult to maneuver without seeing it.

"Get behind me," Imara said. "I'm going to lead you around a pit with rocks." She tiptoed around the path until they had safely passed it. On the map, she wrote *pit with sharp rocks*. She wanted to send the updated map to Abe and Siluk, but without service it was impossible.

They started exploring the passages that branched off from the main path, and it quickly felt like a maze. Each passage was a different length, and they all had their own illusions. Some of the passages connected to paths, and others didn't. At least they had the map from Professor Santini. Without it, they would've been lost in fifteen minutes. So far, none of the tombs had anything inside them except a few stray skeletons.

In one passage, Imara stared at the ground for any illusions, but brushed her hand across the empty tombs in case another illusion was only making them appear empty. On the path ahead, a bit of dirt shined with a silvery glint. Imara stared through the illusion and saw a cluster of short spikes waiting for an unsuspecting foot. Imara pushed Abe and Siluk behind her to get past the spikes and continue on to another passage.

So far, the illusions down on this level were less frightening and less dangerous than the ones above. Still, a close eye was imperative.

They rounded a corner into a corridor. The first half of the corridor was filled with tombs. Halfway through, the tombs switched to crypts with elaborate carvings. Near the end, several passages and paths branched off from the corridor. A large chamber stood at the end of the corridor.

Imara glanced along the floor of the corridor, which immediately shimmered. After a moment, small pits big enough for a foot appeared before her eyes. Silver spikes poked out the sides and bottom of each pit. The foot pits polka dotted the path in a checkerboard pattern.

Imara smiled. Professor Santini was right. With each illusion, it got a little easier to see the truth. It took less than three seconds that time.

"Be careful on this path," Imara said in a hushed voice.

Siluk got serious, but Abe grinned. "Are you just saying that to scare us?"

Imara's head snapped back. "No."

"Are you sure this isn't a normal path?"

Imara raised an eyebrow, testing him. "You don't trust me?" she asked.

Abe shrugged. "What do you see?"

Imara explained about the pits in a checkerboard pattern. Abe asked all sorts of questions about the size and distance from each other. Imara helped him find the edge of a pit so he could feel it with his foot.

Then, to her surprise, he hopped over the pit and landed safely on the other side. He looked to her with a cocky smile.

Imara's eyes widened, but she couldn't help be impressed. "What are you doing?" she said, scolding.

"Jumping," Abe said as he hopped over another pit.

Imara followed after him, and Siluk followed close behind her with short steps.

Imara grimaced. "I told you those pits have metal spikes in them. If you miss, your foot will get pierced with spikes."

Abe smiled and whipped his hair back before hopping over another pit. "Yeah, but don't you think it's cool I can avoid the pits when I can't see them?"

Imara's mouth twitched into a smile, but her breath caught in her throat as he hopped again. "No," she said and pursed her lips to make the point clear. "I think it's dangerous. Why are you so reckless?"

"Because I like it when you make that face."

Imara pursed her lips tighter, trying to keep a pesky smile off her lips. Smiling would only encourage him, and those spikes were sharp. "Get back over here," she chided.

Her lips may have been pursed, but she had no control over the smile in her eyes. She thought he was brave for standing on a floor that looked like a pit of doom, but apparently he was more of a risk-taker than she realized. She tried very hard not to like it so much.

Abe landed one more hop, but this time his toe came to the edge of a pit. His foot fell forward, and he pulled it back just in time.

Imara froze, and again her breath caught in her throat.

Wine spikes of fear poked out from Abe, but they dissipated almost as fast. He took a tiny step backward and turned to Imara with a grin. "All right," he said. "I guess that was a tiny bit reckless."

Imara pulled him behind her. "From now on, I lead the way."

Imara studied the crypts in the corridor but found no illusions. The chamber had stone couches like the ones upstairs in the pit of doom, but nothing else of significance. Imara chose one of the paths leading out from the corridor, and they set off to explore. The more she saw them, the easier it was to see truth under the illusions. Soon it was instantaneous. On each new path, Abe asked what was really there. Imara explained what she saw, and then Abe and Siluk described what they saw.

After awhile they got into a rhythm. Imara up front, Abe next, and Siluk last. With Abe and Siluk behind her, Imara maneuvered through the illusions and kept them all safe. She took careful notes on all of the illusions on her map, and she made Abe and Siluk repeat back the truth so she knew they remembered it.

After a few hours, they rounded yet another corner and found themselves in a tomb-filled passageway. The ground had an oval hole off to one side. It was easy to avoid, and Imara pointed it out, but then she gave out a loud sigh.

"What's wrong?" Abe asked.

Imara frowned and kicked the ground with her toe as she walked. "What exactly are we looking for?" she said. She shook her head until the curls bounced off of her forehead. "We've been searching for hours, and all we've found are traps and passageways and dirt." Imara rubbed her temple. "We need to find people, not passageways."

"Cheer up, Imara." Siluk said. "Darius is never wrong. They're in here; we just have to keep looking."

Imara glowered at Siluk. "Just because they're in here, doesn't mean we're going to find them in time. How do we know we haven't passed them already?"

The tombs in the passageway ended just as the path curved into a bend. As Imara rounded the bend, Abe stepped out in front of her. He wore a cool half smile and walked backward in front of her. She knew he was trying to impress her again. He said, "We'll find—"

Before he could say another word, his foot found the edge of another pit. The pit was so large, it was more like a cliff and dropped into an enormous clearing of stone. Abe's foot slipped over the edge, and he teetered backward.

Without a second thought, Imara clutched his hand and yanked him toward her onto the narrow path. Abe held her hand tight, his fear spikes growing larger than Imara had ever seen them.

Imara gave one last tug, and Abe came back toward her. But all the force she used to pull him back sent her flying over the edge of the cliff. She tried to turn and grasp onto the rock, to Abe, to anything, but it was no use.

Imara struck the bottom of the pit and rolled a few times before she slowed to a stop and tightened her body into the fetal position. She groaned and her knees pricked with pain as she stood. She held up the light from her ring and saw that she was far beneath the path where Abe and Siluk stood.

Abe put his belly on the narrow pathway and reached down over the cliff side. "Grab my hand," he said.

Imara reached up, but there were still a few feet before their hands could touch. Abe's eyebrows lowered while wine-colored fear spikes grew out from his skin. Covering each spike was a raven black rash of anxiety. Next to the spikes dripped mustard yellow guilt. "I'm sorry," he said. "I see the pit, but the path looked wider than it really is."

Imara shrugged. "It's not your fault. It was an accident. Do you have any more rope, Siluk?"

"No."

"Stay there," Abe said. "We'll go back and get the rope from the shaft."

Siluk nodded, and they both turned the corner and were out of sight before Imara could say a word.

"Stop!" Imara called after them.

She waited a moment, but didn't hear a response. She frowned and kicked a small rock into the cliff-side. She didn't like Abe and Siluk traveling the catacombs alone. Even through the paths they already knew. They could probably remember some of the illusions and avoid the traps, but not all of them. Plus, Imara had the map so they were just as likely to get lost.

Imara kicked another rock and shook her head. She had clothes in her backpack. They could have made a rope with the clothes. Or with a belt. She could think of several ways to get out if only they had stayed and used their heads.

Abe, reckless again. And impulsive. But also sweet. She had seen both guilt and fear coming off his skin. He knew it was his fault Imara was in that pit, and he felt awful.

Imara kicked one last rock and turned to stare back at the path above. There was only one thing to do now. She'd have to get out of the pit and find them before they got hurt.

Imara sat down and unzipped her backpack. She took out all of the clothes and tied them together into a makeshift rope.

The last pair of pants she tied to the end. Then, turning the pants into a circle, she tied them in the same spot so there was a loop at the end of her clothes-rope.

Imara hung her now-empty backpack on her shoulders and walked along the bottom edge of the cliff. She examined the cliff side with each step. After a few minutes, she saw something useful. A bit of stone on the top edge of the cliff jutted out into a narrow ridge. Imara swung the rope of clothes around a few times and then threw it up, attempting to land the loop around the ridge.

The first throw fell way too low. Imara threw again, and it was closer. After ten tries, Imara frowned. She wasn't strong enough to throw the rope high enough. She'd have to think of a different idea.

Imara walked and scanned the ground. Then, she looked up and scanned the cliff-side. She tried climbing the cliff wall, but gave that up within seconds. There weren't enough things to grab or step onto, and her fingers weren't strong enough for any kind of rock climbing.

Maybe she could fill her backpack full of rocks and attach the clothes rope to it. Then she could throw it up onto the path and climb the rope. Imara's head hung. But, the weight of the rocks probably wouldn't be heavy enough to support her weight. And she couldn't even throw the rope high enough. There was no way she could throw a backpack full of rocks high enough.

Imara paced back and forth. After a few paces, she tripped on a rock about the size of two fists. She kicked it away annoyed, but then looked back at it. A small half smile formed on her lips.

NINE

ABE AND SILUK STEPPED THROUGH THE passages as fast as they could while avoiding the traps. They stopped for a moment, and Siluk rested his shoulder on a nearby wall.

"Ouch!" he said in surprise. Siluk touched the wall behind him and said, "This is sharp. It's another illusion."

Abe ran his fingers across the wall opposite Siluk and said, "This one's sharp too."

Abe frowned and closed his eyes. He pointed his fingers in different directions and said, "I thought this passage had that brick thing that made you trip and fall."

Siluk shook his head. "No, we turned four to the right, then two to the left. The brick thing is in the path that leads to the winding corridor."

"Then this should be the passage with the line of jagged rocks," Abe said with a grimace. "Imara never said the walls had spikes. She would have told us."

Siluk shifted his eyes back and forth while he tapped his teeth together. His nostrils flared with a big sniff before he said, "We must have taken a wrong turn."

Abe kicked the ground and raised his voice. "How can we get back if we don't even know where we are?"

"Hello?"

Abe and Siluk looked at each other with wide eyes. "Did you hear that?" Abe asked, already drawing his stun gun.

Siluk nodded and pulled a stun gun from his pocket.

"Is somebody out there? Can you hear me?"

A muffled pounding made Abe turn, searching for the direction of the sound. Something about the voice said hostage rather than tagger. But it could have been a trap. They shouldn't have left Imara alone.

Siluk breathed in through his nose and let the air out in a slow breath. He pointed down the passage when they heard the voice again, a little louder.

"Help!"

"It's my dad," Abe shouted and he rushed toward the noise.

"Be careful of illusions," Siluk called after him.

Abe ignored him and walked along the edge of the wall hoping to avoid any traps.

Abe shouted, "Where are you?" After a few shouts, Abe came to the end of the path. The path ended like a dead-end, except through the wall, Abe heard muffled shouts and pounding. His father was just on the other side. Abe dragged his hand across the wall. As far as he could tell, there weren't any spikes or other dangers on the wall itself. Just to be sure he had the right spot, Abe hit the wall three times. A matching three pounds sounded back. "We're right here," Abe said. "We'll find a way to get you out."

Abe grabbed a large rock from the ground and hit the wall as hard as he could. Siluk chose a rock and joined Abe. They pounded the wall over and over, but the stone showed no wear and no change. They heard pounding from the other side of the wall. At least two people on the other side tried to break down the stone. Abe and Siluk continued to hit the wall with rocks, but it seemed to no avail.

At last, Abe's rock hit something, and they heard a loud click. The stone moved to the side and began to open like a door, just like the crypt with the outhouse. Abe and Siluk backed away while some mechanism moved the stone.

With the stone door out of the way, Abe and Siluk faced a small chamber. Inside stood Mr. Nazari and Darius. Mr. Nazari's suit hung limp and wrinkled. This was probably the only time in his life Abe had seen his father so unkempt.

"Abraxas," Mr. Nazari said with a smile. "I thought that was you."

Siluk smiled at Darius as he said, "Dude, I'm glad we found you."

Mr. Nazari stared at the opening. "How did you get the stone to move to the side like that? We tried for hours when we first got here."

Abe shrugged. "I don't know. There must be a button or something. There was a door like that upstairs, but I couldn't see the button. I must have hit it on accident."

Darius shook the bouncy, golden hair out of his eyes. He picked at his facial hair and said, "A button? That was pure stone with dirt from the second century, and then they go and destroy it with modern mechanics. If anyone needed proof that taggers are barbarians, this door alone would be proof!"

Siluk laughed. "Glad to see your priorities are straight after being taken hostage."

Abe gave Darius a sideways glance and asked, "How do you know the dirt was from the second century?"

"My hila," Darius said.

"Oh," Abe said, hoping he didn't look as sheepish as he felt. "What's your hila?"

"Elemental hearing."

Abe stared with a blank expression, and Darius must've realized more of an explanation was needed.

"I can tap on things and hear what they're made of."

Abe's eyebrows raised, impressed. "You can hear individual elements?"

"Technically yes, but it takes an insane amount of concentration to hear things that specific. Don't even get me started on the number of chemistry classes I've had to take."

Darius stepped out of the chamber and scanned the path. "Where are we?" he asked.

"It's the Catacombs of Kom el Shoqafa, just like you said," Siluk said with a grin.

Darius's frown dove deeper, and he shook his head.

"What's wrong?" Siluk asked.

Darius raked his fingers through his golden hair. "Not the catacombs." Darius stroked a nearby stone wall with tangible heartbreak in his voice. "I cannot believe anyone would destroy a place with such rich history. How could someone so brazenly add modern technology to a structure like this? They've completely ruined a treasure. This place is a treasure! Or it was. But now?"

Abe gave Darius another sideways glance, but chose to keep his mouth shut.

Siluk shook his head and laughed again. "It sort of seems like you're more concerned with the catacombs than you are about getting rescued. We risked our lives for you, you know? You could have died down here."

94

"Well," said Mr. Nazari. "We probably wouldn't have died."

"A person can only live three days without water," Siluk retorted.

Mr. Nazari nodded. "True, but look." He pointed back into the chamber. Food and water sat on the floor. "The Judge brought it to us this morning."

"Why?" Abe asked.

Mr. Nazari shrugged. "I have no idea, but I think it's clear the Judge never intended to kill us."

Abe stared at the food and water, searching for the logic behind it. The Judge said they had three days to bow to his demands before he killed the hostages. They all assumed it meant he would let them die of dehydration. They must have been wrong about that.

Darius grunted under his breath. "Maybe the Judge didn't want to murder us, but he still murdered the catacombs."

Siluk grinned. "Come on. We need to get back."

"Back to what?" Mr. Nazari asked.

"One other person came with us," Abe said. "She fell into a pit. We have to find her and then we need to figure out how to get her out."

Siluk took out a tissue and blew his nose. He sniffed a few times and pointed. "I think it's this way."

Abe didn't know what Siluk based this assumption on, but since he had no idea which direction to go, he figured it was as good a place to start as any. Siluk and Darius tiptoed down the path while Siluk explained all about the illusions and traps they had encountered so far.

Abe walked behind them with his dad. Mr. Nazari said to Abe, "How did you figure out we were in these catacombs?"

Abe pointed ahead. "Darius told Siluk about this place, and when you all got kidnapped, Siluk told us."

Mr. Nazari nodded.

Abe turned to his dad. "Do you know a *Meera*? Or *Ameira* maybe. Or *Amara*. She goes to the school."

Mr. Nazari raised an eyebrow. "Why?"

"I synced with her at the graduation party, but I broke the connection too soon and lost her contact info. And... it's a little too late to ask her name now. She has dark brown skin, short hair around the back and sides, but with curls on top. Big eyes. Like, really noticeably big eyes. And they're dark, but with golden flecks."

Mr. Nazari shrugged. "I don't know all of the students personally."

"Her sister was the valedictorian," Abe said.

Mr. Nazari stopped and looked at Abe surprised. In a louder voice he said, "Imara? Imara Kalu, the truth seer?"

Siluk stopped his conversation with Darius and glanced back at Abe.

Abe nodded while a smile tugged one corner of his lips. "Yeah, Imara. I knew I was saying it wrong. So, you know her?"

"Of course I know her," Mr. Nazari said as he continued walking. "I've thought about hiring her. I probably won't since we already have Professor Santini, and truth seers are so rare, but Imara is a good teacher. Her explanations are clear, but captivating. I don't know, maybe I will hire her when she graduates. She can always teach a class on basics."

Mr. Nazari trailed off while he adjusted his cuff links. Abe held back a chuckle at his dad's distraction. Siluk glanced back again, and Mr. Nazari slid his thumbs across the silver cuff links once more, but caught himself. His raised an eyebrow suspiciously and said, "Why do you ask?"

"I kissed her," Abe said with a grin.

Both Siluk and Darius turned around in surprise. Siluk's mouth hung open until he said, "When?"

Abe knitted his eyebrows together, and Siluk clamped his mouth shut, accepting that he wasn't meant to be part of the conversation.

"You really kissed her?" Mr. Nazari asked with narrowed eyes.

Abe nodded, and his smile grew.

"That's going to have some consequences." Mr. Nazari's voice was thick with warning.

Abe clenched his jaw, and his eyes flashed with a sudden anger. "I don't regret it, if that's what you're implying."

Mr. Nazari's raised an eyebrow for the third time. "You don't even know her. How do you know you won't regret it?"

Abe rolled his eyes. "Fine. Even if I do regret it, I still think it was worth it."

Mr. Nazari stared at Abe, clearly more intrigued than anything. Then his face changed to a whole different expression that Abe couldn't place. Mr. Nazari said, "Well, you know she's—"

But then Mr. Nazari stopped himself, and his face changed again. "Never mind," he said.

Abe looked at his dad, startled. "She's what?"

Mr. Nazari shook his head and ignored the question.

Siluk laughed quietly. "You'll find out." Siluk frowned, which he tried to hide with a snarl. "It won't take long," Siluk said as he turned to keep walking down the path.

Abe's gut twisted as he watched Siluk. "What?" he said with clenched fists.

Abe turned to his dad who gave a disapproving glare to the back of Siluk's head. "What is he talking about?" Abe asked his dad.

"Don't worry about it," Mr. Nazari said, and he wouldn't say another word.

Siluk walked with confidence down the path until he reached an intersection. Siluk gave a pointed look in each direction, and his frown deepened.

Abe rubbed his chin. "Do you have any idea where you're going? I thought you said it was this way."

Siluk frowned. "I'm trying to figure out the right way. It's hard in here. It's dusty."

Mr. Nazari pushed to the front of the group. "I'll lead the way. None of you children should even be involved in this."

Darius rolled his eyes and picked at his beard again.

Mr. Nazari was about to lean against the wall, but Abe called out, "Don't touch that!"

Mr. Nazari stood up straight and a miniature look of confusion appeared on his face.

"That wall is sharp, Dad. And we're adults, not children. You and Darius have no idea what to expect in these catacombs. Not to mention there might be taggers around any corner. Siluk and I should lead the way. We've been wandering around all day and know how to avoid the traps... mostly."

Mr. Nazari smiled, but Abe could see his dad's eyebrow twitching with disappointment. He waved Abe and Siluk ahead. "I'll be right here if there is any danger."

Abe tried to hide his smile. "Okay, Dad. Thanks." Then he rolled his eyes so only Siluk could see.

Siluk smiled under a tissue. He blew his nose while Abe surveyed the path ahead. Right, left, or straight. The right side looked more familiar, but he wasn't sure. They all looked so similar.

Siluk turned his head to one side. His chest rose and fell as he took in deep breaths. He pointed to the right and said, "This way."

"You sure?"

"No."

Abe nodded. "Well, I guess that's as good as we're going to get. To the right it is."

They started down the path. Abe guessed this was the passage with spike-covered pillars, but there was no way to be sure. They crept through the passage with their bodies brushing against the tombs in the wall.

"Hey, Darius," Abe said. "Why are you so into history? Shouldn't you be a chemist with a hila like elemental hearing?"

Darius scoffed. "Chemistry is so boring. I study it out of necessity, not desire. But history?" He smiled. "History is about people. Real lives. Real stories. Plus, I use my hila all the time studying history. I can tell all sorts of things about artifacts that most historians only dream of knowing. And since I can hear down to individual elements when I listen hard enough, carbon dating is a breeze."

"*Shh*," Siluk said. "Do you guys hear that?"

Abe reached for his stun gun, but the noise didn't sound like people. It sounded like a great whooshing and churning.

Abe gripped his stun gun as they walked toward the sound. Soon they reached a fork in the road. One side of the fork looked bright and cheery. The walls twinkled as if gems peeked out from the rock, and the light reflected off them. Deep down the path, a bright light shined as if the path led straight outside the catacombs.

Along the bottom of the path were fuzzy white balls that looked like cotton. The noise definitely came from this side of the fork. An inviting *whoosh* came from air conditioners built into the stone. With non-functioning temperature controlled underclothes, they all leaned toward the air conditioners. The cool air beckoned them forward.

The path on the other side of the fork was dark and foggy. There was no brightness and no twinkling. The only light came from hot coals, which covered the entire path. The coals glowed, still hot and burning. The heat from the path was sticky and searing.

Mr. Nazari pushed ahead of Siluk toward the twinkling path with air conditioners. "This way," he said.

Abe grabbed his dad's shoulder and said, "No."

Mr. Nazari laughed and pointed to the path with the hot coals. "Well we can't go that way."

Abe turned to Siluk. "Why would they put air conditioners down here? Nobody uses them now that we have temperature controlled underclothing."

Siluk shrugged. "Maybe it's because there's no service and the temperature controls don't work."

Abe nodded. "True, but still. Doesn't it seem weird that one path is so inviting and the other so scary?"

Siluk brought his hand to his chin and nodded in thought.

Abe turned to the path with the hot coals. "Remember upstairs. The fire looked bad, but it wasn't. And the wooden platform looked good, but it wasn't. I bet what looks good is bad and what looks bad is good."

Siluk nodded, but Darius stepped in between Abe and Siluk. "Are you crazy?" Darius said. "We're not walking on hot coals. They'll burn through our shoes in seconds."

Abe shook his head. "They aren't hot coals. I think. It's just an illusion. There's a projector or something creating the image. We aren't sure how it works, but the coals aren't real."

Darius planted his feet and crossed his arms. "They look real to me. And besides, I can feel heat coming from that path. Either we turn around or we go down the twinkling path. Listen. You can hear the gentle whir from the air conditioners. And the walls sparkle. Illusion or not, that path is safe, and you won't convince me otherwise."

Abe clenched his jaw and narrowed his eyes at Darius. "Fine," Abe said. "I'll walk on the coals myself so you know it's safe."

Abe turned toward the path, but Mr. Nazari stopped him. "Wait!" Mr. Nazari said. "Isn't there something we can put on the coals to test if they're real or not? Something from your bag? If the coals are real, you'll burn yourself."

Abe stopped and unzipped his bag with a grumble. He was certain the coals were fake, but he grabbed his extra shirt and threw it down anyway.

The instant his shirt touched the ground a flame shot up from the coals and engulfed the shirt. Darius gasped and took a step back. Mr. Nazari's eyes widened, his face serious but ready to fight the fire.

Abe shook his head. "You're both looking at the wrong thing. Look down."

Mr. Nazari squinted his eyes at Abe. Abe shook his head again and bent down to pick up the shirt. It was unharmed except for some dirt. "See," Abe said, brushing the dirt away. "The coals are fake."

Abe put the shirt back in his bag and took a step forward. He was certain the coals weren't there, but his thumping heart wouldn't steady. His hands were shaky and sweaty, but he continued until he was on top of the coals. He turned and beckoned to the others. "Come on," he said. "It's warm in here, but there are no coals."

Siluk followed behind Abe. After watching Abe and Siluk get through without burning, Mr. Nazari and Darius followed on tiptoes. They took careful steps across the path and rounded a bend into a small chamber. Inside the chamber, a tall woman with terrifyingly red eyes leapt out at them. She brandished a heavy rod, ready to hit anyone who dared cross her.

Flames shot out from the wall on the left, and Darius screamed. He backed up behind a pillar that jutted out from the wall on the right. Mr. Nazari picked up rocks and threw them at the woman, but she seemed invincible. Soon, he was behind the pillar with Darius.

Abe continued forward, assuming the chamber led out to another path. He took slow and careful steps. "She's not really here. It's just an illusion," he said more to himself than anyone.

Abe lifted his foot to take another step when they all heard a scream from behind them.

"STOP!"

TEN

IMARA'S PULSE POUNDED AS ABE HELD A foot in the air, ready to step forward. She held her breath until he turned to face her. She let out a puff of air in relief, and then closed her eyes and shook her head. When she opened her eyes, she raised a pointed finger. "No one is allowed to go anywhere in these catacombs without me. Ever again. Understood?" She tried to sound authoritative, but her voice shook in fear.

Wine-colored spikes of fear grew out from Abe. He took a step closer to Imara and stooped down. "What's wrong? Is she real?" Abe pointed to the woman with the rod.

Imara pushed past Siluk. "No, that's just a statue. But this is real."

She kicked the rock in front of Abe.

"What is it?" Abe asked.

"It's a rock. And you would have tripped over it if you took another step. And these," Imara grabbed onto tall spikes, which she knew must look strange to Abe since he couldn't see them. "These are spikes. Huge and dangerous spikes that could kill you if you tripped onto them."

Abe gulped and took another step backward.

"What were you doing in this chamber anyway?" Imara asked.

"We were trying to find you," Abe said.

"Why would you go here? This chamber ends with these huge spikes so you couldn't have come through this way. Why did you think this would lead you back to where I was?"

Abe's mouth dropped open, and he scratched the back of his head. "Um," he said. "Because we're idiots." Abe turned and said, "Siluk?" He hoped Siluk had a better explanation.

Siluk looked down. "I thought this was the right way." He tucked his head down farther. "I thought I could tell."

Imara pointed an accusing finger at Abe. "You are reckless and impulsive." She shook her head. "You both have to do everything I say from now on. No more running off without me."

Abe grinned, and his amusement for Imara's concern was more than apparent. Not an ounce of regret showed on his face. Imara tried hard to not like it since she was trying to be serious.

Imara shook her head and turned. With a start she said, "Mr. Nazari!"

Mr. Nazari stood up from behind the pillar, still looking toward the statue in fear.

"And we found Darius," Siluk said with a smile.

"Just those two?" Imara asked.

Abe touched her shoulder. "Just those two so far. We'll find your sister."

Imara looked at Mr. Nazari. "Wasn't Naki with you when you got transported? How did you get separated? Do you know where she is?"

Mr. Nazari frowned. "The Judge transported Darius and I to that chamber and transported away immediately. He must have taken Naki somewhere else."

Imara nodded while a lump formed in her throat. She turned to Darius who crouched behind the pillar. In a gentle voice, she said, "You can come out. It's safe. Just don't go that way." Imara pointed toward the spikes that only she could see.

Darius gulped and gave a suspicious glance around the pillar. But he didn't say a word as he stood to join the rest of the group.

Imara led them back out of the chamber when Abe nudged her in the arm. He said, "We were supposed to save you, not the other way around."

Imara smirked. "Your technique needs a little work."

Abe laughed and he flashed a quick smile at Imara.

In the middle of the path, Abe stopped and pointed at an opening. "We were trying to do what you would do. See, we chose this path instead of that one because this one looked scarier, and we thought that meant it was safe."

Imara narrowed her eyes in confusion. "What other path?"

Siluk pointed. "That one with the light at the end."

Imara turned to see Siluk point at the same opening as Abe. She squinted her eyes.

"Were we wrong?" Abe asked. "Is that path safer?"

Imara shook her head. "No, that isn't a path. It's an opening that drops off into a river. A fast river. You probably would have drowned if you went that way." She shook her head. "Can't you hear it?"

Abe's face screwed up in concentration. He lowered his eyebrows. "We did hear it, but it looked like there were air conditioners built into the stone. And I'm just now realizing how stupid that sounds. Can you even build air conditioners into stone?"

Imara shook her head. "You cannot go through these catacombs without me."

Mr. Nazari pushed his way toward Imara. "You can see through the illusions with your hila?" he asked.

Imara nodded. "It took a lot of concentration at first, but it's instantaneous now."

"How'd they get a river in here?" Siluk asked.

Imara shrugged, but Darius answered without hesitation. "They must've created it when they built the dams to stop the flooding." He shook his head and grumbled. "Yet another way these catacombs have been destroyed."

Abe turned to Imara while mustard drips of guilt fell from his skin. "I'm sorry I made you fall in that pit. And I'm sorry we left you. Taggers could have showed up, and we got lost in about thirty seconds, so it was obviously a stupid idea. Are you hurt?"

Imara allowed herself to relax and shook her head. "No. Just some bruises. I'll be fine."

"How did you get out of the hole?"

Siluk turned toward her with anxious curiosity in his eyes.

Mr. Nazari looked down the path. Darius stroked the walls again, every so often tapping them and listening.

"I made a rope with the clothes in my backpack," Imara said. "Which we could have done if you two stayed, and it would have been a lot easier to get out."

Siluk's eyebrows shot up high on his forehead. "You made a rope out of clothes?" He did a half smile and said, "Fresh."

Imara ignored his compliment.

"But what did you attach the rope to?" Abe asked.

"There was a narrow ridge jutting out from the top of the cliff. I made a loop at the end of my rope to catch on the ridge, but I wasn't strong enough to throw the rope that high. So, I tied a rock inside the loop at the end of my rope, which made the rope go up higher when I threw it. It took several tries, but I caught the loop on the ridge, then I climbed out of the pit."

"You're pretty resourceful," Abe said impressed. He shrugged with a playful smile. "You know, for a truth seer."

Before Imara had a chance to roll her eyes, Darius yelped in pain. A small gasp escaped Imara when she saw Darius. She ran to his side and helped pull his foot out of a trap with silver spikes. She lowered him to a safe spot on the ground. Darius groaned while white-hot strings of pain whipped out from his foot.

Two short spikes stuck to Darius. One was lodged in the rubber sole of his shoe. Imara couldn't tell if it went through the sole to his foot. The other spike speared his ankle. A long line of blood above Darius's ankle dripped where the spike had scratched before it stuck inside his skin. Imara grabbed onto the spike in Darius's ankle. Before she could tug it free, Abe said, "Wait."

Apparently he could see the spikes now that they were out of the foot trap and away from the illusion. Abe bent down and asked Darius all kinds of questions like, "Where does it hurt?" and "Describe the pain. Stinging or cutting?"

Imara backed away since Abe seemed to know what he was doing.

While Abe was busy, Siluk unzipped his backpack. He said, "Darius loves baba ganoush, but he didn't get any from the party yesterday."

Siluk pulled out an oxy-gone container with six triangles of pita bread topped with baba ganoush. He opened it and took a few whiffs. He narrowed his eyes and studied the appetizers for a moment. He sniffed twice more then pulled three small bottles with spray tops from his pocket. He spritzed two sprays from the first bottle, five from the second, and one from the last. He breathed in one more time and did a small half smile. He put the bottles away and said, "I'll tell him they're as fresh as they were last night at the party. He won't know it's just the smell."

Imara glared at Siluk as he passed her. He said defensively, "Oh, come on. It's a white lie. It's not hurting him."

He turned his back on Imara and went to Darius's side. Darius welcomed the distraction from his ankle and chose an appetizer. He brought it close to his mouth, but stopped and did a long sniff. "These smell divine," he said. He took in a deep breath. "Those oxy-gone containers work better than I thought at keeping things fresh." He took a bite and said, "They're delicious."

Siluk chuckled while Darius gobbled up the rest of the baba ganoush.

Darius's shoe sat next to him as Abe worked. The spike that had been stuck in the shoe sole was pulled out and tossed to the side. Abe shimmied the second spike out of Darius's ankle and immediately covered the cut with a wad of gauze. When the bleeding stopped, Abe procured cleansing wipes from his backpack and cleaned the entire ankle. Next, he smoothed ointment from a tub onto Darius's cut, rubbing it in some sort of pattern. When that was finished, Abe covered the cut with a small square of clean gauze. He took the extra shirt from his bag and ripped off a long strip from the bottom hem. He used the strip of cloth to wrap Darius's ankle and foot.

Abe nodded to himself and helped Darius to his feet. "See if you can put your weight on it. I want to make sure you didn't twist your ankle."

Darius nodded and took a gentle step. He winced, and a few white-hot strings of pain whipped out from his foot. But after a couple more steps, the strings faded away.

Imara glanced at Abe, intrigued by everything he had done. Abe swung his backpack over his shoulder and said, "Hey Siluk, can you give your stun gun to Darius? With an injured ankle, he'll need a quick way to defend himself."

Siluk pulled the stun gun from his pocket and tossed it to Darius.

Abe said to Darius, "You'll have to stand at the back of the group and listen for any sign of the taggers. We haven't run into them yet, but we can't let our guard down."

Darius nodded and pocketed the stun gun. Mr. Nazari stood at the head of the group with his head held high. "We need to make a map of these catacombs. Without a map, we will get lost. Does anyone know how to draw?"

"We already have a map," Abe said.

Mr. Nazari's eyebrows flicked up. "Oh. Of course you thought of that, Abraxas. How clever of you."

Abe chuckled. "It wasn't my idea. Imara got a map from Professor Santini that the city made when they opened this exhibit twenty years ago."

Mr. Nazari nodded. "Oh good." But his face changed, and he put his hands on his hips. Looking at Imara, he asked, "Did she hack into the Egyptian Council to get that map?"

Imara squished up her mouth and averted her eyes.

Mr. Nazari laughed. "Well, at least we know where you learned your resourcefulness, Imara."

Mr. Nazari chuckled again, and Imara opened the map to show Mr. Nazari the parts of the catacombs they had already explored.

After some discussion, they went back to the chamber where Mr. Nazari and Darius were held hostage. Imara examined the door to figure out how Abe got it open. The door had an illusion over the button, but it was trickier to see past than the one on the outhouse crypt upstairs. It took a few minutes before she spotted the button Abe had pushed by accident. After studying it, she was certain she could pick out the same illusion if she saw it on another door.

Mr. Nazari decided they should go back through the part of the catacombs they had already explored, trying to find another door. If they couldn't find one there, then they would start exploring the new paths. Imara was grateful neither Darius nor Mr. Nazari protested when she asked them stay and help look for the other hostages rather than leave right away. Though Imara suspected Mr. Nazari had another motive.

Soon they were off again. Imara led the way, and everyone walked behind her. Except Abe, who chose to walk by her side.

Abe glanced back and said in a low voice, "Does my dad always do this? Act like he's in charge?"

Imara held in a laugh. "At the school, your dad *is* in charge."

"True."

Imara tried to hide her smile. "But, yes," she said.

Abe shook his head, amused.

Imara glanced back at Darius who complained again about how the taggers destroyed the catacombs. No trace of white-hot strings of pain came from his ankle. Imara narrowed her eyes in thought. She turned back to Abe and said, "You're a healer."

"What?"

"You fixed Darius's ankle."

Abe shook his head. "Oh no. I'm not a healer, I just have medical training. I told you, I'm mashimo, just like my dad."

Imara smirked. "I know you don't *think* you have a hila; I'd be able to tell if you were lying."

Abe smiled and Imara continued. "I'm saying I think you're a healer and you never realized it."

Abe shook his head. "I'm not. I have medical training."

"Why? Are you studying to become a doctor?" Imara asked.

"No, I'm an entrepreneur, remember?"

Imara nodded, noting that Abe failed to answer her first question.

Abe shrugged. "I know how to clean a wound, that's all. Oh, and I did a massage-like technique because I'm pretty sure Darius did twist his ankle."

Imara stood up taller and turned her head to point at Darius. "Look. Darius is no pain. Just because you cleaned the wound and massaged his ankle doesn't mean the pain would disappear. I've never seen pain dissipate like that."

Abe frowned. "What about Siluk? He gave Darius that baba ganoush. Maybe Siluk is a healer."

"He's not. He's a smell master."

Abe narrowed his eyes. "How do you know that?"

"He's my classmate," Imara said. "I've known Siluk for years."

Abe tilted his head to the side. "You two act like strangers. You barely speak to each other."

Imara tightened her jaw. "That's because I don't like him, and he knows it. He's a liar."

Abe glanced back at Siluk. Imara knew Abe and Siluk got along well. She could tell Abe was full of conflict looking at Siluk now. He wasn't sure what to make of this new information.

Abe shrugged. "Maybe Darius's ankle wasn't as bad as we thought."

"I can see pain," Imara said. "The pain was bad, and it stopped fast. I've never seen anything like that. I think you're a healer."

Abe sighed, and a single cobalt blue drop of sadness pelted off his skin. "I wish I was. I really do. I spent years wishing I had a hila. I spent every day for an entire year concentrating on any weird abilities I had, trying to figure out what my hila might be. I tried to invent a hila, tried to pretend I had one, but I got nothing. Trust me, I'm mashimo. If I had a hila, don't you think I would know by now?"

Imara turned his words over in her mind before she asked, "How old were you when you tried to invent a hila?"

"I don't know. Eleven, maybe. Why does that matter?"

"Most hilas aren't manifested until puberty. You were probably too young at eleven to even have a hila."

Abe frowned again. "Maybe," he said. "But I still wished for a hila when I got older and I never got one."

Imara shrugged. "A hundred years ago, no one thought they had hilas. People thought they were just strangely good at mundane things. Like someone who never got in a car accident despite being close thought they were extra lucky. Really, they had 4D vision. And someone who was good at judging time thought it was their internal clock, but really they were a time feeler. It wasn't until people recognized their abilities as a special power that they became hilas. It takes a lot of practice to control and manipulate a hila. Some people believe everyone has a hila, mashimos just haven't discovered theirs yet."

Abe smirked and nudged Imara in the arm. "That's what the taggers say. You're not one of those fanatics are you?"

"No," Imara said with a scoff. "If I was a tagger, do you think they would have taken my sister hostage?"

Abe snickered. "I'm just teasing you."

Imara looked to the side in thought. "I know taggers have wild ideas, but they might be right about mashimos."

Abe leaned toward Imara. "It would be fresh if I were a healer." Abe broke his gaze away from Imara and stared ahead for several seconds. "How did you know you were a truth seer?" he asked.

Imara bit the inside of her cheek while she thought. "It started out as a gut feeling. I didn't know for sure when someone was lying, but I could feel it in my gut. The more I listened to that feeling, the more sure I became. Then I started to see it with my eyes. Skin would look dull, almost gray, when someone lied, and then it would turn glowy and bright when they told the truth."

"But you said you can see feelings and motivations too."

Imara nodded. "I can, but that didn't come until later. After training. The truth and lie thing was how I knew I was a truth seer." Imara smiled. If he kept asking questions like this, Abe might realize she was right.

ELEVEN

IT WAS LATE SATURDAY EVENING. AFTER ONE full day in the catacombs, Imara found several empty chambers, but no Naki. Everyone begged Imara to go back upstairs so they could sleep for the night, but Imara kept insisting they check just one more passage.

Finally, Mr. Nazari put his foot down. "The Judge gave Darius and me food and water. Why wouldn't he do the same for Naki and Headmaster Bello? Besides, we have three days to find her, and it's only been one. We're going to bed now. We can look again in the morning."

Imara conceded because as much as she tried to ignore it, she was tired too. On the way back to the shaft, they ran into a wall a little taller than Mr. Nazari.

"Is it an illusion?" Darius asked.

Imara slid her fingers across the wall, feeling for any inconsistencies. "It's real," she said.

She pressed her palm against the stone and slid it across the wall trying to feel something. Anything other than stone. Imara held her eyes on the stone for several long seconds and then scanned the entire wall quickly, but nothing. There were no illusions as far as she could tell.

"This wasn't here before," Imara said.

Abe nodded. "That's what I thought."

"Want me to blow it up?" Siluk asked. "I brought explosives. I know how to position them so they don't hurt anyone. I can break down the wall and leave everything else intact."

Abe looked at Siluk with a hint of unease. "Why do you have explosives?"

"I'm from Alaska. We use explosives in my family for hunting and building and stuff. It's very useful."

Darius nodded. "Yes, yes. Explosives are fresh. You can do amazing things with them. But I'm going to pretend you didn't suggest blowing up a wall in the Catacombs of Kom el Shoqafa. We are not going to destroy this place!"

"What is the wall made of, Darius?" Imara asked. "I don't think it's original to the catacombs."

Darius nodded and approached the wall. He leaned his ear in close and tapped the wall with his fingernail.

"What's this?" Abe asked.

"*SHHHHHHH!*" Darius lowered his eyebrows, deep in concentration.

"Sorry," Abe said, and Darius tapped the wall again.

Imara turned to Abe who had a small, white square in his hand. The square was thin and folded in half. Imara's eyes went from the white square up to Abe's eyes. He shrugged with a frown.

Darius turned. "The stone is manmade and less than a year old. You can blow it up. Is that paper?" Darius said with a start.

He grabbed the square from Abe and slid his fingers across the white surface. "This is fresh!" he said. "I haven't seen paper in years."

"Let me touch it," Siluk said.

Abe looked at the paper with narrowed eyes. "How did it get in here?"

Mr. Nazari wore a blank expression, though Imara could see he was intrigued. "Whoever put up the wall must have dropped it," he said.

Darius unfolded the paper with pure bliss. His mouth dropped. With a smile in his eyes, he said, "There's writing on it. There's actual writing on this paper. By hand!"

Mr. Nazari snatched the paper from Darius. "Let me see that." He masked his curiosity with a patronizing look. "You children. Getting excited over paper. It used to be commonplace, you know."

"What does it say?" Imara asked. "The writing?" Mr. Nazari looked down, and Imara said, "Read it out loud."

We all have secrets we want to hide,
Maybe you're embarrassed, or maybe you lied.

One among you has a secret past,
The truth of it I'll reveal at last.

He stole a scholarship from his best friend,
And now the friendship may never mend.

You will see that tagging is just,
For now you know who you cannot trust.
The Judge

When Mr. Nazari finished reading, Darius laughed with a cynical shake of his head. "Please. The only person here who

117

ever applied for a scholarship is Siluk. And I didn't steal the scholarship from him. I didn't even apply. I was going to, but that was before... Before the rules... Wait a minute."

Imara stole a glance at Siluk, and her mind shot back to five years earlier.

ଽଠଽଠଓଽଓଽ

Imara walked into Headmaster Bello's office to return a holographic geo dome she had used for a lesson with Professor Santini. When she walked in the door, Siluk sat in Headmaster Bello's chair, busy working on the transparent hologram. He worked for several more seconds before Imara cleared her throat. He jumped at the sound and immediately exited the programs he was using. It made no difference since Imara had already seen what he did through the transparent hologram.

Siluk had altered the rules for the scholarship. He sent the changed rules to Darius and only to Darius, but made it look like an email that went to the whole school. Siluk changed the rules to say a grandchild of an employee could not receive the scholarship. Which meant Darius was no longer eligible.

"What are you doing?" Imara asked.

Siluk smiled and pointed to Imara's hands. "Hey, is that the geo dome Professor Santini invented herself?"

"Don't try to change the subject!" Imara snapped back.

Siluk gulped. "Headmaster Bello asked me to do that for him." Siluk's skin turned a dull gray. Lie.

Imara scowled at him in response. "You can't lie to a truth seer."

Siluk stood from Headmaster Bello's chair and sneered at Imara. "They won't take your word over mine just because you're a truth seer. That's illegal."

Imara frowned and her gut twisted in a knot. She hadn't expected Siluk to turn on her so fast. It wasn't like him to be rude, even to her. "I know," Imara said as she tilted her chin up. "But I know what you did. I can tell Darius."

Siluk pushed past her and laughed. "Darius won't believe you. No one likes you because you're mean to everyone. But people love me. I'm getting away with this, and there's nothing you can do about it."

He reached for the door opener, but Imara grabbed his hand. She looked him square in the eyes. "I know you did it." She threw Siluk's hand away from her. "At least I know you can't be trusted."

Siluk scoffed and opened the door. "You don't trust anyone."

꽍뙓꩜��03꩜03

Siluk turned on Imara with fire in his eyes. "Who did you tell?" he accused.

Imara looked back, her stare unwavering. "I never told anyone. But you just did."

The confused look on Siluk's face lasted only a moment before his face fell. The color drained from his cheekbones as his head turned to face Darius.

Darius's jaw dropped, and he said in a hush, "This is true? You cheated me out of that scholarship?"

Darius tore his eyes away from Siluk and stared at the ground. His shoulders slumped, and he swallowed hard with

119

a frown. "I was happy for you when you won." Darius's voice broke, and his eyes glistened. He squeezed his eyes shut, obviously embarrassed that his emotion was so visible. He clenched his jaw and smothered his pain with an anger Imara could see. "I didn't realize you stole it from me," he said.

Imara's eye twitched at these words. *Stole it.* Those were the exact words Keiko used with the tagger boy about her scholarship. The poem also said *stole*, but the coincidence was suspicious nonetheless.

Darius sniffed then curled up his lip. "How could you do that to me? I'm your best friend."

Siluk raised his hands in defense. His face was pale, and his eyes appeared to sink into his skull. With a tortured expression, he said, "I hated myself after I did it. I wanted to admit to it, but I was afraid you would never forgive me. I never did it again."

"Lie."

Everyone turned to Imara surprised.

Mr. Nazari's lip twitched, but his neutral expression soon returned. He asked Siluk, "What was the lie? You never lied to Darius again or you never committed scholarship fraud again?"

"Well obviously—" Siluk stopped when he glanced at Imara. "I never...Well you see..." Siluk stuttered.

Imara folded her arms in front of her chest and glowered at Siluk. "I met a girl named Keiko last night whose scholarship essay was corrupted with a scrambler. Did you do that?"

"No," Siluk said with such sincerity, everyone almost smiled.

Imara's frown only deepened, and she spoke through her teeth. "You can't keep lying, Siluk. Not when I'm here."

Siluk turned to Imara. For an instant his sincere expression turned to rage. It was gone a moment later when he looked at Darius. "Okay," he said. "I did it more than once, but not every year."

"Siluk!" Imara said.

He huffed like a bull ready to charge when he caught Imara's eye. But to her surprise, he looked down, and mustard drips of guilt fell off his skin. "Fine. I've done it every year since."

"Why?" Darius asked with a sullen face. Imara knew Darius was hurt and had no idea how to cope with the feeling. Siluk and Darius were as close as best friends could be. They'd fought before, but never about something so real. Darius tightened his hands into fists, again masking his pain with anger. "Why did you keep doing it? You got the scholarship five years ago. Once you have it, you don't lose it unless you get suspended. If you already had the scholarship, why did you keep committing scholarship fraud?"

Siluk shrugged exasperated. "Well it's not like I was getting paid to do it."

"Lie." Imara's nose crinkled in disgust. "You lie all the time, and everyone believes you because you're friendly. But they deserve to know the truth about who you are. Darius should have found out about this years ago."

Siluk swallowed and scratched the back of his head. He kept his eyes on the ground while he spoke. "I'm not a bad person. The first time I did it for myself, but only because I needed the scholarship. My parents couldn't afford tuition, and the less expensive hila school they wanted to send me to was crap. Darius didn't need the scholarship as much as me. I hoped it wouldn't matter to him when he couldn't apply." Siluk rubbed his arm with a guilty frown.

Blood red flames of anger shot out from Mr. Nazari, but his face revealed no emotion. "How did you do it?" Mr. Nazari asked in an even tone. "I had no idea this was going on at my school. How did you commit scholarship fraud without getting caught?"

Siluk kicked a rock with his shoulders slumped. "Every year I got a list of two or three names. Those were the people I needed to sabotage. I did lots of different things. I gave them really bad advice for their essays. I hacked their emails so they got the wrong topic. I bribed the teachers who chose the winners. Sometimes I just distracted them so they never had time to write the essay. I had to get creative."

"Wait a minute," Darius said with a frown. "Is that why you dated Navya Malouf for like a week last year?"

Siluk pulled his head down and tucked his chin to his chest. "Yes," he said.

Darius rocked his head from side to side while his jaw tightened to a stiff clench. "I thought I could trust you."

So far, Abe remained quiet. But now he looked at Siluk, more curious than anything. "Someone *paid* you to sabotage scholarship applications?"

Imara's eyes shot up as she tilted her head to the side. She was so busy arguing and being angry, she had forgotten about that. "Who paid you?" Abe asked. "And who gave you the names?"

Siluk sighed. "I did get paid, but it wasn't much. And it was for a good cause, I promise. I only sabotaged scholarship applicants who had enough money and didn't need the scholarship. That way, someone with greater financial need won the scholarship."

"Who could possibly decide who had enough money and who didn't?" Imara asked. "Did you have access to financials?"

Abe turned to Imara and asked, "Was Siluk lying when he said he was doing it for a good cause?"

The constricting anger inside of Imara relaxed while she thought back. "No, that was true. But maybe he didn't know what was really going on. Maybe he only thought it was for a good cause. Either way, it's still abominable."

Mr. Nazari asked, "Who paid you?"

Siluk pinched the bridge of his nose. "The year after I won the scholarship, it was scholarship time again, and I got an email explaining how some applicants were more financially deserving than others. The person who sent the email asked for my help, since I successfully manipulated the results the year before. I agreed to help, and then I got a list of names. The money deposited straight to my bank account after scholarships were awarded. The email was from a fake account. The name was *Defender of the Poor* or something stupid like that. It didn't have a real name on it."

Abe looked to Imara again. "Truth," she said.

Abe rubbed his chin in thought. "You didn't know who sent the email at first, but did that ever change? Did you ever find out who it was?"

"No." Siluk responded without thought.

"Lie."

Siluk huffed. His face flushed with anger as he pointed. "This is why no one likes you, Imara. You get in everybody's business when you shouldn't. I bet you're the one who wrote this note, not the Judge."

Imara rolled her eyes, unaffected by his accusation. "I don't even know how to write on paper. You should have known your lies would catch up to you at some point. Don't blame me."

"Who was it?" Mr. Nazari asked. "It sounded like you said you found out who gave you the names. Who was it?"

Siluk gulped. "I don't want to say."

"You have to now," Darius spat out. A forest green corkscrew of jealousy twisted away from Darius. Imara thought it was strange that Darius would be jealous of the attention Siluk got when it was all so negative. But then, Darius got jealous about a lot of things.

Siluk picked at the pale skin around his thumbnail. "I'm afraid I'll get in trouble if I say who it was."

Imara laughed. "You're already in trouble. You should have thought of that before you committed fraud."

Siluk's eyes flashed with guilt, but he closed them before anyone else could tell. "I was trying to do a good thing. I know it was wrong, but I did it for the right reason."

Mr. Nazari's face stayed calm, but Imara saw turmoil surrounding him. His ever-present burnt orange prickles of greed grew to enormous lengths. Imara knew he didn't appreciate his school being used like this. As always, he feared how it would affect his bottom line. "If someone paid you to commit scholarship fraud, I need to know about it. Was it a student, a teacher, an employee?"

Siluk swallowed hard. He rubbed the back of his neck, and his eyes darted across the ground. "I'm not going to say who it was. I only found out by accident."

"You'll tell me if you want to keep attending my school," Mr. Nazari said with teeth gritted together.

Siluk lowered his eyes as reality set in. It only took a moment to make his choice. "It was Headmaster Bello."

Mr. Nazari's eyebrows shot up. He was silent for several seconds, but to Imara's surprise, he let out a soft chuckle. "Oh, Jabari." Mr. Nazari smoothed his jacket sleeves and made them even with his shirt sleeves. "Unfortunately that doesn't surprise me one bit. He's always been a bit of a vigilante."

Imara caught her jaw before it dropped.

"Don't get me wrong," Mr. Nazari said. "He'll be punished, but it's my own fault for not keeping a better eye on him. I guess I need to take away his access to student financials."

There was a moment of stunned silence while everyone blinked at Mr. Nazari. Darius broke the silence with a question. "Do you think the Judge got the scholarship story out of Headmaster Bello after taking him hostage?" A wrinkle formed between Darius's eyebrows as he brought them together. "Or maybe Headmaster Bello is the Judge. Technically none of us saw him get kidnapped. He wasn't in the room when the Judge was there."

"Of course he was," Mr. Nazari said.

"Actually," Imara said. "Darius is right. Headmaster Bello ran after that tagger with the scar on his head, and neither of them was seen again. The police told everyone the tagger with the scar must be the Judge, but I guess we don't know for sure."

Mr. Nazari shook his head with an intensity that surprised Imara. "Jabari is a little crazy sometimes, but there's no way he's the Judge."

"Why?" Imara asked with sincerity.

Mr. Nazari opened his mouth, but it hung open, and no words came out. He closed his eyes and gave his head a vigorous shake. "We're all tired. Let's get past this wall and go to bed. Things will be clearer in the morning when we've had a chance to rest."

Siluk nodded and unzipped his backpack. "Right. Let me get the explosives."

"No." Darius glared at Siluk. Darius's eyes were full of rage, his mouth in a deep frown. "How can we trust you with explosives now that we know you're a liar? What if you get too much? What if you're trying to hurt us?"

"What?" Siluk said. Cobalt blue drops of sadness pelted off his skin. "Maybe I committed scholarship fraud, but I would never hurt you guys."

Darius scowled, and Imara put her hand on Darius's shoulder before he could speak again. She said, "We don't need the explosives. We can help each other over the wall. It's not that tall."

Darius raised his eyebrows pointedly at Siluk. "See. We don't need you anyway."

TWELVE

IMARA WOKE UP SUNDAY MORNING TO SILUK
and Darius bickering. Siluk had tried to help Darius with his
sleeping bag, but Darius said, "Don't."

"I'm sorry," Siluk said under his breath.

"You should be," Darius hissed back.

Imara jumped out of her sleeping bag and went straight
for the crypt room. Once there, she filled her water bottle
and drank it while examining the crypt along the back wall. It
was the only one so far that hadn't been opened. She
narrowed her eyes and looked at all of the cracks and
roughness in the stone. She touched the top of the crypt,
making note of the warm and rough texture. Carefully, Imara
ran her fingers over the crypt, searching as she touched.

Imara heard footsteps, and soon Abe stood next to her.
He leaned against the crypt with bright eyes. "Hey," he said.

Imara dropped her hand with a twinkle in her eye.
"Morning," she said.

Abe frowned. "Just morning? Not good morning?"

Imara bit her lip with a grin.

"How about now?" Abe asked as he took her hand in his.

Imara enjoyed the heart-leaping sensation and leaned
toward him, but then her smile vanished.

"What's wrong?" he asked.

Imara turned her eyes down and frowned. "I just hope we find Naki today."

Abe rubbed his thumb across the back of Imara's hand. "We'll find her today. I know we will." He held his free arm out in front of her. "Look at my skin. You can tell I'm not lying. I really do think we'll find her today."

Imara smiled with gratitude, but knew her eyes still drooped.

Just then, Mr. Nazari, Siluk, and Darius entered the crypt room. Abe pulled his hand away from Imara, and a flash of violet embarrassment shot from his skin. Mustard yellow drips joined the embarrassment.

Imara turned back to look at the unopened crypt. For someone as impulsive as Abe, it seemed strange he would be embarrassed about showing affection in front of others. But it was in front of his dad, and she didn't know what their relationship was like in that regard. Imara narrowed her eyes at the crypt and pressed her fingers against it.

Abe whispered to her while everyone else filled their water bottles. "Do you really think it's that bad what Siluk did? He was just trying to help students who didn't have enough money."

Imara frowned and picked the hair on the back of her neck while she thought. "What he did to Darius was the worst thing. Darius has always trusted him and stood up for him. He never expected to be betrayed by his best friend."

"Yeah, I guess," Abe rubbed his chin in thought. "But it seems like Siluk regrets it. Can you tell if he really does?"

Imara stole a glance at Siluk. "He is sincere about some things," she said. "I think he's sincerely afraid of losing his friendship with Darius. I think he regrets what he did because of that, but I don't think he regrets his actual actions."

Abe nodded.

Soon they were done filling water bottles and went down the shaft to the lowest level of the catacombs. They set off to search for Naki and Headmaster Bello. When they reached the wall from the night before, Siluk again offered to use his explosives to break it down.

"We already told you," Darius said. "We don't trust you anymore."

Siluk groaned. "Don't you get it? The Judge tagged me, and you're all falling for it. You're treating me differently just because you know about something I did five years ago."

Darius narrowed his eyes. "This is not the same as tagging. And you did it this year too. Don't try to justify it."

Mr. Nazari directed them over the wall, but the bickering didn't stop. Imara stood at the head of the group as they went down the path. Abe joined her and said, "He is right, you know."

Imara cocked an eyebrow up in confusion.

"Even the Judge said he was tagging Siluk in that note."

Imara shrugged. "Then I guess taggers aren't so bad after all."

Abe laughed until he recognized the note of sincerity in Imara's voice. He said, "Are you serious? What about their demonstrations? What about the asterisks? The Judge took hostages to get what he wanted."

"I agree their methods are wrong, especially the hostage thing." Imara shrugged. "But I don't think their core belief is evil or anything."

Abe leaned back on his heels and opened his eyes wide. "Wait a second. You're talking about the actual tagging. You don't think tagging is that bad?"

Imara blinked and said, "No."

Abe shook his head in disbelief. "Are you kidding me? Tagging is easily the worst thing about taggers. You think people should be tagged?"

"No," Imara said. "But it's not the worst thing you could do to a person."

"It's one of the worse things," Abe said while maroon mounds of frustration piled onto his skin. "Tagging is like... it's like branding cattle. You're branding them. For life! They'll forever be defined by their mistakes. No achievement will be as strong as the tag." His fingers were stiff, with a raven black rash of anxiety coming off them.

Imara sighed. "I get why people think it's unfair. I do. But that's how I always see people because of my hila. I can see if people are liars or thieves or abusers. Maybe it wouldn't be so bad if everyone knew who they could trust."

Abe's fingers relaxed and he looked to the side in thought. "I never thought about that. I guess you do see everyone's mistakes." He rubbed his chin, staring away as he put his thoughts together.

He frowned and said, "For you, everyone is tagged." He turned and looked at her through the side of his eyes. "That must be hard."

Imara almost tripped as she walked. She was used to people being intimidated by her. She was used to people being jealous of her hila. She wasn't used to sympathy. She didn't like admitting how much she appreciated it. She pulled her head down. "It was hard at first. But I'm used to it now."

"I can see why you don't think tagging is that bad. But I have to say, I disagree."

Imara narrowed her eyes, impressed that Abe could disagree without being offended by Imara's opposite opinion. Abe said, "You don't see past mistakes with your hila. You see who people are at that moment. The problem with tagging is redemption. When you tag someone, you take away their chance to change."

Imara let out a hollow laugh. "Most people don't change. No one knows that better than me."

Abe nodded. "That's exactly what makes tagging so bad. Once a person is tagged, they'll always be defined by their mistakes. They'll never have a chance to change even if they want to. You might as well execute them."

Imara watched the colors of many emotions sputter and fly off Abe at increasing intervals. She couldn't help but smile as she said, "You're a pretty passionate person."

Abe laughed. "Yeah, I know. It gets me into trouble sometimes."

ಬಾಬಾಀಀ

Hours passed. Imara tried to ignore the panic rising inside her. Darius had taken to calling out Naki's name every once in awhile. It seemed sweet until Imara realized he only did it to avoid conversation with Siluk.

Imara stared hard at the map and rounded a bend into a long corridor. They had searched this corridor twice already. Imara didn't know how this time would be any different, but she ignored that thought and marched forward. She would just have to look even harder and not miss anything this time.

"You seem tense," Abe said out of nowhere.

Imara turned to him with a start. "Sorry." Then she shook her head. "Did you just ask me something?"

Abe laughed. "Uh, that was awhile ago." He chuckled again. "Don't worry about it. Do I need to cartwheel down this path to get you to smile?"

"No," Imara said with her eyes focused on a tomb. "This path is dangerous."

Abe gave Imara a half smile, trying again to cheer her up. Imara sighed. "I thought we would find her by now. I'm trying not to panic, but it's hard."

"We have three days," Abe said. "That means we have until tomorrow night. And the Judge probably gave her water anyway so we actually have more time than that."

"I know. But if we don't find her today, I can't start my new job tomorrow. Which is stupid. Finding Naki is more important. I'm sure they can extend the deadline considering the circumstances. But I'm still stressed about it. Though not as stressed as I am about Naki."

"You're supposed to start a new job tomorrow?"

"Yeah, my dream job." She paused and squinted at the wall next to her. The tombs had ended, but there were several feet of plain, stone wall before the corridor branched off to a path. "This spot right here. It's not right." Imara pointed and everyone gathered around her.

"You see something?" Mr. Nazari asked.

Imara shook her head. "No. It's the map. It's darker in this spot as if there's supposed to be an alcove or a crypt, but the wall is flat."

"Maybe it leads to a secret passageway!" Siluk said, jumping forward with a smile.

A micro-smile appeared on Darius's mouth, which he buried with a glare. "Catacombs weren't built like that. It's just a cemetery. There's no reason the ancient Egyptians would build secret passageways into a cemetery. That would be weird."

"But this wall doesn't match the map," Imara said. "Maybe taggers built a wall over an alcove to create a secret room. Listen to the wall, Darius. Does it sound like it's as old as the rest of the catacombs?"

Siluk sniffed and leaned toward the wall.

"I'll do it, Siluk," Darius said with another glare.

While Darius listened, Imara concentrated hard on the wall. She couldn't see anything. But when she turned to hear Darius say the wall was only a year old, she saw it again. She'd noticed it on a few walls. She saw something from the corner of her eye, but no matter how she concentrated there was nothing there.

"Of course!" Imara slapped her forehead. "It's not a projector illusion, it's an optical illusion. Well, both, I think."

Imara turned away from the wall and looked at it from the side of her eye.

"So the key is to ignore the wall?" Abe asked.

Imara chewed the inside of her lip, desperate to concentrate. "No, not ignore it. You know at night when you see a star out of the corner of your eye, but when you look at it properly it disappears? When it's dark you see with the rods in your eyes instead of the cones. But the center of the eye is filled with cones and the edges are filled with rods. So you can see the star with the side of your eye, but not the center."

Imara shot her hand out and said, "Gotcha."

She stuck her thumbnail under part of the stone and lifted a camouflaged metal cover. Under the cover sat a black button.

"Finally," Imara said. "Now we're getting somewhere."

She pressed the button, and the wall slid to one side to reveal a small alcove. Imara held her breath, ready to see Naki, but the alcove was empty. A secret room, but still. Empty.

Charcoal balls of panic bounced from Siluk's skin. Imara lifted her chin. "It's okay. She's not here, but I know how to see past this illusion now. We'll go back through the catacombs and find the doors we've missed. There must be more."

Imara started down the passage, pushing her fear deep under a veil of confidence. "Come on. We'll find Naki and Headmaster Bello in no time."

Silence rang through the passage. Everyone was afraid to say anything that would make Imara's surety waver. Four paths and another empty room later, Mr. Nazari risked a question.

"What could you see on the Judge, Imara? Did you recognize the..." Mr. Nazari made a motion with his hand as if he was grabbing onto a string and pulling it. "Thingies," he said. "You know, the color stuff you see off people? Did you recognize it?"

Imara stared at the empty room and shook her head. "I saw desire for power. I've never seen someone with that much of it before."

Abe turned to her. "Do people always look the same to you? Don't you see different emotions depending on how they feel at the moment?"

Imara nodded. "Yes, but some people, especially people I know well, have consistent emotions I always see. It's like I can see their personality. The current emotions are at the forefront, but I can still see the others."

"But the Judge was in disguise. If you knew the Judge, would you know who it was based solely on the emotions? Or is your hila subjective? Based on your interpretation?"

Imara felt the muscles in her shoulders tense as she cross her arms. "Truth is truth," she said. "My opinion of a person doesn't change what I see." The frown on Imara's face dove deeper. "And why do you assume it's someone I know? I don't make a habit of hanging out with extremist groups. I've only met one person with that much desire for power and I always try to avoid him."

"Do we know him?" Siluk asked.

"Who?"

Siluk raised his eyebrows and said, "The person you avoid."

"Oh," Imara said. She shook the thought away and started walking down the path. "Yeah, it's—"

Imara stopped with her foot in the air. Her eyes went wide before she realized she was holding her breath.

"Who is it?" Mr. Nazari asked.

Imara gulped as she lifted her hand to pick the hair on the back of her neck. "Um," she said, her voice shaking. "It's not necessarily the same person. He has desire for power, but I'm sure he's not the only one in the world."

"Who is it, Imara?" Darius asked.

"Um." Imara tapped her fingers against her leg and tried to keep her breath even.

"Headmaster Bello," Mr. Nazari said. It wasn't a question.

Imara nodded, and Mr. Nazari looked down with a sigh. He covered his eyes with one hand and shook his head while blood red flames of anger erupted from his skin.

Siluk shuddered. "I've been working for the Judge?"

Imara frowned. "We don't know Headmaster Bello is the Judge. He could be a hostage just like the others. Maybe the Judge transported Headmaster Bello down here before the Judge came back to the graduation party."

A shiver ran down Imara's spine as she turned to walk down the path. But before Imara could take a step, Darius lowered his voice and said, "Guys, I think I hear something."

Imara turned toward him just in time to see a large rock flying through the air. Darius pulled out his stun gun, but the rock hit him in the shoulder and the stun gun dropped to the ground.

In the next second, several things happened all at once. Darius dropped to his knees, trying to retrieve the stun gun. Siluk raised his arms over his face. Three taggers appeared from around a corner. But Abe clenched his jaw and looked ready to act.

Abe said, "Form up."

Darius got up and stood at Abe's side. His eyes darted across the ground still looking for the stun gun. Siluk stood on Abe's other side and grabbed the large rock that had hit Darius in the shoulder.

Abe glanced back and pointed to Imara with his thumb. "Dad, get her out of here."

In the chaos, it was hard for Imara to tell what was going on. All she knew was when Mr. Nazari grabbed her by the elbow, she yanked her arm away and bent over to grab a rock. By the time she looked up again, two taggers were unconscious on the ground, several feet ahead of their group. Abe must have stunned them.

Siluk was in a hand fight with a tagger, and it looked like he was winning. Darius tried to get his stun gun, but a tagger threw a rock at it and broke it. Imara pushed forward and threw her rock at four more taggers charging toward them. Abe aimed his stun gun, and a tagger dropped to the ground unconscious. But another tagger was close behind, and Abe now had his attention on Siluk.

Imara ducked and grabbed a handful of dirt. She threw it into the eyes of the tagger who was ready to attack Abe. The tagger dropped and grabbed at his eyes. Abe jerked toward the tagger then looked back at Imara surprised.

A short tagger woman emerged from behind the corner. She had thin eyes and long, silky black hair. "Get that stun gun, and regroup!" she screamed.

Two taggers attacked Abe at once and wrested the stun gun from his hand. The black-haired tagger woman dropped to her knees and touched all three unconscious taggers with her arms. The other taggers ran to her and grabbed onto her shoulders. She looked Imara straight in the eyes and said, "We'll be back."

In the next instant, they disappeared.

THIRTEEN

IMARA BLINKED AT THE EMPTY PATH, HER head still reeling from the chaos. Abe frowned and looked ahead. "We need to get to a path that's difficult for them to navigate. I think we can assume they see the illusions and not the truth. Imara?"

Imara nodded and searched the map. She marched forward and said, "The checkerboard of foot paths."

Everyone followed behind her. As soon as Abe got close enough, she glared at him and said, "Why'd you try to send me away? You think I'm a liability?"

Abe's eyes narrowed in confusion. "You're mad that I was trying to protect you?"

Imara shook her head and looked back at the path with a deeper glare. "I'm mad that you think I'm incapable of helping."

"I don't," Abe said.

Imara jerked her head toward him.

"You're the only one who can see through the illusions. You're an asset. We need you and I was just trying to keep you safe."

"Oh," Imara said.

Abe looked over his shoulder. "Darius?"

"No sign of them. At least not yet," Darius said.

Imara rounded a bend and entered a passage that would lead them to the corridor with the checkerboard of foot pits.

Abe glanced at her. "You're not one to back down from a fight, huh?"

Imara shrugged. "You were in trouble."

Abe brought a corner of his mouth up into a smile. "That was a resourceful idea to throw the dirt in his eyes. Do you know how to fight?"

Imara turned into the corridor with the checkerboard of foot pits. Abe pointed to the tombs on one side of the wall. Imara nodded and climbed backward into an empty tomb. She said, "I took a self-defense class when I was sixteen. But I don't really remember anything from it."

Abe eyed her curiously as he climbed backward into his own tomb. When he got settled, he said, "You have some good instincts."

For the next several minutes, Abe detailed what they would do when the taggers returned. The stun gun caused people to stay unconscious for seven to fifteen minutes depending on the person, so he estimated the taggers would be back no sooner than that.

But twenty minutes came and went, and the taggers were nowhere to be seen. It was possible they hadn't guessed where they were hiding, but Imara had a feeling it was more than that.

While they waited, all Imara could think of was Naki withering away in an empty crypt. To get that thought out of her mind, she asked Abe, "Why do you want to stop the Judge?"

"Because I think tagging is wrong," Abe said matter-of-factly.

"But do you think taggers are a real threat?" Imara asked.

"Taggers have resorted to more and more ridiculous tactics. Adding asterisks to names. Taking hostages. Remember a couple months ago when they exposed that guy for robbery and he turned out to be innocent? It's only a matter of time before things get violent."

Imara watched Abe's skin, looking for only one color. Those turquoise blue smoky swirls of hope danced out from him. She hadn't seen him without them yet. Some small blood red flames of anger burned, probably anger for what the taggers did. Then there were tumbling golden squares. Justice. Imara searched, but couldn't find the color she sought.

Imara stretched her legs back to ease the aching muscles in her thighs. She propped her chin up with her fist and hoped this position would be more comfortable. "You actually think you can save the world? You think you alone can make a difference?"

Abe shook his shoulders out and glanced down the empty corridor. "One person *can* make a difference. Buddha, Gandhi, Nelson Mandela, Noah Nguyen. The world only changes if we change it."

Imara squinted at Abe's skin. The turquoise smoky hope swirled, but no new colors appeared. She chewed her lip before she said, "Most people change things for selfish reasons. I find it hard to believe you want to change the world purely for the sake of others."

Abe shrugged. "If I make the world a better place, don't I get to live in a better world? I'm doing it for me as much as for others." He turned his eyes from the corridor to focus on Imara. "And if someone like you happens to be impressed, then so be it." And then he winked so fast, Imara almost missed it.

Imara grinned and averted her eyes. But as her eyes fell away, the color she was waiting for suddenly appeared. Almost transparent, but there. Red orange whips fighting their way through Abe's turquoise hope swirls.

Selfishness.

She liked Abe for all his hope and passion, but she knew he couldn't be perfect.

"Maybe I'm an optimist," Abe said. "But I do think people are good at heart. Tagging would make it difficult to see things that way."

Imara nodded. She wasn't sure she agreed, but she also didn't disagree. As much as she hated to admit it, Abe had a point.

Abe glanced back through the corridor again. Imara listened for footsteps or voices, but heard nothing. Abe turned back to her and said, "Hey, what job are you supposed to start tomorrow? You called it your dream job."

"Oh," Imara said while a smile overtook her face. Excitement burst out before she could stop it. "I'm going to be a consultant for the police in Kenya. Kenya has grown immensely since hilas were discovered there a hundred years ago. There's been economic growth and developmental growth, but also criminal growth. Especially in the last fifteen years. I'm going to use my hila in interrogations to catch criminals. They can't use my hila like a lie detector, but I can use what I see to ask the right questions."

A mischievous smile appeared on Abe's lips. "So. You want to save the world just like I do."

Imara chuckled. "Just Kenya for now. I'm a realist. I know I can't save the entire world." Imara squished her mouth down into a frown. "And I don't actually change anyone. I just catch them. I wish there was a way to persuade people to be good."

Abe shrugged. "People are already good. If you believe in them they believe in themselves."

Imara scoffed. "People are not always good. And you can't control their actions just by believing in them."

"I know, but people usually rise to your expectations whether good or bad. If you expect them to do something bad, they are more likely to do it. But, expecting greatness from people causes them to expect it from themselves. It's called *optimism*. You should try it sometime. It's much more fun than realism."

Imara caught the grin before it appeared on her face. She tried to remain unimpressed, but Abe's hope was intoxicating, especially when she was so worried. Imara tapped her ring to check the time. Fifty minutes had passed since the taggers appeared. Imara glanced at Abe.

He frowned and shook his head. "They said they would be back. We can't let our guard down."

Imara tugged on her raspberry shirt collar. "I know, but..." She pulled herself forward and stuck her head out of the tomb. Still not a footstep or voice to be heard. She looked back at Abe and hoped her eyes contained the pleading in her heart. "My sister," Imara said.

Abe's face fell, and he gulped. He looked down and nodded. "Fine. But we have to be extra cautious as we look.

The Judge and the taggers know we're down here. And we don't have the stun guns anymore."

ᏮᏮᏅᏅ

More time passed as they trudged through the catacombs. Imara knew it was late Sunday evening, but she refused to look at the time. She didn't need another reason to panic.

Mr. Nazari cleared his throat, and Imara saw Abe nod back at him. Abe narrowed his eyes at the map and said, "You know what I don't understand? If these catacombs are the tagger's hideout, where do they do stuff?"

Imara gave him a sideways glance. "They probably just talk. They can do that anywhere down here."

"Then what's with all the traps? I get the ones upstairs. They stop people from getting into the catacombs. But why are there traps down here? They have to be hiding something."

"Hiding more hostages?" Darius asked from behind them.

Abe shrugged. "I don't know, maybe. Remember the Judge had that transporter? He built it somewhere. Don't you think he has a workshop or an office or an evil lair or something?"

Siluk laughed, anxious to get on anyone's good side since Darius was still angry. Siluk said, "Dude. The Judge strolled into a party wearing all black. He wrote an ominous note in rhyme. You know he has an evil lair."

"Exactly," Abe said. "We should look for it. It could help the police catch the Judge. Especially if we get that transporter."

Imara gritted her teeth. "We shouldn't waste time looking for a lair when we still haven't found Naki."

Abe shook his head and put his hand on Imara's arm. "No, I don't mean instead of looking for her. I mean while we're looking. If we happen to stumble upon it."

Mr. Nazari said, "We should actively look for the Judge's lair. We need to find it before we leave the catacombs. The more we know about that transporter, the better. We have to end this fight before it gets out of hand."

Imara filled her lungs with air, willing herself to stay calm. Now it was clear why Mr. Nazari was so quick to stay and look for the other hostages. He did have an ulterior motive as she had suspected. Imara stomped her foot. "I did not come down here to get involved with some terrorist group. I want to find Naki and go home. The rest of you can look for an evil lair if you want, but I have a life. My dream job is already on the line. I don't need any more distractions."

Mr. Nazari said, "Yes, but you were supposed to start tomorrow and you'll most likely miss that deadline. So, why not stay another day or so to help us find the lair?"

Imara turned and looked at Mr. Nazari through narrowed eyes. "How did you know I was supposed to start tomorrow?"

Mr. Nazari pursed his lips and glanced at Abe through the corner of his eyes. A micro expression that Imara didn't miss. Her eyebrows lowered. "You two thought of this together? You thought you'd ambush me and force me to help? This isn't my fight. I just want to find my sister and go home. I don't want to get involved with the Judge."

"It wasn't supposed to feel like an ambush," Abe said while mustard yellow drips of guilt fell from his skin. "And we're not forcing you to help. But we can't get through the catacombs without you. You definitely don't have to fight the Judge or anything. We just want to find the lair. It could have important stuff in it."

Abe looked at Imara with eyes filling full of hope. "Anything in the lair could be useful, but the transporter is key. If we're going to stop the Judge or at least slow him down, we need that transporter."

Imara turned and stomped down the passageway.

Abe had to jog a few steps to keep up with her. "But we'll find Naki first. That's the number one priority."

But an hour later, they were still searching, and Imara had lost every ounce of patience she had. Imara found a camouflaged cover using the trick she had discovered earlier in the day. She lifted the cover and pushed yet another black button. The door slid open to an empty chamber. Imara slammed her fist against the wall and let out a scream.

"Nothing is happening!" she said. "We have been searching all day, and we haven't done anything!"

"Calm down, Imara," Siluk said. "What is your problem?"

"I want to find my sister! Why is Naki so well hidden when the others weren't?"

"Look at this," Darius said, pointing to a plaque on the wall of the empty chamber. "They made a monument for the people who died in the flood."

"What flood?" Imara asked, curiosity defeating her anger for a small moment. "The one that closed this place twenty years ago?"

Mr. Nazari raised an eyebrow. "Do you know how the taggers started?"

Imara shrugged. "Some person decided he was better than everyone else and found followers by being charismatic?"

Mr. Nazari shook his head with a frown. "No. There was a time when all of us agreed with the taggers."

Imara's eyebrows raised at this unexpected phrase.

Mr. Nazari continued. "These catacombs were closed for years because of a flood almost a hundred years ago. But in 2101 the Egyptian Council decided to dam the water and reopen the catacombs. They hired a contractor, and the exhibit opened a few months later. There was a grand opening with fireworks, food carts, carnival games. No expense was spared. But then the dams broke and people drowned only a few days later."

"Wait a minute," Abe said confused. "Drowned? I thought they had the Nguyen method in 2101."

Mr. Nazari nodded. "They did. And they used it. They saved a lot of people, but there were too many people and not enough time. And anyway, that's not what this story is about. The people drowning, that was horrible of course. But then everyone found out the flood..."

"Wasn't an accident." Darius finished.

Mr. Nazari looked to the side. "Well, it wasn't exactly on purpose. But the contractor knowingly cut corners on supplies and construction in order to pocket the extra money. As investigations went deeper, they found out it wasn't the first time people were injured because of that contractor's shoddy workmanship. He did the same thing in Italy only a year before, though that time nobody died. As you can imagine, people were upset. Everyone was mad that he'd gotten away with the same thing twice."

"That's when they had the idea for tagging?" Imara asked.

"Yes," Mr. Nazari said. "What started out as reasonable quickly escalated. A particular faction took it upon themselves to make his name known in the entire world. He went to prison for involuntary manslaughter, but when he got out, his sentence didn't end. Everyone knew his name everywhere in the world. No one would hire him and he was forced to move to Alaska and live off the grid."

"But hey," Siluk said. "Not everyone in Alaska lives off the grid to hide from the world. We have lots of normal people there, too."

Imara reached up to tug the hair on the back of her neck. "He killed those people. He deserved what he got."

Mr. Nazari shrugged with one shoulder. "When he got out of prison, he couldn't get a job anywhere in the world. He couldn't feed himself. He was homeless. He almost died of starvation, and the media rejoiced. That's when people started to think that faction went too far. He moved to Alaska and everyone realized what they had done to him. His life was destroyed. He was alive, but he had no way of living."

Imara felt a small twinge of sympathy for the man. But when she frowned, all she thought of was Naki. She sniffed and finally checked the time on her ring. It was well past one in the morning. Mr. Nazari suddenly insisted they were going to bed for the night.

Imara tugged the hair at the back of her neck all the way back to the shaft. In the crypt room, she was the last to fill her water bottle, and Abe hung back to talk to her.

"Are you sure you want to risk your dream job for Naki?" he asked.

Imara looked at Abe surprised. "I wouldn't expect a question like that from you."

"I'm not saying you *should* give up on Naki. She's your sister." Abe shrugged, "But you don't seem especially thrilled with your decision."

"Of course I'm not thrilled with it. This is what I've wanted to do ever since I found out I was a truth seer. I'm sure they'll extend my deadline, but even if they don't, I'd sacrifice anything for Naki. There's nothing more important than family, which ironically I learned from Professor Santini, not from my family."

Abe laughed. "So everything you know you learned from Professor Santini, huh?"

Imara narrowed her eyes. "I learned from my family too. My parents love us and sacrifice for us and all that. But one time Professor Santini missed an entire week of school when her mother was in the hospital. Your dad fired her for it, and she didn't even blink an eye."

Abe's eyes widened. "He fired her? For taking care of her family?"

Imara looked at Abe amused. "Are you really surprised by that? Your dad is a ruthless businessman. It makes the school successful, but he's not afraid to do whatever it takes to get it there."

"But what happened? Professor Santini still works at the school."

Imara laughed. "Oh, the replacement truth seer was a joke. It lasted about two days before he begged Professor Santini to come back. I think he even gave her raise."

Imara glanced at the unopened crypt one last time before leaving the crypt room. A fresh wave of fear thrummed through her veins. This wasn't over yet. She still had one day to find Naki.

One more day.

FOURTEEN

ANOTHER DAY CAME AND WENT WITH NO sign of Naki, Headmaster Bello, or the taggers. Imara thought Headmaster Bello was the Judge anyway, so she stopped worrying about him. And Abe was worried about the taggers enough for all of them, so Imara didn't worry about them either. But it was Monday night, and a deep panic had settled into Imara's stomach. Everyone reassured Imara that Naki would be safe because the Judge must have given her food and water, but this didn't calm Imara at all. Nothing could calm her until she saw Naki safe. On top of that, she now had to worry about her dream job, which may or may not be on the line.

Imara's feet ached with each new step. She was fairly active, but walking all day for three days straight took its toll. She wasn't the only one either. White-hot strings of pain whipped off everyone's feet. Imara tried to ignore the growing balls of panic bouncing off everyone. It was hard enough when the panic inside her was so strong.

"Stop showing me the statues, Siluk," Darius said. "I know you're only trying to get on my good side."

"Maybe if you cared about something other than history, it wouldn't be so difficult to get on your good side," Siluk said under his breath.

"What did you just say?"

Imara dug her toe in the ground and squeezed her fists until her nails dug deep into her palms. "Stop fighting. I can't concentrate."

Mr. Nazari groaned. "I just ran out of water. Does anyone have some?"

Abe dug through his backpack for his water bottle.

Darius huffed. "And don't you spray me again, Siluk. I can't smell that bad."

"We've been down here for three days. We all smell bad."

Imara slammed her fist against the wall until she felt the imprint of stone on her hand. "We. Are. Missing something!"

Mr. Nazari grunted at Siluk. "Maybe if you stopped sniffing so much, it wouldn't smell so bad."

"You're out of water too?" Abe said from behind Imara.

Imara stared at the map again, trying to see something new. Her foot tapped on the ground at an increasing speed until she let out an exasperated grumble.

"Maybe it's time we go back upstairs," Abe said.

"No," Imara said turning toward the rest of them. "I'm not giving up. If she hasn't had water, we only have a few more hours."

"Maybe we can take a quick break to refill our water and then come back," Abe said.

"What if there really is a secret passageway?" Imara said, resisting his suggestion. "Maybe the taggers built one. Darius can listen to the walls and see if there's anything that sounds new."

Darius rolled his eyes. "You want me to listen to every single wall in the catacombs? That would take—" Darius paused when Abe glared at him. Darius gulped. "That would take more than a few hours."

Mr. Nazari frowned. In a cautious voice he asked, "Do you think maybe she's not down here? The Judge must have noticed Darius and I were gone, and maybe he took Naki somewhere else. You know how to see past all the illusions, don't you?"

It took forty-eight hours, but he was finally brave enough to voice the fear all of them had, including Imara. She ignored his words because there had to be something she could do for Naki.

There had to be.

Imara's eyes shot up. "What if it's not an illusion? I've been looking past projector illusions, but what if there's a secret passage that's blocked by an actual object like a statue or something?"

Abe nodded. "Maybe the fork in the road with the river on one side and the dangerous path on the other. Why would it be that dangerous if it wasn't hiding something? It looked like a chamber that ended with the spikes, but maybe there was a path behind the spikes."

Imara nodded and let his hope encourage her. "Yes! I never checked if it went beyond those spikes, I just assumed."

"And what about that one passage that had the man with a feather and staff?" Darius suggested. "You said that was a statue."

Imara nodded again and walked forward, grateful to be doing something new. "We'll check the statue passage first

151

because it's closer. And then we'll check the fork in the road. If we think of any other ideas, we'll check those too."

For the first time in a day, Imara marched with a clear purpose in mind. When they reached the passage with the statue at the end, she reminded everyone to stay to one side so they would avoid the spikes coming out from the tombs in the wall.

Imara got to the end and stared at the statue until her eyes watered. It looked like all the other statues in the catacombs, more of a carving than a statue. "Listen to it, Darius. Is it old?"

Imara turned and saw Darius flinch along with the others. "Sorry," he said. "It looks like it's swinging the staff at us. I know it's fake, but—" He flinched and closed his eyes. "It's hard to ignore."

Imara grabbed his hand and led him forward so he could keep his eyes closed. "I need complete silence," Darius said. "Everyone stand still. Don't breathe or make a noise. I have to concentrate."

Darius planted his feet and relaxed his entire body. He wrapped one hand behind his ear so the sound would be amplified. Then he tapped the statue with his fingernail.

Darius squinted and stood still for an entire minute. His breath was frozen in his lungs. He put his head down, afraid to say the words. "It's as old as the catacombs."

Imara hit the wall with her fist. She clenched her jaw and said, "Let me check one more thing before we go. This is carved into the wall like all the others, but I want to see...wait a second."

Imara pushed her fingers behind the statue with a flutter of hope. "It's not carved into the wall. It's pushed up against it."

The stone warmed her fingers as she pulled the statue to get it away from the wall. "It's stuck," she said. "There must be a mechanism keeping it in place."

Imara slid her finger along the edge of the statue and the wall. She concentrated as she looked, but her fingers were ready to detect any change in texture as well. She felt all the way around the statue. "I wish you guys could look. I must be missing something."

But then Imara noticed a silvery shimmer from the bottom of the statue. She reached for it without a thought. Imara didn't know as much as Darius, but she was pretty sure ancient Egyptians didn't put metal in their statues.

Imara found the metal, but pulled her hand away with a start. "*Ow!*"

"Are you okay?" Abe said, stepping forward.

"It's fine," she said. "There's metal, and it burned me, but it's not bad. It surprised me."

Annoyed yet again by the lack of working temperature-controlled underclothes, Imara reached for the metal. She knew it wasn't a button, so this time she tried sliding it to one side. She pushed one side of it and nothing. She pushed another side, and it didn't budge. But on the third side, it jiggled. She pressed harder, and the metal moved to one side about an inch. At the same time, the statue scraped against the back wall as it slid to one side.

"Whoa!" Siluk said.

Imara jumped up expecting danger. "What happened?"

Everyone stared at the statue with wide eyes.

"What?" Imara asked again.

"The illusion is gone," Abe said. "We heard a scraping noise, and then the jumping man turned into a statue. Look!" Abe said pointing back.

Imara turned around. The statue had moved all the way to the side. An opening sat behind it, but only a small one. It was no wider than a fist and as tall as the statue.

"How are we supposed to get through that?" Mr. Nazari asked.

"I don't know," Imara said frowning at the stone. Something about it wasn't quite right. It looked flat.

She reached into the thin opening. Her arm went through all the way to her shoulder. "There's something weird about this stone." Imara rested her hand on the flat stone and started when she felt it move. "It's a curtain," she said.

Abe took the curtain and ran his fingers over it. "That's incredible," he said. "It looks like stone."

Imara took the curtain back to drape it over the statue and out of the way. "Let's go," she said.

Imara stepped into the secret passageway. It was narrow and short with a crypt on one side and a dead-end wall at the end. "Naki!" Imara yelled.

They heard a quiet voice right away. "Hello?" it said.

Imara's eyes widened and she yelled Naki's name again. The answering voice came from the other side of the dead-end wall. Darius and Siluk pounded on the wall, trying to open it with sheer force.

Imara shook her head. "Do you really think that's going to work?"

"Then you open it," Siluk said stepping back with a frown.

Imara pushed Siluk out of the way and readjusted her hologram so the flashlight shined over the whole wall. Her eyes glided over the surface of the stone, looking for anything that seemed strange or felt weird to her eyes. One spot was blurry. "Right here," she said as she lifted a cover to press the button.

Imara stared until the door was fully opened. Leaning against a wall with a tear-stained face was Naki, still wearing her sapphire blue graduation robe. Her heels were askew on the ground beside her. Imara released a breath she had been holding in since Naki was taken hostage. The air filled Imara's lungs with calm. The relief relaxed every muscle in her body, and Imara allowed herself a small smile. Another sigh escaped her when she saw a plate with food and a water bottle only half empty.

Naki and Imara made eye contact, and gratitude seeped out from every pore of Naki's skin. Naki opened her mouth to speak, but before she could say a word, Imara did a short nod and reentered the passageway. She leaned against the wall and looked back in at Naki.

"Thank you," Naki said bursting into tears. Darius ran forward, and Naki held him in a tight hug. Siluk was there a moment later, and Naki released Darius only to wrap her arms around Siluk. Her sobs slowed and were soon replaced with a fit of giggles. "You have no idea how happy I am to see you guys."

Siluk stepped away from Naki, and she embraced Mr. Nazari before he could protest. "Thank you," she said. Naki wiped her tears with her fingertips then breathed out with relief. She grabbed her heels and walked into the narrow passageway. "Let's get out of here."

155

Naki started when she noticed Abe. "Who are you?" she asked happily.

Mr. Nazari put his arm around Abe and gave a proud smile. "This is my son, Abraxas."

Naki grinned. "That's fresh. It's nice to meet you. I'm Naki." She turned toward the others. "Thank you all for rescuing me. Even you, Abraxas."

Naki held her temples as she shook her head. "If I had to wait another minute in that vault, I swear I would have died of boredom. I'm so glad to be with people again. You have no idea how terrible it is to be alone for that long. I started talking to the wall." Darius laughed, and the others smiled.

Imara stood with her back to the wall, waiting for the pleasantries to end.

Naki lowered one eyebrow and licked her lips. She opened and closed her mouth several times. Imara's heart beat faster as she asked, "What is it?"

Naki held her tongue out then closed her mouth around it. "I don't know yet." Naki hooked her arm around Siluk's. "How come you all smell good? Do you have your sprays?"

Siluk nodded and sniffed around Naki before pulling the bottles from his pocket.

"Thank goodness," Naki said. "I thought I was going to die of smell and of boredom."

Siluk spritzed her with some bottles and laughed. "You were dying of boredom?"

Naki tossed her ponytail full of tiny braids back behind her. "You know how I am, Siluk. I hate being alone. I'm so glad you finally found me." She pulled Siluk and Darius in for a group hug, and they both grinned.

Naki licked her lips again but then shook her head dismissing it. Naki's eyes went wide when she looked down at her clothes. Her face fell into a deep frown. "I don't know how useful I'll be in this robe. And I only have my heels from the party. I have no idea how I'll manage these halls."

Imara took the backpack off her shoulder and handed it to Naki. She said with a blunt voice, "I packed clothes for you. And shoes."

Naki looked at the bag in surprise and breathed a long sigh of relief. "Oh good," she said, turning back to Darius and Siluk. "I guess I better change. Is there a good—"

Naki licked her lips with frantic speed. "We need to get out of here," she said. Imara started toward the statue, but everyone else stared with blank expressions. "NOW!" Naki yelled.

Everyone scrambled to the entrance of the secret passage when a mist shot out from the ground near the crypt in the secret passage. "Hurry!" Naki said, the panic in her voice rising.

Everyone made it through the passage opening, but the mist flowed through it. Imara bent to close the opening with the metal piece in the statue. "Ow," she said as a deeper burn surged through her finger. With her mouth open, Imara gulped in a huge breath of the mist. She shut her mouth, but her face was full of the mist as the statue closed, and it still came in through her nose. Imara's peripheral vision disappeared. She blinked, trying to regain her vision, but within seconds, everything went black.

"Cover your mouth and nose with your shirt collar," Siluk said. "It will stop some of the particles from getting in your body."

Imara grasped at her shirt collar, but it was too late. Too much mist had entered her system. She stumbled, and her gut tightened. Her knees hit the ground, and a pain shot through her thighs. She held her arms over her stomach, trying to ground herself. The voices around her were distant and hollow. Her head hurt trying to focus on them.

"What was that stuff?" Darius asked. His voice bubbled as if he was under water.

"It smells like sleeping gas," Siluk said, his voice as fuzzy as Darius's. "We use it in animal traps sometimes, but that had another smell I don't recognize."

"Do something, Siluk!" Naki's voice was louder than the others. Her voice shook with fear. "She's dying!"

The voices faded to mumbles while Imara's mind clouded over. Imara coughed, which tightened her stomach in another knot. Imara doubled over clutching the slippery fabric of her shirt. For a moment, she considered giving in to the pain. The effort to resist it was too much.

A short spray came out under Imara's nose that caused her to take a sharp breath. She sat up so fast she almost hit her head on the wall behind her. Siluk sprayed again, and Imara took in another sharp breath. Her vision started clearing, and she focused on everyone huddled around her. She blinked and let her breathing return to normal. Air rattled through her lungs, but the knot in her stomach loosened with each breath.

"You were right, Abe." Siluk said. "That spray isn't exactly like smelling salts, but it did the trick."

Abe helped Imara to her feet while she shook her head to clear it. She took several deep breaths before the muscles in her body stopped tensing. Imara leaned against the wall and pinched the bridge of her nose. She shut her eyes tight and opened them wide a few times before the world stopped spinning.

Just as her breathing evened, Abe took her hand and turned it so the palm was up. "What happened to your hand?" he asked.

His hands were soft against hers. A sudden flutter in her heart careened Imara back to reality. "Oh, I burned it," she said while her ears filled with heat. "It was nothing compared to that mist."

Abe rubbed the pad of her pointer finger with his thumb. "This one?" he asked.

Imara shook her head to remove the cloudy feeling inside it. She looked down at the finger Abe indicated and nodded. "Yes, but I'm sure it's fine."

She went to put her hand down, but Abe held it fast. "I have some ointment," he said. "Will you let me put it on?"

Imara stopped resisting and nodded with a hint of a smile. Her body still felt weak from the mist, and the anxiety of the last three days threatened to collapse her on the spot.

Abe rubbed her finger once more then pushed down on it with gentle pressure. "Sometimes burns go deeper than you think. The surface is okay, but the inside isn't. The ointment will help."

Imara nodded, and Abe dug through his bag. Imara grinned and whispered, "If you're not a healer, then how did you know the burn went deeper than the surface?"

Abe shook his head with a quiet laugh. "I have medical training, remember?"

"Why?" Imara asked.

Abe opened the ointment and smeared it over her finger. "You need the ointment because it heals the skin several layers deep."

Imara cocked her head to the side. "No. Why did you get medical training? You never told me."

"Because I wanted to," Abe said cryptically. He finished by wrapping Imara's finger in a soft gauze. She leaned into the stone wall to keep from falling over.

While he put the supplies back in his bag, Naki wiped her forehead and said, "I guess I better go change." She started down the path and went straight for a spike coming out from a tomb. Without a thought, Imara lunged in front of Naki to protect her from the spike.

Naki stepped back in fear, and Darius patted her on the shoulder. "There are illusions down here, and only Imara can see past them. You almost walked into a spike."

Naki put her hand over her heart and sighed with drama that could rival a soap opera. "This place is the worst," she said. "How do I get through this hall without being impaled by a spike?"

Imara stumbled back against the wall while Mr. Nazari showed Naki where to walk. Soon Naki was around the corner.

The moment she was out of sight, Abe turned to Imara and said, "What happened?"

"What?" Imara asked, wondering if her head was more muddled than she thought.

Abe looked at her like it was obvious. "Did you get in a fight with your sister at the party or something?"

Imara shook her head with closed eyes, trying to understand. "What? No," she said. "Why would you think that?"

Abe narrowed his eyes. "You barely spoke to her. You didn't hug her or greet her at all. What happened?"

Imara shrugged it off. "It's fine. We're sisters."

160

"This is how they always are," Siluk said.

Imara glared at Siluk and spoke through her teeth. "Nobody asked you."

Siluk rolled his eyes. "Abe asked. Maybe not me, but he did ask."

"Mind your own business," Imara said with a clenched jaw.

Abe glared at Siluk and stepped in front of Imara, acting as shield between her and Siluk. He looked into her eyes and said, "Are you okay?"

Imara's heart sank as she turned her eyes to the ground. "Yes. It's fine. Siluk is right, this is how it always is. I love Naki more than anything, but we aren't close."

"Why not?" Abe asked.

But then Naki came back around the corner in the clothes Imara had packed. With the backpack flung over her shoulder, Naki looked ready to take on the world. "Which way are we going?" she asked.

Everyone turned to Imara. She glanced at the map and said, "I guess we better check the fork in the road. We might find Headmaster Bello." Imara shrugged with apprehension. "Or the evil lair."

Naki started talking as soon as they started down the next corridor. "I'm so glad you finally found me. There were a few times I heard your voices, but just as I was going to call out, the Judge would come and move me to another room."

"He moved you?" Siluk asked.

"Yeah," Naki said. "You were right outside my door one of the times."

"We were so quiet at first, but we stopped being careful. He must have heard us when we got too close." Darius said.

"Why do you call the Judge a he?" Naki asked. "It could be a woman."

"The taggers say 'he.'" Imara said. "Although maybe that's to throw us off."

"What did the Judge do when he moved you?" Siluk asked.

Naki shuddered. "It was so creepy. He spoke in my head with my own voice just like at the party."

Mr. Nazari slapped his forehead. "Of course! The Judge is a telepath. I forgot. That means Jabari can't be the Judge."

Naki gasped and clutched her heart. "You thought Headmaster Bello was the Judge?"

"It's a long story," Darius said.

Imara narrowed her eyes at Mr. Nazari. "There's no such thing as telepaths."

Mr. Nazari shrugged. "That's what I thought too, but how else could he talk in our heads like that?"

"Maybe it's technology."

Mr. Nazari shook his head with surety. "That kind of technology doesn't exist. I heard my own voice inside my head. Who could make my own voice speak to me? He has to be a telepath."

"I guess you're right," Imara said, and she turned to keep walking. "Let's see if we can find Headmaster Bello at the fork in the road."

FIFTEEN

AFTER A FEW MINUTES, THEY CAME TO THE fork in the road. Imara stood in front of the fork, making notes on her map to describe the illusion while Abe explained what he saw. Naki blabbered on about how she could taste the humidity and how hard it was to be in a place with such extreme temperature. She walked as she talked, but no one noticed when she started toward the side of the fork that looked like a twinkling path.

Imara glanced up and saw Naki at the part of the path that opened into a river. "Stop!" Imara screamed.

Naki turned around, but took a step backward toward the river. Her foot brushed the edge of the path, and her body teetered backward. Her eyes grew wide, and her hands clutched the empty air around her. Naki couldn't see the river or the edge of the path, but she knew she was about to lose her balance.

Abe ran forward and grabbed her hands. He tugged her back onto the path, but his own foot slipped over the edge. Imara tapped her ring to close the map, and her legs shot forward in a run. Abe leaned away from the river, but it did no good.

Imara was still a few steps away when his other foot slipped off the path. His back hit the edge of the cliff-side. His arms flailed out, grasping at the empty air.

He slid further down the cliff when Imara finally reached him. She yanked his hand high so he could grip the cliff-side. She found his other hand and pulled with all of her strength. After a few anxiety-filled moments, they were both safe on the path, huffing with uneven breaths.

Imara shook her head as they got to their feet. "Reckless," she said under her breath. "You should have waited for me. I can see the cliff, and you can't."

She held his hand tight in hers, squeezing as her heart raced. She let out a long breath and noticed something coming from his skin. Red orange whips.

Selfishness.

Not transparent like they were when she asked him about making the world a better place. Now they were heavily pigmented and whipping wildly. Imara swallowed and took a step away from him, staring at the whips. It wasn't lost on her that they reappeared only minutes after Naki was back in his presence. Naki ran up to him, almost toppling him over with a hug. "You saved my life!" she said.

Abe ran his fingers through his hair, clearly enjoying the attention. He didn't seem to mind the hug either. He grinned and puffed his chest out before he waved his hand. "It was nothing," he said.

Imara clenched her jaw and spun around. Her body felt shaky as she walked away. "I'm going to check the path with the spikes."

Imara marched forward, and the others stayed behind while Naki commanded their attention. "I was so scared," she said. "What was over there?"

"It's a river," Siluk said. "It looks like a path, but it's really a river."

"Why didn't anyone warn me? I could have died." Naki said.

Everyone fawned over her, apologizing for not telling her about the illusion. They asked if she was okay and wanted to check her foot to see if it was injured.

Abe jogged up to Imara just before she rounded the bend in the passage. He said, "What's wrong?"

Imara grunted. "Nothing. What are you talking about?"

"Why are you mad at me?" Abe asked, half jogging, half walking just to keep up with her.

"Who said I was mad?" Imara said, her eyes facing forward with fierce determination so she wouldn't have to make eye contact.

"Imara," Abe said in exasperation.

Imara turned to him with a tight jaw and clenched her fists. She lowered her voice so no one else could hear. "You risked your life for Naki. You want her just like you did at the party."

"What?" Abe's eyes opened wide. "No."

Imara tightened her jaw until her veins popped out. Her body still felt weak from the mist. She said through her teeth, "You can't lie to me. I know you want to be with her."

"Is that what you see?" Abe asked. "What do you see?" Abe put his palms up and reached his arms in front of Imara.

The red orange whips were there as strong as ever. Imara's nose stung and her eyes warmed from tears. She swallowed and tried to keep her expression neutral. "You saved Naki for selfish reasons. I can't see why. But I don't have to see because I already know." She sniffed and hated herself for letting it get to her. "You want to be with her. Just go and do it already. I don't care."

"No." Abe let his hands fall as he shook his head. "I did it for you." Abe put his hand over his forehead to cover his eyes. "I was trying to impress you." Abe wrapped his fingers around Imara's hand. "Because I care about you," he said.

Imara wrenched her hand away and burrowed her eyebrows over her eyes. "I see only selfishness. I don't see care or desire or anything for me."

Abe gritted his teeth and his eyebrows twitched. "Then you see only the bad and not the good."

"Just because it's bad, doesn't mean it's not true." Imara folded her arms across her chest and turned away from him. "The truth hurts."

When Abe spoke, his words were filled with anguish. "It doesn't have to. I do care about you. If you can't see that, then you're ignoring it."

Imara stopped and turned toward Abe with fire in her eyes. "I know how to use my hila," she said louder than she meant.

Naki's incessant chatter stopped, and Imara realized everyone's eyes darted to her and Abe. She turned her back to them and lowered her voice to a whisper. "You're just upset because I know your intentions. Stop making excuses."

Abe looked at Imara and threw his hands in the air. A sound came from his throat, but he clamped his mouth shut to stop the words from coming out. He gave a final exasperated stare before he turned around and joined the others.

From behind her, she heard Siluk say to Abe, "This is what your dad was talking about. I told you it wouldn't take long to find out."

Abe huffed. "Just shut up, Siluk."

Imara turned, ready to round the bend in the path. She clenched her jaw. It would be difficult to concentrate on the spikes while she was this upset. And the tears in her eyes blurred her vision, which she desperately tried to ignore. While she waited, she became aware of a conversation she hadn't noticed earlier.

"You betrayed me, Siluk. Stop acting like it was no big deal."

"I said I was sorry. What more do you want?"

Imara heard what must be Siluk stomp toward her to get away from Darius.

Naki rushed onto the path next to Siluk and said, "He's just angry right now. Give him time, he'll forgive you. It was one mistake."

Imara's nose crinkled, and despite her better judgment, she turned to join the conversation. "It's not one mistake. Siluk is a liar. He lies about things all the time. Darius and everyone else should have found out a long time ago. Siluk doesn't deserve to be forgiven."

Naki turned to Imara and rolled her eyes so far back, Imara was almost impressed. "Sometimes you should care more about people than the mistakes they make."

Imara scoffed. "Are you saying you want to be best friends with a liar? The relationship justifies the lies? That sounds like an unhealthy relationship to me."

167

Naki shook her head with another eye roll. "Oh, I'm sorry, I didn't realize you were the expert on relationships. When was the last time you had a best friend?"

Naki glanced toward Abe and lowered her voice. "You and your boyfriend or whatever he is are having issues already and it's been what? A couple days?"

Imara swallowed, and her lip quivered. She pursed her lips to hide it and made fists with her hands. "Mind your own business."

Naki turned with a whip of her ponytail. "That's what you always say," she said as she walked off.

Siluk knitted his eyebrows together. "You're just jealous of Naki because she can keep a boyfriend and you can't."

Imara's nostrils flared. She clenched her fists so tight, her nails dug into her skin. "I'm not the jealous one," she said. "And it's not Naki's fault I can't keep a boyfriend, it's mine. Don't act like I blame her because I don't."

Siluk glared for a moment, but turned away as if she wasn't worth the effort.

Imara frowned and let her eyes wander back to Abe. He was sad, genuinely sad. It was the first time she saw so many cobalt blue drops pelting off his skin, and Imara knew it was her fault. He was trying to be cute, and she yelled at him. She usually ignored the guilt when she offended people because she always felt justified. But this time it was different. Abe was different.

Reckless, but selfless. He cared about the world. He cared about people. And he cared about her. He said he did. She didn't see the feeling, but she saw that he wasn't lying. And there was one more thing tugging at her, no matter how she tried to ignore it.

She liked him.

A lot.

It had only been a few days, but everything about him intrigued her. His passion, his hope, his skills. She had never met someone like Abe before. He sacrificed himself to help others, just like Imara did. And he wanted to make the world a better place. How could she not be attracted to that?

Imara let her head fall to her chest. She fiddled with her fingers while she thought. She tried to find an easy out, but there wasn't one, and she knew it. She stuck her bottom lip out in a frown. The decision was made, and now she had to follow through.

Imara plodded over to the others. "I need a break," she said to them. "I'm too tired, and the illusion around the spikes is tricky. I can't tell if there's anything behind them."

Imara tried and failed to catch Abe's eye. His hands were deep in his pockets, and his eyes stuck to the ground.

Mr. Nazari stood tall, using every ounce of his authority. "We should go upstairs and sleep for the night. We can come back in the morning after we've rested and gotten water."

"No," Imara said, her focus drawing away from Abe for a brief moment. "We have to find Headmaster Bello tonight. I only need a break. If the Judge didn't give him water, we only have one hour left."

Naki looked at Siluk and Darius with narrowed eyes. "One hour? Why one hour?"

Darius answered with a smug expression. "A person can only survive three days without water."

Naki gulped. "Not down here."

"What does that mean?" Siluk asked.

Naki frowned. "It's hot down here. When it's hot, you sweat more." Naki slid her tongue across her bottom lip. Then she closed her mouth and tasted. "In these conditions I estimate someone could survive forty-two to fifty-four hours without water, depending on the person."

A lump hardened in Imara's throat. It had been seventy-one hours since the Judge took the hostages. Guilt swam through Imara's veins and stiffened the muscles in her body.

After a long silence, Abe said, "The Judge gave you food and water, right?"

"Yes," Naki answered.

"Then I'm sure he did the same for Headmaster Bello. Why wouldn't he?" Abe stood tall and rolled his shoulders back. "Let's go to bed and Imara can get past the spikes in the morning."

Abe walked next to Imara and allowed their eyes to meet for a moment. He pointed his hand ahead with his palm up. "Lead the way."

Imara nodded, but held her breath as she starting walking forward. She was relieved when he walked with her. Still, it took more effort than she expected to get the words out of her mouth. "I'm sorry," she said.

Abe frowned, and her eyes widened when she saw mustard yellow drips of guilt dropping away from his skin. "I didn't mean to imply you don't know how to use your hila. What do I know? I'm mashimo."

Imara held her mouth open and reached up to tug the hair on the back of her neck. She never expected Abe to apologize. She was the one who yelled at him and accused him. In a moment of weakness, a confession tumbled out of her mouth. "Seeing the truth isn't always straightforward. It's

170

easier for me to see the dominant emotion than the background ones." She tucked her head down and bit her lip. "I shouldn't have been so quick to accuse."

Abe shrugged. "You weren't wrong about me saving Naki for selfish reasons. You've saved us all multiple times. For once I wanted to be brave like you. I was trying to impress you with my heroics." He gave her a half smile and said, "I'm still kind of hoping it worked."

Imara averted her eyes and let out a soft laugh. "Do you always throw yourself toward cliffs to rescue people? You did that when I fell into that cliff pit."

Abe scrunched up his face. "Like you can talk, Miss I'll-use-myself-as-a-human-shield-between-people-and-any-danger-whatsoever."

Imara raised an eyebrow. "Any danger whatsoever? That's an exaggeration."

Abe counted off on his fingers, "That boy at the party and the hover cart. Siluk and me and that faulty rope. Naki and that spike, which happened right after you almost blacked out, by the way. I could go on. Plus, you saved me from that cliff pit before I tried to save you."

Imara's stomach quivered with a wave of delight. She couldn't believe he paid such close attention. She tugged harder on her hair, trying to maintain some level of sanity. "Someone had to do something. I was the only one who could in all of those situations. That's not impressive."

"Yes, it is," Abe insisted. "Especially when I was falling over that cliff just now. Aren't you afraid of heights?"

"Terrified."

Abe's smile disappeared as his face grew serious. He locked his eyes on Imara and said, "I'm not interested in Naki."

Imara watched as his skin turned glowy and bright. That was the only reason he said this. He knew with a direct statement, Imara could tell if it was truth or lie. In this case, truth. His words and actions should have been enough for her, but she appreciated his statement all the same. She couldn't deny the truth when she saw it like this.

Imara turned her head to the side while the corners of her eyes crinkled. "It wouldn't matter even if you were interested in Naki. She doesn't like my leftovers."

"What?" Abe asked while one eye narrowed.

Imara brought her head down. She shouldn't have said it because now she had to explain. "Naki won't date anyone who has showed interest in me," Imara said. "I guess I don't know why, but I'm pretty sure she thinks less of them for considering me worthwhile."

Abe's lip curled up. "Wow, that's... sad." He looked into her eyes and feigned concern, but it was pity, and Imara knew it. She let out a silent sigh. This is why she shouldn't have said anything. Pity was what people felt for an inferior, not an equal.

Abe glanced behind him at Naki. Imara thought it was strange timing, but it didn't bother her. At least not until a grass green thread of desire flew out of Abe, straight toward Naki. Abe turned back to Imara, and in a panic, she smiled. The thread of desire was thin enough that Abe probably wasn't even aware of it. And there was no way he knew Imara could see it. So she smiled and pretended she couldn't.

But she could.

Grass green. It wasn't romantic so it didn't matter. So what if he wanted something from Naki? It could be anything. Sure, grass green desire often turned to scarlet romantic desire. Sure, it often took hours instead of days for the desire to turn when it was directed toward one person like that. Imara pushed the thoughts away with stubborn determination. That logic wasn't making her feel better. Abe just told her he wasn't interested in Naki. For now, she wouldn't worry as long as the thread of desire stayed thin.

SIXTEEN

THE NEXT MORNING, ABE SLEPT IN LATER than any other morning so far. Now that Naki was safe, and they had a good guess where Headmaster Bello was hidden, the urgency wasn't as strong. Abe was about to follow Imara to the crypt room, but had to go back for his water bottle. On one of the stone couches, Naki was rolling up her sleeping bag. Abe took advantage of the moment and dug through his backpack, pretending to be busy. This was just the chance he was waiting for. Darius sat fussing with his hair and beard, but once he left, Abe could talk to Naki alone.

Naki said to Darius, "Where did you get that?"

"I've had it the whole time," Darius said. "It was in my pocket when the Judge took us hostage."

"Don't let Imara see it," Naki said in a solemn tone.

"She already knows I have it. Obviously I don't use it when she's in the room. I'm not stupid. I don't need her yelling at me."

Abe turned to sneak a glance. Darius had a small, round object in his hand, but Abe couldn't see it. Curiosity got the best of him, and he asked, "What is it?"

Darius turned and held up the object. "It's just a mirror," he said.

Abe lowered his eyebrows in thought, but Naki jumped up and left the room so fast, it was almost a jog. Abe zipped his backpack and tried to mask his disappointment. He would have to catch Naki alone another time. It would be tricky, but he was convinced this was the best way. Abe heard Imara yelp, and his back shot up straight. But by the time he got to his feet, he heard Siluk yell and Imara started gagging.

೮೦೮೦೮೩೮೩

Imara filled her water bottle, drank from it, and then filled it up more. As she drank, she saw Siluk frowning at the unopened crypt. She dropped her water bottle and joined him as quick as she could. He sniffed as he looked at the crypt, the corners of his eyes pulled down.

"You smell something?" Imara asked.

Siluk nodded.

Imara shook her head and pointed at the crypt. "It's this spot right here. It's been bothering me since we got here, but I can't figure it out. This crypt should open, the others do. But the opening doesn't make any sense. The only way to open it is to stick my hand in this hole, which only I can see, and turn a knob. But if I do that, my hand will get butchered by the stone as the crypt opens. But my hand has to be there to squeeze the knob, otherwise it won't open. It doesn't make any sense. Who would design an opening that's meant to hurt you? There has to be another way, I just can't figure out—"

"Imara," Siluk said, his eyes serious.

"What?" Imara was annoyed by his interruption until she saw the look in his eyes. "What is it?" she asked. "What do you smell?"

"Death."

Imara sucked in a breath, and her eyes opened as wide as they could. She shot her hand into the hole. She squeezed the knob, which then made the stone scrape through several layers of her skin just as she thought it would. She yelped in pain, but held her hand fast to the knob, thinking of Siluk's single word.

The crypt opened, and the smell of death rushed into Imara's nostrils. Before she finished turning away, vomit spewed from her mouth.

Siluk yelled at the sight of the body. Imara coughed, trying to settle her stomach. The moment she took in another breath, she vomited again.

Siluk looked at her, then pulled a bottle from his pocket and sprayed it ten times. Soon the smell of death was covered by the scent of evergreen trees.

Imara gagged and grabbed her stomach, trying to calm it. She wiped her mouth clean with the fabric on her shoulder, and now that smell made her gag. She closed her eyes and took deep breaths. She heard footsteps running into the room. No one said a word, but everyone stood near.

"Pine?" she heard Darius ask. "I thought you could neutralize smells."

"I can." Siluk said with a biting tone. He wiped Imara's shoulder with a cloth and sprayed her shoulder with a few sprays. Within seconds her stomach stopped churning. "Imara was throwing up so I sprayed the first thing I could think of. I'll fix it once the pine wears off."

Imara stood up and faced the crypt. She chewed the inside of her cheek bracing herself for the sight. She knew what was there, but she had to look anyway. Her eyes landed on a body, bulging and bloated with blood leaking from the mouth and nose. Still in his party clothes.

Headmaster Bello.

The smell was bearable, but the sight alone was enough to make her queasy. But it wasn't just the sight. She felt the weight of his death deep in her bones. She sat down in the middle of the room while breaths came out in rapid succession. Sweat dripped down her back. She felt a tingle of anxiety start in her fingertips and spread through her whole body.

"This is my fault," she whispered.

She felt everyone turn toward her, but she didn't address them. She stared ahead, making eye contact with the air. "I figured out how to open the crypt yesterday morning, but I thought I missed something. I ignored what I saw because it didn't make any sense. I knocked on the crypt and listened for a voice. But I never expected somebody to be inside."

"It's not your fault, Imara," Naki said with tears already welling in her eyes.

Imara continued, almost unaware of Naki's voice. She spoke to the air in front of her, ignoring everything in the room. "We found Mr. Nazari and Darius in the third level. And Naki too. I thought everyone would be down there. But I shouldn't have assumed. I should have tried it anyway. This is all my fault."

Imara squeezed her eyes shut and brushed away the tear that fell.

Imara heard Abe step forward. He said, "What happened to your hand?"

Imara shook her head, ignoring Abe. "I should have tried it anyway. I should have known."

"That's how she opened the crypt," Siluk said to Abe. "She had to hold onto a knob while the stone scraped across her hand. She knew it would destroy her hand, which is why she didn't try it earlier. She thought there had to be another way."

Abe grabbed Imara's hand to look at the cuts on the back of it.

Imara offered no resistance. Instead she muttered to herself, hardly aware of his presence. "We could have saved him if I wasn't so selfish. My hand isn't as important as a life. I should have tried it anyway."

"Hey," Abe tried to look Imara in the eye, but she stared off seeing nothing. "This isn't your fault. Anyone would have done what you did. How were you supposed to know that hurting your hand was the only way?"

Imara shook her head slow at first, then faster. She shut her eyes tight. "It didn't make any sense. But I know better. The truth always hurts." With her eyes closed, Imara's mind wandered back to her first year of hila school.

ଔଔଓଔଓଔ

Sweet, thirteen-year-old Imara sat at her desk in a hila beginnings class. The room was filled with all the thirteen-year-olds no matter their hila. Imara's ears were perked up, every muscle attentive to the lesson.

Professor Santini stood at the front of the class, pointing to a puzzle on her hologram. She said to the class, "Hilas are enhanced when you apply logic to them. When you look at the world in a new way, it will become natural to use your hila."

Imara stared at the hologram. A puzzle blinked from the screen. To solve it, they had to draw a certain number of lines to connect all the dots. This one had nine dots arranged in a square.

Imara stared until her brain ached. She tugged the hair on the back of her neck and blinked until a smile appeared on her lips. Imara threw her hand into the air. "Could you repeat the instructions?"

Professor Santini nodded and said in a gentle voice, "Of course. Please connect all the dots using only four straight lines. Your finger can never lift off the screen, and you can't backtrack over a previous line."

The smile on Imara's face grew with confidence. Professor Santini mirrored the expression. "Do you think you can solve it, Imara?"

Imara nodded, and Professor Santini moved the hologram screen in front of Imara. Imara used her finger to draw an arrow through the dots. She had to draw outside the square the dots created. The arrangement itself was the trick. The square of dots was meant to limit her thinking. Only when she drew outside the square, could the puzzle be solved.

Professor Santini's eyes gleamed. "Well done, Imara." Professor Santini moved to address the entire class. "When using hilas, we must expect the unexpected. Don't limit yourself because you don't understand."

Imara heard mocking whispers from behind her. "What a brown noser." "Professor Santini just likes her because she's a truth seer." "She's so annoying and ugly with those weird-looking eyes."

A pit dropped in Imara's stomach. Her victory squashed as she touched the corner of her eye. They were just jealous probably. She couldn't see emotions yet, but it had to be jealousy. People weren't mean like that without a reason.

But the words still hurt no matter what she told herself. She shoved the pain from her mind. It didn't matter anyway. She had made friends here. Real friends. She wasn't going to let some random insults get her down.

After class, Imara got up to get a tissue while the other students filed out of the room. When she got there, Siluk was the only other student left. Imara smiled at him. One of her true friends.

Siluk gave Imara a lopsided grin. "Those other kids are dumb. They shouldn't have said those things just because you figured out the puzzle."

"Yeah," Imara said as she reached up to touch her eye.

"I don't think you're annoying at all," Siluk said.

Imara looked up with a grateful smile. Siluk smiled too, but Imara's stomach dropped. His skin dulled from a lie. Imara forced her smile back. He said *at all* didn't he? Everyone was annoying sometimes. Maybe he only thought she had been annoying once. That would make his statement a lie.

But Siluk opened his mouth again. "I think you're really smart, Imara."

Lie.

"Those other guys are dumb if they're jealous."

Lie.

"I think you're pretty too," he said with a broad grin.

Lie. Lie. Lie. Not one of his statements true.

"See ya." With perfect nonchalance, Siluk turned and left the room.

Imara's lip quivered as soon as the door shut. Not even pretty? Were her eyes as bad as everyone said? Imara pressed her eyelids down, trying to suppress the memory. Siluk was supposed to be her friend. Warm tears slid down her cheeks. She sniffed and brushed her nose with her wrist. With a clenched jaw, she turned to get another tissue.

Professor Santini stood next to the counter, holding a tissue out to Imara. "I saw that," Professor Santini said. "I'm so sorry."

Imara took the tissue and blew into it. She shed a few tears and thought that was the end of it. But with Professor Santini there, the sadness bundled up inside her. More tears fell and her shoulders heaved with a sob.

Professor Santini wrapped an arm around Imara and said, "You poor thing. Puberty is too young for truth seers. No one knows what we have to endure day in and day out. You shouldn't have to see these things at such a young age."

Imara sobbed again and buried her face into Professor Santini's shoulder. "My mom did the same thing to me last night. She said I was such a good cook." A sob shook in Imara's throat. With a sniff she said, "Even my mom is dirty liar."

"Imara." The scolding in Professor Santini's voice was tangible.

"I know, I know," Imara said bobbing her head up and down. "Mothers are better than teachers or whatever it is you always say."

"A good mother is worth a hundred teachers."

Imara blew into the tissue and squeezed her eyes until she saw stars behind her eyelids. "I do have a good mother. She loves me and she tries. I know that." Imara put her head back into Professor Santini's shoulder. "But I'll never forgive her for lying. Not Siluk either."

Professor Santini patted Imara's head. "I suppose some things may be unforgivable, but only drastic things like murder. Everybody lies. You need to forgive your mother."

Imara's voice broke as she talked. "But the lies hurt so much."

Professor Santini squeezed Imara a little tighter. "I know, Imara. Trust me, I know."

Another sob escaped and then Imara said, "They don't understand me like you do. No one does." The truth was heavy, and sometimes Imara didn't want to see it. Professor Santini let Imara cry into her shoulder until the sobs subsided.

Professor Santini patted Imara's shoulder before letting her go. "You have a gift. Not just a hila, but a gift. Few people are truth seers, and even fewer are able to achieve greatness with it. You are one of the few, I know it."

Professor Santini took Imara by the shoulders. She looked Imara in the eyes and said, "The truth hurts. But if you can accept it, it will make you stronger."

�������

Abe's voice brought Imara back to reality. His words were shaky and strained. "This is really bad, Imara. The cut goes down to the bone in two different places. And the entire back of your hand is covered in cuts."

The cuts stung, but the pain seemed so far away. Her body numbed with guilt. The smell of death mixed with pine danced into her nose. All she could see in her head now was Headmaster Bello.

"I killed him," she said. "I knew better. Expect the unexpected."

Imara stared ahead, barely aware of Abe's frantic search through his backpack. He dug out supplies, throwing things left and right. "I thought I had cleansing wipes. I can't find them," he said.

"Can't you use water?" Naki asked. Imara heard their voices, but they seemed distant compared to the reality of her guilt.

"I need clean water," Abe said.

Water *whooshed* as Mr. Nazari threw his water bottle to Abe.

"No," Abe said. "This is only clean because of the filter. But the filter is in the straw. It's not clean until it's in your mouth. But once it's in your mouth, it's not clean anymore."

A light wind rustled Imara's hair as Siluk dropped to his knees beside her. He rummaged through the things Abe had thrown from his bag.

"The water looks clean. How bad could it be?" asked Darius.

Abe hissed through his teeth. "There is dirt in the wound. It will get infected if the water isn't clean."

Imara heard Naki stumble to the water-filled crypt. "I can tell if the water is clean or not." She smacked her lips several times. A shot of panic lined her voice when she spoke again. "It's not clean."

Abe's head blurred in Imara's vision as he turned his head every which way. "Then we'll have to boil some water. If we go outside the catacombs maybe we can find wood or something. Or we can burn our clothes. I need a pot to boil it in."

"Are these the cleansing wipes?" Siluk asked.

Abe turned to him with a start. "Where did you find those?"

Siluk pointed to the pile next to Abe's backpack. "You threw them out with the other things. You must have missed them."

"Thank you," Abe said as he took the wipes from Siluk. He tore them open and pressed into Imara's wound with gentle pressure.

Imara's fists contracted from the sting of alcohol. She clenched her jaw, but kept speaking to the air in front of her. "Of course it was going to hurt. The truth always hurts. I should have opened it earlier."

Abe shook his head as he cleaned. "You need stitches, Imara. I can't do stitches. I have training on it, but I'm not that good. Plus I don't have the materials with me. I can dress the wound and get you through the next couple days, but you'll have to see a doctor."

Imara sat silent as a stone. Her eyes glazed over and her muscles went limp. A frown fell deeper on her lips while her eyelids drooped.

Abe cleaned the wound, but huffed in frustration every few seconds. "I can't see this and clean it at the same time. I need it to be… unless…"

Abe sat up with a start. "Darius, get out your mirror and hold it here for me."

At the mention of the mirror, Imara's entire body shook. She clenched her toes inside of her shoes and tried to pull her hand from Abe. "No," she begged. "No mirror. Not right now. I can't."

Abe held her hand fast. "I need you to cooperate, Imara. Quit pulling your hand away, it's making the cuts worse."

She relaxed the hand Abe held, but pressed the fingers of her other hand into the ground, trying to grasp the stone. She moved her head side to side and sucked her lips into her mouth. Staring out ahead she said, "Not a mirror. Please."

Darius stood frozen.

Abe gritted his teeth and furrowed his brow. "Darius, get the mirror now!"

He turned to Imara's hand and his gentleness returned. "Imara, I'm sorry, but I need to clean this wound or you'll get an infection. Just close your eyes if you have to because I'm using the mirror."

Darius held the mirror over Imara's hand. It didn't reflect on her face, but she could see her skin in the reflection. Her own emotions were invisible to her, except through a mirror. She tried to close her eyes or look away, but it was no use. Her eyes were drawn to the mirror like a magnet. She couldn't deny the truth she saw. And when she looked in the mirror, she saw it all.

Selfishness. The selfishness that killed Headmaster Bello. The red orange writhed and whipped in angry twists. Guilt. The mustard yellow bubbled and popped and splattered everywhere. Anger. The blood red flames festered and pulsed like pus filled boils. Every bad thing she had ever done or felt screamed at her through the mirror. Judgmental. Mean. Greedy. Selfish. Her eyes watered from staring so much, but

185

no matter how hard she tried to look away, the mirror compelled her to look back. Why was she so flawed? Why did the truth have to hurt with such intensity?

Abe pushed into her wound with the cleansing wipe and shook his head. "Really Imara, do you have to keep sacrificing yourself for other people like this?"

For the first time since opening the crypt, Imara came out of her trance. With wide eyes she said, "What?"

Abe stole a glance at her before going back to her hand. "It's a good thing," he said. "But this is the second time in twenty-four hours I've had to fix up this hand. Can you try to sacrifice other body parts next time?" Abe smiled at himself, but Imara's eyes left Abe and went back to the mirror.

She did sacrifice for others. Abe teased her about it since they met. Sacrificing was a good thing. Imara stared into the mirror again, searching through the colors. Maybe she was selfish for waiting to open the crypt, but she was selfless too. In the mirror she saw every emotion she ever felt, not just the current ones. So where was selfless? She stared back at the mirror and realized other colors were missing too. Where was love? She loved Naki and did everything she could to save her. So why couldn't she see it in her reflection?

Imara searched, but every emotion staring back at her was negative. It made her insides boil with hate. A self loathing she had learned to ignore.

At last, Abe said to Darius, "I'm done. You can put that away now."

The moment Darius pulled the mirror away, Imara's muscles relaxed with a sigh of relief. Her chest no longer constricted, and the churning in her stomach eased.

Abe dug through his supplies again. He slathered ointment onto Imara's wounds with a tender hand. Now that she was out of her trance, the pain hit her all at once. The pain cut like a knife, but suddenly reduced to nothing more than a dull sting. Imara jerked her head toward her hand. "The pain is almost gone," she said.

Abe nodded. "There's pain killer in the ointment. I'm almost done." Abe turned to put the ointment away and stared at it with a frown. "Wait, this ointment doesn't have pain killer." Abe looked around and saw another tub at his side. "Oh, this is the one with pain killer. Did I put this one on you?"

Imara closed her eyes for a moment. With each breath, the tension inside her unraveled. She rubbed the back of her neck and said, "You must have used that one if the pain is gone."

Abe squinted at the ointment, but tried to shrug it off. "Yeah, I must have."

Abe finished wrapping her hand while Imara looked around the room. She saw Siluk first. Dull skin. Liar. That's how she always saw him. She never expected to see anything else, and she rarely did.

She turned to Mr. Nazari. Burnt orange prickles surrounded him. He always had the greed. It made him a good businessman, but he had a constant desire for more money.

Darius with his never-ending forest green corkscrews of jealousy. Jealous for attention. Jealous that Siluk had helped with the smell. Jealous of Naki's charm.

Then Naki. Fear, anger, guilt. All frequent emotions. Imara looked down. But Naki was kind. She was a good friend. She was passionate and loved people fiercely. Imara knew that from experience, but she didn't see it. Why?

Imara stared harder at the colors, willing herself to see more. After several long seconds, she saw something. A wisp of light pink fluff. Care? Not romantic or platonic. It wasn't even strong, but it was there. Her eyes danced around the room again. Her mouth fell open when she noticed they all had it. The light pink fluff wisped out and blew toward her. She watched everyone, and with the clues in their faces, she pinpointed the emotion. Sympathy. They all felt bad about Imara's hand.

"Done," Abe said.

She looked over, and even he had the light pink fluff. More than anyone else in fact. Why hadn't she noticed it before? She had never seen this pink fluff before in her life. It was new. But the more she looked, the more obvious it became.

Abe helped Imara to her feet. He checked the bandage one last time. "I'm serious, Imara. No more hurting your hand. I'm not a doctor or a healer. My skills are limited."

Imara nodded, but glanced back at the crypt with Headmaster Bello. All of her excitement at the discovery of the light pink fluff diminished. Imara held her breath as sorrow washed over her. She didn't even like Headmaster Bello, but she never wanted him dead. She couldn't fathom how any human being could take the life of another. How could hate grow so strong?

"What do we do now?" Naki asked.

Imara swallowed and straightened her back. "Now we go to the police. They're afraid of this place, but we should be able to convince them to come down here once they see that we've been down here for days without dying."

Abe stared at the body with narrowed eyes. "Why would the Judge kill Headmaster Bello? Why give everyone else water and not him?"

Mr. Nazari shook his head. "Does it matter?" His face was somber, but it managed to hide most of his grief. Cobalt blue drops of sadness pelted off his skin like a rainstorm. Imara ached for him, but knew there was nothing she could do.

Abe said, "If we can understand the Judge's motivation, we'll know how he thinks. That will make it easier to catch him."

"Come on," Imara said. "We can discuss this in the bubble car. We have to go to the police."

Just then, a loud clatter and the sound of tumbling rocks filled the catacombs.

SEVENTEEN

IMARA HEARD CRUMBLING, SCRAPING, AND crunching as she climbed the short flight of stairs outside the crypt room. She hurried past the shaft and stopped with a start. A huge pile of rocks covered the entrance to the catacombs. Not a beam of light from the outside shone through them.

"It caved in?" Darius asked.

Siluk kicked a boulder with his foot and scanned the rock pile. "It looks like this was deliberate. Maybe with explosives or something like it. The rocks fell from the same spot."

"Maybe it's an illusion," Darius said.

"Not all of it is an illusion otherwise I couldn't kick these rocks." Siluk's eye twitched, obviously annoyed that Darius still insisted on disagreeing with everything he said.

Despite Siluk's protest, everyone turned to Imara.

Imara looked at the rocks, trying to ignore the anxiety pulsing through her veins. "It's not an illusion, but—"

Imara crouched down, examining the rocks from every angle. She pushed a pile of rubble to the side to clear the way of a boulder. She scanned the boulder through narrowed eyes. After staring, she pressed her shoulder against the boulder and pushed as hard as she could. With all her effort, the boulder only moved a smidgeon. She anchored her feet to try again when Abe bent down to help.

Imara nodded and showed him where to push. "There's a light just past this boulder," she said. "It's a blue light, though, from technology, not the sun."

With Abe's help, the boulder slid away as if it were nothing more than a pebble. Imara wiped the dirt off her hands and added inhuman strength to her mental list of Abe's impressive qualities.

"You've got to be kidding me," Abe said when he looked at the ground. "Just another pile of rocks."

"Now *that* is an illusion," Imara said. The triumph would have made her smile in normal circumstances. But with Headmaster Bello lying dead in the other room, it did nothing. She got down on her hands and knees and climbed into a tiny opening that glowed with blue light.

"Ah ha!" she said. "A door, just like I thought."

"Can I come— *Ow*," Abe said with a grunt.

Imara turned back to see Abe rubbing his forehead. She frowned apologetically. "Sorry. It's a small opening. There's only enough room for one person at a time. I should have mentioned."

"Oh, it's fine." Abe backed away and stood up to join everyone else.

Imara readjusted her flashlight, determined to find the illusion to open the door so they could all leave. They had found all the hostages. The police could catch the Judge themselves. And Imara could go home. She would give them her map and explain about the illusions and maybe come back with the police for an hour or so, but that was it. Finally she could go home and work everything out with her new job. If she still had one. All she had to do now was figure out how to see past the illusion on this door.

Imara stared with deep concentration, but thirty minutes later Imara still sat in the same spot. Sweat lined her brow, and she wore a deep frown. After all this time, the only thing she learned was she had no idea how to open this door. She huffed and decided to check on the others.

As Imara crawled back through the small opening, her ears filled with hostile bickering. She got to her feet and said, "Can't you all find something useful to do?"

"Like what?" Siluk said with a snap, angry blood red flames burning around him. "You're the only one who can see the illusions. Naki still has to close her eyes to get past them."

"Shut up, Siluk. I only saw them for the first time last night. You've had a lot longer to adjust."

"Well excuse me if—"

"Hey!" Imara said as an idea struck her. "You guys can turn off the illusions."

Darius slapped his forehead. "Oh yeah. Good call, Imara. Let me just pull out my illusion turner-offer. I can't believe I didn't think of that earlier. I've had it in my pocket this entire time."

Imara rolled her eyes, but rolled them back and tried to remain calm. "I'm serious. We know the illusions are from projectors. Probably in the ceiling somewhere. We never bothered to look because we were too busy finding the hostages. But the police won't be afraid to come down here if the illusions are gone. Then they can find the Judge's evil lair or the transporter or evidence or whatever."

"Brilliant!" Mr. Nazari said. Imara knew he only agreed with her because he thought she would be more likely to help him find the lair if he was on her side.

"Yeah, good idea, but how are we supposed to find the projectors?" Darius asked. "It's not like there's a bright green arrow pointing to them." Darius picked at his golden beard and now she saw he was jealous of Imara's good idea.

Imara slowly formed a fist in one hand as she released a long breath. "Use your hila, Darius. Listen to different spots on the ceiling until you find a foreign object."

"That will take forever!"

"Well," Imara's shoulders slumped. "This could take awhile. It's not like the other doors."

Imara ducked back into the opening before anyone could protest. She stared at the door until her eyes watered, but saw nothing. Imara tapped her teeth together and her eyebrows drew close together. Everywhere she looked, a blurry square sat in front of her eyes.

She tried looking out of the corner of her eye. She tried covering one eye at a time. She tried to see through her blind spot. But nothing.

Imara tried opening her eyes wide and pushing her face toward the wall, but it made no difference. Everywhere she looked was the blurry square. This door was nothing like the other doors in the catacombs. None of her tricks helped. She tried to expect the unexpected, but that got her nowhere. After several more minutes, she was still lost.

Imara closed her eyes and tried to rub out the dryness. She'd been staring so long, her eyes were getting tired.

"Hey, Imara," Abe said through the opening.

Imara crawled back, grateful for the chance to take a break. Abe grinned, and smoky turquoise swirls of hope surrounded him. "We found a projector. Well, the general area anyway. We're hoping you can see it and knock it down."

Imara followed Abe down the short staircase to the landing with the snake statues. Darius stood atop the oval table-like structure in the middle of the landing. His palm rested against the ceiling.

Imara stared at his hand while she climbed onto the stone table. Now that she knew where to look, she hoped it wouldn't be hard to find the projector. But just like with the door, there was nothing.

"Do you see it?" Abe asked.

Imara frowned, angry that this was the second time her hila wasn't helping. "I don't see anything out of the ordinary," she said. "It's all just stone. There's a bit here that comes out from the wall, but—"

"I couldn't see that," Darius said. "It felt like there was a bump or something, but it looked smooth."

Imara felt a corner of her mouth perk up. "Get me that rock."

Naki turned to grab a rock from the ground, but she backed into the wall with a gasp. She closed her eyes and reached back, grasping for something to hold.

Imara frowned. "Sorry. I forgot you still see the illusion. Can someone get me a rock from the crypt room?"

Naki turned away from the snakes before she opened her eyes. Her chest fell with heavy breaths. Abe glanced at her for a moment before he walked into the crypt room. Imara saw his grass green thread of desire again. It wrapped itself around Naki's wrist while another transparent green thread started wrapping around her arm. Whatever Abe wanted from Naki, his desire was growing.

Imara shook the thought from her mind. Now wasn't the time to worry about that. Abe came back from the crypt room with a rock the size of his fist.

Imara used it to hit the part of the ceiling that stuck out. She hit it several times, but nothing changed. She moved her body to the side, trying to get a better angle on it. With every ounce of strength she had, she hit the stone again. This time it jiggled. It took a few more hard hits, but the stone piece broke away from the wall. It fell to the ground with a clunk and Imara saw something black inside.

"Did it work?" Imara asked.

They nodded, and Imara allowed herself to appreciate the small victory. Darius stepped toward the crypt room, his face filled with awe. Instead of pouncing snakes, he now saw the snake statues carved into the wall. He slid his fingers over them with a look of euphoria.

"This is incredible," Darius said. "Serpents like this represent Agathodaimon, which is a good spirit from Greece. And these crowns on their heads are traditional Egyptian double crowns. But they're holding this winged staff, which is a Roman insignia called *kerkeion*."

"What does that mean?" Abe asked.

Darius turned, his palms up and his eyes bright. "It means, this place is fascinating. These catacombs were in use between the second and fourth centuries. Alexandria was a melting pot of culture at the time. It's incredible to see Egyptian, Greek, and Roman influences within the same structure. Alexandrians welcomed different cultures and incorporated their ideas and art into their society. These snakes are proof of that. They were accepting of all sorts of people." Darius laughed to himself. "It sort of seems against what the taggers believe, which is ironic."

Siluk chuckled. "That's hilariously ironic. But it's awful how the taggers ruined this place with all the stupid illusions and stuff."

"Right?" Darius agreed. "It's a scandal. An atrocity!"

Siluk did a small smile, which Darius matched for half a moment. But then he turned away with a scowl. "Stop pretending like you care, Siluk."

Imara glanced back up the stairs, and Abe nudged her with his elbow. "How's the truth seeing?"

"It's not going well." Imara frowned and wished she could cover her face with her hands. "I don't know if I can get us out."

Naki fell to the ground in a heap. "What are we going to do now?"

"We find the transporter." Abe spoke the words so fast, it was obvious this wasn't the first time he had the idea.

Imara squinted. "But the Judge uses the transporter. He has it with him."

Abe nodded. He'd obviously thought of that too. "The Judge, or at least the taggers, have been down here several times. Someone dropped the note about Siluk. The Judge moved Naki to different rooms. The Judge must have been the one who blocked the entrance with those rocks. We know the taggers can transport too, but I don't think they have a transporter like the Judge. I saw something red in that one tagger's hand. I'm guessing they can't transport anymore and that's why we haven't seen them again. But the Judge can with his golden transporter. So, all we do now is find the lair and wait for the Judge."

Imara bit her lip. She wasn't sure she was ready to search for the lair.

"Brilliant," Mr. Nazari said. He was acting more agreeable than ever, which made Imara's heart wrench. She wondered if anyone else knew it was all an act.

Siluk pounded a fist into his palm. "Let's take the Judge down!"

Imara frowned.

Darius said, "We can start looking at that fork in the road. We never finished checking it out last night. Let's find that evil lair."

"And then what?" Imara asked. "Are you going to kill the Judge?"

"He killed Headmaster Bello," Siluk said. Imara was surprised that he found the idea so justified.

"Do you want to be a killer?" Imara asked.

"Do you always have to be a buzz kill?" Siluk said under his breath.

Abe glared at Siluk then said, "I know you don't think tagging is that bad, Imara. And I know you don't want to get involved in this, which is fine. But if we don't stop the Judge, he's going to destroy Alexandria as we know it. And then Egypt. And then maybe other territories, including Kenya. We don't know when he'll stop. You don't have to fight the Judge, but we do need your help to find the lair."

Here was Abe as hopeful and optimistic as always, but somehow his words weren't enough to sway Imara this time. She was annoyed about the two grass green threads of desire still drifting over to Naki.

"I'm not killing anyone," Imara said with finality. "And there are a few projector illusions we should break before we look for the transporter. If the police ever get down here, some of the illusions are too dangerous for them, even with the notes on my map."

Imara watched as jagged indigo waves of annoyance broke off Abe's skin. The tightening of his jaw was far more subtle. "Good idea. We'll take down the illusions first and then go find the lair. Either way, we need the transporter. Both to stop the Judge and to get out of here."

Imara swallowed hard and walked to the shaft. Now Abe was annoyed with her. He knew she was stalling, but she didn't care. What was so wrong with what she said, anyway? She just said she didn't want to kill the Judge. And why should they? Sure the Judge was dangerous, and sure Headmaster Bello was dead. But the Judge gave Naki food and water. He didn't kill all the hostages, so why should they kill him? She already had enough guilt about Headmaster Bello. She wasn't about to add straight-up murder to the list.

As Imara lowered herself down the shaft, her frustration only grew. Maybe tagging wasn't perfect, but this wasn't her fight. She wouldn't fight anyone unless she had no other choice.

Imara hopped off the rope and leaned against a wall. Abe came down next, but didn't join Imara by the wall. He paced the ground and stared at his shoes as if he suddenly found them to be the most fascinating things in the world.

Imara's nostrils flared, and she ground her teeth together. Maybe it would be easier to go along with Abe's ideas if those grass green threads weren't growing thicker.

EIGHTEEN

IMARA MARCHED TO ONE OF THE MOST dangerous illusions in the catacombs. It was the corridor with a checkerboard of foot pits filled with spikes. It wasn't hard to guess where the projector hid. A long spike came down from the ceiling in the middle of the corridor.

Imara climbed Mr. Nazari's shoulders and pulled the spike off the ceiling with a hard tug. Darius climbed onto Siluk's shoulders and tapped the ceiling where Imara pointed.

"What is this thing?" Abe asked, taking the spike from Imara's hand.

"It's a spike. It's about half the length of an arm."

Abe stared into the distance as he slid his fingers across the spike. He led his fingers along the smooth texture with careful attention. When his fingers felt the end with the point, he rubbed his thumb across to test the sharpness.

"It's right here, Imara," Darius said.

Imara used a rock to hit the ceiling where Darius indicated. Imara's arm was already tired after knocking down the illusion upstairs, but she couldn't give up now.

Abe tossed the spike in the air and it spun a few times before he caught it again.

"Can you see that?" Imara asked.

"Nope."

Abe tossed the spike again.

Imara scoffed, but she was too annoyed with Abe to muster up any argument. She hoped a disapproving glance would be enough to stop Abe. He ignored the glance and tossed the spike again.

Imara tried to ignore him while she hit the projector. It took longer than upstairs, but she got it to jiggle. Imara slammed the rock against the projector, releasing frustration into each hit.

Just as it broke away from the wall, Abe threw the spike into the air. Imara clutched the rock in her hand as the spike began its descent. Every other time Abe's aim had been perfect. But this time the spike fell point down, straight for his face. Abe stared forward with perfect indifference. He wasn't even aware that the projector was broken and the spike visible.

"Watch out!" Imara called out. But even as she said it, she knew it was too late. Abe didn't have enough time to look up and react. Before she finished yelling, Imara threw her rock at the spike. She watched in horror as the rock flew through the air, and all she could do was hope her aim was true.

Abe looked up, and his eyes grew wide with terror when he saw the spike hurtling toward his face. His hands started to come up, but as Imara guessed, he couldn't react in time to do anything.

A loud clang emanated through the passageway when Imara's rock hit the silver metal. The spike veered off its course just enough to miss Abe's face. It fell with a clatter at Abe's feet.

Imara clambered off Mr. Nazari's shoulders and punched Abe in the arm. "Are you trying to kill yourself?" she asked.

She meant it to be sarcastic, but it ended up sounding more sincere than anything.

Abe swallowed, but didn't say a word.

Imara shook her head while heavy breaths heaved in her chest. She turned around and saw a color shoot out from Mr. Nazari's skin. Periwinkle. A sparkling glint of periwinkle, almost like starlight. Imara caught her breath when she saw it. Another new color. Imara glanced at Mr. Nazari's face and saw right away what the color meant.

Worry. But not just worry. It was protective. Not the possessive or jealous kind of protective. This was pure and caring. Protective because of love. Protective worry for Abe.

Mr. Nazari adjusted his cuff links, and though Imara had watched him do it a thousand times, she saw something different this time. That same protective worry was directed at his cufflinks. Along with cherry red puffs of love. Only love for an object, not a person, but still. It was rare for Mr. Nazari to love anything besides Abe and money. She had never realized those cufflinks were so precious to him.

Imara turned and walked down the corridor for the next illusion. She took heavy steps, trying to stomp out her confusion. Two new colors in one day. First sympathy and now this protective worry. Both of them positive emotions too, which she rarely saw. If she was such a good truth seer, then why was this the first time she saw these colors? Why now?

The catacombs were new, and she often saw new emotions with new experiences. But sympathy? Was this really the first time in her life someone around her felt sympathy?

Abe caught up to her, and before she could stop herself, she said, "I saw a new emotion."

"For real? That's fresh. A new emotion no one knows about?"

Imara shook her head. "No, sorry. Just a new emotion I've never seen before. I do see new emotions, especially when I do something new, but it's been awhile."

Abe smiled. No trace of the indigo waves lingered around his skin. "Either way, that's fresh. How's your foot?"

"What?"

Abe pointed to her left foot. Now that he pointed it out, it did seem to ache a little. He said, "When you got down to punch my arm —*ow* by the way— you landed on your foot pretty hard. Doesn't it hurt?"

"A little." Imara tried to bite her tongue, but as she passed the tombs they used earlier to hide from the taggers, she lost the desire to hold back. "Abe, why do you refuse to believe you're a healer?"

Abe narrowed his eyes to tiny slits then shook his head. "I don't refuse to believe it. There's never been any evidence that I'm a healer."

Imara turned down a path that branched off to several passages and a large cavern. "Then how did you know my foot got hurt?"

Abe waved off her remark. "It looked like it hurt when you fell. I wanted to make sure you were ok. That doesn't mean I'm a healer."

Imara stared off in thought for several seconds. When she looked back at him she said, "Do you know how hilas were discovered?"

"Yeah yeah," he said. "I know the story. It was in Kenya. A girl dared to believe she had a superpower. Once she treated it like a superpower, it became a superpower. I've heard it tons of times."

Imara nodded. "A trick she called it. She had reflexes like a cat. Her body moved away from punches before her brain even registered them. But the more she developed it, the more powerful she became. Through studying probability, she could anticipate moves in a fight, people tripping, and even objects falling off tables. Predictive reflexes. That was the first hila." Just before the cavern, Imara entered a tunnel that led to a short passage full of tombs.

"Yeah, then everyone in Kenya started getting their own hilas."

Imara nodded. "Once everyone saw what she was capable of, they started to believe too. It's not a coincidence hilas began in Kenya then spread to the rest of the world. It wasn't until people believed in their hila that they could use their hila. Training and knowledge makes it easier to use."

"What does that have to do with me?" Abe asked.

"If you believed you were a healer, you might realize you actually are. I think if hilas manifested before puberty, people would have figured out thousands of years ago that we have hilas. But you don't get hilas until after puberty, right at the age when you stop believing in things. Imagination is a powerful thing."

Abe tugged at his teal blue collar. "I don't know. It seems farfetched to me. I think people have hilas because of evolution, not imagination. Evolution hasn't caught up to all of us yet."

Imara thought for a moment. "Imagine this. The human body is capable of swimming, right? But if you never saw a body of water large enough for swimming, you'd never know you could do it. Not only that, you'd never even imagine that swimming exists. That's what it was like with hilas. We couldn't do it until we realized it was possible, and we tried. It takes a lot of knowledge and practice to be hila wasomi. I know more about cones and rods in the eye than anatomy professors. But I was a truth seer before my training. The potential was always there." Imara wiped her brow as she finished.

"That is a compelling thought," Abe said. "But I think I would know by now if I had a hila." Abe glistened with sweat as he gave Imara a sideways glance. "Wait a minute. I thought you were supposed to be the realist. Why do you believe in imagination over evolution?"

Imara shrugged with a smile. "I'm layered."

Abe laughed and rubbed the side of his head across his t-shirt. "Siluk's going to have to spray us again. I'm sweating like a pig all the sudden."

Imara twisted her mouth up to one side. "It could be both," she said. "Imagination and evolution." A drop of sweat slid down the back of her neck.

"Yeah." Abe nodded.

"It's so hot in here," Siluk called out. "You guys have no idea how torturous it is to move to Egypt, in the summer no less, when I live in Alaska the rest of the year."

Abe's eyes shifted from the ground to the ceiling and then down the passageway. He rubbed his chin with a furrowed brow. "It's not just hot. It's getting hotter."

Naki smacked her lips together then licked each one. "It tastes like it's raining, but it's way too hot. Well, that and we're underground."

Imara's stomach tangled in a knot. Apparently uneasiness was now a constant feature of the catacombs. She stared at her map to find an explanation for the sudden rise in temperature. Imara wiped her forehead while Abe panted beside her. Imara held onto her lip with her teeth. She reached for the back of her neck and tugged the hair. She moved her eyes from the map to the catacombs, searching her surroundings for some kind of answer.

She turned to face the others. She saw nothing in the air or walls, but when she glanced at the ground she saw it. Creeping up the path behind them was a puddle of water.

Imara pointed, and everyone turned around.

"What the?" Darius said as he stepped toward the water. "Where did that come from?"

"Don't touch it!" Naki said pulling Darius back. She leaned toward the water and licked her lips. "We need to get out of here."

Naki ran forward, and everyone followed without question. When Naki caught up with Imara, Imara asked, "What's wrong with the water?"

"It's boiling hot. If anyone touches it, they'll burn." Naki smacked her lips, and her voice rose in a panic. "There's more coming!"

Imara pointed to the map. "We need to backtrack, but we'll have to go a different way than how we got here. The checkerboard corridor has a chamber at the end with stone couches. We can stand on top of them."

As they ran, the ominous sound of rushing water followed behind them. The water licked the bottom of their shoes, and everyone started running faster. Imara got to the chamber first. One corner of a couch stood slightly higher than the rest. Imara pointed and tried to ignore what would happen if there was enough water to cover it.

Imara huddled everyone together on the highest spot. No matter how much she glared at it, the water kept rushing into the chamber, faster and faster than ever. Imara curled her toes when the water rose to the edge of the stone couch. The water reached the soles of their shoes and it showed no sign of stopping. The boiling water would soak through their shoes in mere moments. Imara panted and wiped the sweat from her face. She tapped her fingers against her thigh. She watched the water when suddenly her eyes widened and she stopped mid tap. She snapped her fingers and grabbed the strap on her shoulder.

"Put your backpacks down!" Imara said.

Everyone with a backpack threw it near their feet on top of the stone couches. They all climbed onto the pile of backpacks before the water seeped into their shoes. This bought them a little time, but the water was still rising, and Imara was out of ideas.

"What are we going to do when the water rises past our backpacks?" Darius asked.

"Burn," Naki said. "This water is boiling hot." Naki's reactions were always extreme, but this time her face was somber and unmoving. It unnerved Imara more than the water rising around them.

Naki swallowed and closed her eyes. "If we don't get out of here, we're all dead."

Sweat dripped down Imara's face and back. She shook her head to keep the drops away from her eyes. Her mouth hung open with heavy pants. Imara shifted and pushed Naki to a higher spot. Even with the backpacks, it wouldn't be long now. Imara watched the water and felt silly that she had worried so much about her job. She should have worried about her life. She thought of her parents. Professor Santini. If only she'd been given one last chance to say goodbye.

Abe took her hand and squeezed it, and Imara felt a rush of emotion. Maybe she was wrong for fighting against him. Apparently the Judge was willing to kill them after all. She breathed out long and hard, but it did nothing to calm her. Imara leaned into Abe in as much of a hug as she could manage.

He dropped his head down against hers just as the water lapped up to their shoes for the second time. Everyone seemed to close their eyes at the same moment. Imara knew it wouldn't hurt any less with her eyes closed, but it felt better to close them all the same. Imara heard Naki's lips smacking together.

Imara held Abe's hand tighter, waiting for the water to seep into her shoes. She braced herself for the pain and imagined what it would feel like to burn from the bottom up. Sweat dripped off her eyebrows, and each second seemed to last a lifetime. Imara waited.

And waited.

Still she waited, almost impatient, which was strange considering she waited for her death. Imara peeked at the water through one eye.

At the same time Naki said, "The water is receding."

"What?" Darius said as his eyes shot open.

"We'll be safe in a few minutes," Naki said. "Our bags are wet, but I guess it's a fair trade off."

Siluk sniffed loudly and wiped the sweat off his forehead.

"Yeah, yeah," Darius said. "We smell awful from sweating. You don't need to rub it in."

"I'm smelling out the complementary scents so I can spray us after the water recedes. I wasn't complaining," Siluk said.

After a few minutes, the water receded enough that they could climb off their backpacks. Imara lifted her backpack with one hand while Abe held fast to her other. With her nerves frayed and her body weak from the heat, his comfort was grounding. It felt even better knowing this was the first time he was brave enough to hold her hand in front of everyone else.

Siluk stared down at the chamber opening where the water receded. He grimaced and said, "They should have made that construction guy who caused the flood live down here for a week. That alone would be enough punishment for anyone. It's better than how he lives now, that's for sure."

Darius's fingers fidgeted with his water bottle. The air around him was thick with a raven rash of anxiety. His nose crinkled, and his anxiety came out as anger. "You don't know anything about how he lives now."

"Yes, I do," Siluk said, increasingly annoyed that Darius's default emotion was now anger. "He lives in Alaska, forty-five miles outside my hometown. He's an outcast. People use his name like an insult. 'Don't *masud* that up. Don't be a *masud* about it.'"

The water in the chamber had receded, and they all stepped down off the couches. Abe's thumb caressed Imara's hand as he held it.

Siluk let out a long breath as he shook his head. His frustration with Darius turned to sorrow. "He doesn't even own the land he lives on. I think it belongs to a family member of his. He gets zero sympathy from anybody. It's Masud Ganim, right?" Siluk turned to Mr. Nazari.

Mr. Nazari let out a soft laugh. "That's his name now. He had a terrible reputation after the first time his shoddy workmanship led to injuries, so he changed his name. His given name was Marco Santini."

Imara whipped around to face Mr. Nazari. "Santini?" Imara looked to the side and pinched her chin with her thumb and forefinger. "Is that a common name in Italy? You said he was from Italy, right?"

Mr. Nazari shrugged. "I have no idea how common it is, but he is related. He's Professor Santini's brother. I wouldn't be surprised if Carlotta bought the land for him."

Imara didn't know how to take this news. She was so determined to not join a fight that wasn't hers. But now she knew who the taggers were against, and that changed things. A flash of guilt swept through her. Imara forced herself to look at the conflict with fresh eyes.

Just as the thoughts started spinning in her head, Mr. Nazari looked at Abe and Imara's hands, and then he glanced at Abe's face. He looked away, and the moment was over faster than it began. His face was calm and expressionless, and even his emotions gave nothing away. But Abe's discomfort was immediate. He shifted on his feet, and his fingers twitched. Imara felt his commitment wither away. She almost wished she could share his embarrassment, but she didn't. Maybe she had been mad that he wanted her to find the lair, but things were changing. He questioned her hila more than she liked. He still wanted something from Naki, which bothered her. But despite everything, she was addicted to his hope and passion. She was more than willing to see his point of view.

Again her thoughts got interrupted by Mr. Nazari's voice. "You know, the Judge is more sadistic than I realized. I thought death by boiling water was cruel enough, but to only make us think we were going to die and then not actually hurt us. It's—"

"Weird," Abe finished.

"It doesn't make any sense," Imara said. "When I saw the Judge, the only emotion I saw was desire for power. His actions don't seem congruent. He gave you all food and water, and he stopped the boiling water before it got too close. But he also trapped us in here and told us about Siluk's lie."

"And killed Headmaster Bello," Mr. Nazari said.

Imara frowned and nodded with reluctance. "And what happened to the taggers who were here? It doesn't make any sense."

Abe narrowed his eyes, and Imara squirmed under his inspection. He said, "All you saw was desire for power? No background emotions or anything?"

It was a simple question, but it felt like an accusation. Imara had the sudden desire to rip her hand out of Abe's grip. Why did he always question her ability? She couldn't see everything in the world, but she was a talented truth seer. Maybe she hadn't figured out troxler puzzles, but Professor Santini said most people didn't master them until their last year of hila school anyway. She hated that with one simple question, Abe could make her question everything she thought she knew about her hila.

Imara relaxed the tension in her jaw. She was determined to be reasonable. But when she saw Abe's skin, the tension hurtled back, stronger than before. Grass green threads flew out and grasped onto Naki. Thicker. Thicker. Thicker they grew. All toward Naki, and none toward her.

Imara did pull her hand away now. She tapped her ring and kept both hands busy pulling up the map. "Is it safe to walk through the catacombs yet, Naki?"

"I think so. I'll be able to taste if the water is coming again."

Imara walked out of the chamber and started down the corridor without looking back. "Good," she said. "There are two more illusions I want to break before we go to the fork in the road."

Imara stomped forward, angry that Abe got to her without trying. Incensed that she even let herself be offended. She didn't want him walking next to her like always. She needed to clear her head. She said it over and over to herself, but when everyone followed and Abe didn't catch up to her, Imara's heart sank. She glanced back, and her hands tightened into hard fists. Abe chatted with his dad and walked like everything was normal, but Imara knew what he was really after.

What did she care anyway? He wanted something from Naki. The desire was so strong now, Imara was certain it would turn into romantic desire. That was fine with her. She got along just fine before Abe ever came around. She didn't need him. He could have Naki if he wanted her. He was nothing to Imara.

Nothing.

She kept saying it to herself as she marched forward, knowing Abe was behind her getting exactly what he wanted.

NINETEEN

ABE WATCHED AS HIS DAD POINTED TO A passage leading out from the corridor. "That passage has the spinning spike. And around the bend is the zigzag path. And up to the left is the enormous middle pit passage."

Abe laughed, "Did you name all of the illusions like this?"

"Of course I did. It helps me remember."

Abe rubbed his chin with another chuckle. "You have the most amazing memory, Dad. As always. I wish you would have passed some of that on to me."

"I passed on my good looks, didn't I? You've always seemed to enjoy that."

Abe smiled, but his mind turned to the three things he wanted. One, to sleep in a normal bed and not in a room that looked like a never-ending pit. Maybe that one wasn't as important as the others, but the cramp in his shoulder kept reminding him of it. Two, find the lair. To do that, he simply had to humor Imara with destroying these illusions. It was pointless since the police would never enter the catacombs in a million years. But it was important to Imara. And to get to the lair, they needed Imara.

Maybe she was crazy for not thinking the Judge was a psychotic terrorist, but he did respect her for not wanting to kill anyone. Once they found the lair, they would get the transporter and stop the Judge for good.

And three. Well, three was special. This was what he wanted most of all. A fact that still surprised him. The urge inside him grew beyond his control. Not that he wanted to control it. A smile played on his lips for half a moment. He was actually enjoying it. But it meant he had to talk to Naki.

He had his mind made up this time. He would corner her, and he wouldn't give up until he had what he wanted. Abe knew this conversation was the key. Abe chatted with his dad so Imara wouldn't be suspicious. He didn't want Imara knowing what he was up to. But once she glanced back and saw Abe talking to his dad, Abe was sure she wouldn't glance back again. Now he could go for a new goal. The real goal.

Abe waved his dad forward as he took off his shoe. "I got something in here. I'll catch up in a bit."

Mr. Nazari nodded, and soon Abe watched Darius pass by alone. From behind him, Abe heard Siluk and Naki talking.

Siluk said to Naki, "Why'd you ask Imara to stay for the graduation party anyway? Nobody likes talking to her."

Naki huffed out a loud breath. "Just because you don't like talking to her doesn't mean nobody does."

Siluk laughed. "You don't like talking to her either. If her own sister hates talking to her, what hope does she have? She's so annoying."

"Don't you talk about Imara like that in front of me, you jerk. She's my sister. I don't mind talking to her and I'd rather talk to her than to you. Don't be stupid." Naki pushed Siluk away from her. "Go bother Darius, and leave me alone."

Perfect, Abe thought to himself.

Siluk jogged up to Darius, and Abe put his shoe back on. He picked at his fingernails, trying to make the whole thing look like a great coincidence. Naki was thoroughly unconvinced. When she caught up to him, she looked him straight in the eye and said, "No."

Abe rocked back on his heels and tilted his head to the side. "What? *No* what?"

Naki flicked her ponytail behind her back. She looked at the ceiling and said, "I know I hugged you when you saved me from the river, but it didn't mean anything. I'm a hugger. I hug everybody."

Abe's mouth hung open, and he stared at her through squinted eyes. "I have no idea what you're talking about."

Naki leaned forward and spoke through her teeth. "I don't date guys who have dated my sister."

Abe tried to keep his nose from crinkling too much. "You don't date the leftovers?"

"What?" Naki asked.

Abe frowned and looked away. "That's what Imara said."

Naki's mouth dropped, and she turned her head to the side, before shaking with an angry jerk. "Unbelievable!" she said. "I try to do something nice. I try to ignore guys who reject her so she doesn't think they want me instead of her. I try to be a good sister, and somehow she turns it against me. I can't ever make her happy."

Abe slid his thumb across his chin. "You were trying to be nice?" he asked. He sort of felt guilty that he never considered the possibility.

"Of course I was. I don't know why. It never makes any difference." Naki turned back to Abe. She looked him over and said, "Oh well, my answer is no anyway."

"I didn't come here to ask you out," Abe said, hoping Naki would realize how annoyed he was.

Naki clenched her jaw and enunciated every syllable. "Then what do you want?"

Abe tried to soften his expression. "I need something from you."

"What?" The distrust in Naki's eyes was evident as she looked at him through a furrowed brow.

Abe pressed his thumb into his chin as he rubbed it. "It's about Imara. She has a wound."

Naki gasped. "Why didn't you tell me? Is she okay?"

Naki was ready to run off, but Abe stopped her. "No," he said. "It's not that kind of wound."

Abe rubbed his eyebrow, thinking carefully about each word before he said it. "It's something from her past, but she holds onto it."

Naki swallowed, and a flash of fear crossed over her eyes. But then she rolled her eyes and huffed. "It sounds like you have it all figured out. Why do you need me?"

Her reaction was strange, but Abe had a feeling she knew exactly what he was talking about. He tried to stay calm. "I can't fix it. Only you can."

"Me? Why me?" Naki stared at him from the side of her eye, which Abe hoped was guilt.

Abe frowned and spoke without thinking. "Because you're the one who caused it."

Naki's mouth snapped shut. She turned her head away from Abe, but he saw her lip quiver and tears form in her eyes. He took it as a good sign. But without warning, her body went rigid. She clenched her jaw tight and crinkled up her nose. "If Imara is holding onto something from the past,

215

that's her problem. Not mine. She should just forgive and forget."

Abe resisted the sudden urge to punch a hole through the wall. This was going to be harder than he thought. "Obviously that's not going to happen. Please, tell me about the wound." For emphasis he added, "It's hurting her."

Naki jerked her head toward Abe at these words. "How do you know that?" she asked. She swallowed and spoke barely above a whisper. "Did she tell you?"

"No," Abe said. He looked to the side, still trying to make sense of it himself. "I just have a gut feeling."

Naki scowled, her face switching back to anger in less than a second. "A gut feeling? It's not in your gut; it's in your head. She sees the worst in people and you're trying to give her an excuse, but there isn't one. That's the person she is."

"Come on," Abe said frustrated. "Something happened between you two. I know you love each other, but you can't look each other in the eye. Why?"

Naki huffed. She folded her arms across her chest and jutted out her bottom lip. "I have no idea why," she said. "Because she's mean. She doesn't trust me."

Abe nodded. "She doesn't trust me either. I'm sure it's because of her wound." He looked at Naki and dared himself to hope. "If she can learn to trust you…"

Naki laughed before Abe could finish. "Good luck getting her to trust anyone. I've been trying to do that for years. You'd think she could trust everyone with her hila, but instead she trusts no one."

Abe's jaw tightened. He tried to relax it since he didn't want to ignite Naki's anger any more than he already had. "What happened between you two?"

216

Naki flipped her hair back again and turned away from Abe. "I have no idea. We're sisters. We've both said things we don't mean. How am I supposed to know which fight 'wounded' her?"

Abe looked at Naki, a smile growing beneath his lips. "So it was a fight?" he said. "Something you said that hurt her?"

Naki's eyes went wide, and she clamped her mouth shut. She shook her head, flustered. "I don't know. I have no idea." She bumped Abe's shoulder as she pushed past him. "Just leave me alone," she said as she ran forward. She grabbed Darius's arm and asked him about the snake statues. Darius started talking with a grin, and Abe's chance was gone.

Still, it wasn't a complete loss. He knew more than he did earlier. Abe scratched his chin and considered once again whether or not he should just ask Imara. But again, he decided against it. Imara was already on edge around him. He didn't need another reason for her to dislike him. Which meant one thing. He would have to talk to Naki again.

TWENTY

IMARA STOPPED IN A PASSAGE WITH TWO spike pits on either side. It was difficult to get through the passage with the pits so close together. This made it one of the most dangerous illusions, which was why she wanted to find the projector for it.

Imara pointed to a suspicious spot on the ceiling, and Siluk helped Darius up onto his shoulders. Imara stared hard at the ceiling, doing her best to ignore the sting in her nose. When she felt water in her eyes, she poked at them pretending it was nothing more than dust.

Ok. She didn't want Abe to fall for Naki. She didn't need him or anything. Who said she even wanted him? But yes. It would hurt if he wanted Naki. Hadn't Abe turned to Imara when the boiling water was coming? Didn't he grab Imara's hand? That had to count for something.

Abe walked up to Imara, and she was afraid her sigh of relief was a little too audible. He pushed his hair back and cocked up an eyebrow.

"It's going to be weird when we finally get out of here, don't you think? I don't know if I'm looking forward to it."

Imara tried to smile, but it felt forced, and she was sure Abe could tell. "I guess. Though I am excited to have working temperature-controlled underclothes again."

"True," Abe said with a laugh. "That part will be nice. And sleeping on a bed instead of stone."

Imara nodded, happy they had something to agree on.

Abe shrugged. "I meant it's going to be weird going back to regular life with regular responsibilities."

Imara nodded again, but her mouth squished up when she remembered her job. She hoped they would still accept her late paperwork because of the circumstances, but she hated that this was their first impression of her.

"Plus," Abe said. "What am I going to do when I'm not hanging out with you every day? That does not sound fun at all."

Imara turned to Abe, surprised. He was flirting with her? Of all the things she expected, that was not one of them. She thought he would confess that he wanted Naki. Or he would admit that he regretted holding Imara's hand. Or at the very least, that he would pressure her into looking for the lair instead of bothering with these illusions.

But his brown eyes were bright, and he chewed the inside of his lip, trying and failing to hide a smile.

Imara's ears burned up, and she found herself mirroring his expression. She smirked and said, "You could come visit me, you know. Kenya isn't that far from Egypt."

"What city in Kenya?" Abe asked. He rubbed his eyebrow, which brought Imara's attention to his eyes. A deep russet brown. But now that she looked closer, she noticed the outside edges of his eyes were a bright olive green. Where the two colors converged, miniscule specks of maroon dotted between the colors. Rather than blending, each color was distinctly russet brown or olive green. Not similar, yet perfectly complementary. The longer Imara stared, the more green she saw. But how could his eyes look brown when there was so much green?

Imara cleared her throat and smiled. "Nairobi," she said.

Abe nodded with a serious face. "Well I do need to check on the cuts in your hand. I have to make sure you find a doctor who's good at stitches. I'll need to check the cuts for at least the next couple weeks. Purely for medical reasons."

Imara tilted her head to the side and slid her finger along her neck. She liked flirting with Abe. "Do you have an airport pass? It's only forty points to get from Alexandria to Nairobi. It might be even less from Cairo to Nairobi."

Abe ran his fingers through his hair and laughed under his breath. "I don't have an airport pass. I actually have my own jet."

Imara gaped then shook her head. "Why does that not surprise me?" She rolled her eyes. "I bet you do all sorts of dangerous stunts with it."

"You know I do," Abe said while tangerine pride glowed from his skin. "I'll take you sometime."

Imara held a pointed finger in front of her chest. "That is never going to happen. I'm terrified of heights, remember? I have a hard enough time on a plane. I'm not getting into a jet with someone reckless like you."

"It's fun," Abe said. "You can do it." He shrugged. "You just have to trust me."

Imara smiled, but turned her eyes to the ground. The grass green threads were easier to ignore while he was flirting with her, but they were still there. Just trust him. He said it like it was an easy thing. Didn't he understand how hard he was making it for her?

Imara put her hands behind her back and leaned against the wall. "I told you a secret about me. Now it's your turn. What do you want more than anything?" She hoped it wasn't too obvious. If Abe knew how strong his desire looked to Imara, he might have said something by now. But it had been there too long, and more threads flew out every few minutes. If she could ever trust him, she needed to know what he desired.

Abe raised an eyebrow. "You never told me a secret about you."

"I did," Imara said. "Our first night here. In the pit of doom, remember? I told you I have nightmares about that banister in the school."

"Oh yeah," Abe said. He leaned forward, and his olive green and russet brown eyes looked straight into hers. "That was right before I kissed you."

Imara's stomach twisted into a knot, and her ears burned hotter than ever. It wasn't like it was new. She was there when it happened. But for Abe to acknowledge it, with a smile on his face no less, it caused an emotion Imara hadn't felt for a long time. She remembered how much she treasured that kiss. So short and yet so powerful. She had only known Abe for a few hours at the time, and somehow he'd kissed her like no one ever had.

Imara's smile grew to an embarrassing width. "Yeah," she said with a stupid giggle. How Abe kept his cool while she swam in emotion, she didn't know. But she did know things were different that night. Simpler. But that was before the catacombs. Before the grass green threads of desire.

221

Before Naki.

Imara pursed her lips and focused her mind back where she wanted it. "Right," she said with a nod. "I told you a secret, now tell me one."

Abe shrugged. "I don't have any secrets."

Imara rolled her eyes.

"All right, all right," Abe said. "You know that's a lie." He rubbed his chin with his thumb. "I do have a good one."

Abe glanced up at Darius who still tapped on the ceiling with ear pressed against it.

No one was listening to their conversation, but Abe pulled Imara away from the others anyway. He pushed his eyebrows together, and Imara felt a silly giddiness when he touched her arm.

After a few seconds of thought, Abe leaned in close and whispered, "My dad wants to stop the Judge. Maybe not kill him, but definitely stop him for good."

"Yes, I know."

Abe nodded and lowered his voice. "Well, it's not because he thinks tagging is wrong." Abe tilted his head. "Well, he does think tagging is wrong, but that's not the main reason he wants to stop the Judge." Abe lowered his voice once more and Imara leaned in until he was practically breathing in her ear.

Abe said, "He wants to stop the Judge because it's affecting enrollment at his school. He doesn't want to lose money because of some fanatic." Abe straightened his back and raised one eyebrow, expecting Imara to be impressed.

Imara frowned making no attempt to hide her disappointment. "I already knew that."

"Really?" Abe asked.

"Yes. And that wasn't your secret anyway. That was your dad's. I want to know a secret about you. I asked what you want more than anything."

Abe ignored her and said, "How did you know that already?"

Imara shrugged. "I see his greed every day. He cares about some people, but he cares the most about his bottom line. You're the only one who's more important to him than money. He's not the worst person in the world or anything, but greed is his defining quality."

Abe's lip curled up, and he gritted his teeth, clearly fighting not to glare.

"What?" Imara asked.

Abe shrugged, but it wasn't casual like he probably intended. "He's a shrewd businessman. It makes him successful. I guess greedy sometimes, but—"

Abe turned to Imara, and an annoyed huff escaped him. The jagged indigo waves of annoyance were back stronger than ever. He lowered his eyebrows and said, "You really think greed is his defining quality? More than anything else? He has good qualities too."

A bubble of anger burst inside Imara. She knew Abe was defending his dad, but the way he said it rubbed her the wrong way. Yet again, he questioned her hila! Imara tried to be reasonable. She didn't mean to insult Abe. She wore a strained smile and said, "He does have good qualities too. Nobody is all bad."

"Yeah, but does he have more greed than anything else? He makes money from the school, but he wants people to know how to use their hilas. That's important to him. He didn't start the school just to get money."

"How do you know?" Imara asked. The anger boiled up faster than she could control. Why did he have to fight her on everything? He wasn't even listening.

Imara took a deep breath, trying to calm herself. "The school has been around for almost twenty years. How old were you when he started it? Three? Four? You don't know it wasn't for the money."

"And you do?"

Imara relaxed her jaw, but curled her toes inside of her shoes. "The school is a business. Why else do you start a business? I do think he started it for the money."

Abe frowned, and blood red flames of anger burned out from his skin. She swallowed, hating that she let her anger win over reason. But what was she supposed to do? Abe questioned her hila almost every time she talked about it. He was mashimo. Why should she take criticism from him? He knew nothing. Imara pursed her lips, determined she wouldn't take back a single word.

Abe folded his arms in front of his chest. "I think you're wrong."

And that was it. He was mad. She was mad. They were flirting one minute, and now Imara was sure she never wanted to speak to him again.

He hadn't called her yet, but Imara walked over to Darius and asked about his progress. Imara turned back and stole a glance at Abe. Right on cue, grass green threads flew away from Abe and twisted around Naki's arms. Imara almost screamed out loud. What did he want from Naki? And why did his desire always grow after they fought with each other?

Imara tried to calm her racing heart. She tapped her toe until her muscles ached. Abe was a waste of time. He was probably one of those guys who had a new girl every week. Imara could usually pick those out a mile away, but maybe she was blinded by his stupid beautiful eyes. Either way, she was determined he wouldn't make her feel any emotion ever again. At least not any positive one.

She should have known his stupid hope swirls were too good to be true. What she needed more than anything was to get out of these catacombs.

TWENTY-ONE

IMARA CURLED HER TOES AND TAPPED HER fingers against her thigh. Why was it taking Darius so long to find that stupid projector? Imara had pointed out the spot at least ten minutes ago. Or maybe it was the wrong spot. She was beyond irritated with these stupid catacombs. She didn't want to find the stupid Judge or the stupid lair, but she did want to get out. Maybe Abe was right. Maybe it was time to get the transporter.

Aghhh! But she didn't want Abe to be right either. She was mad at him and nothing would change that. Imara pulled her water bottle from her backpack and grimaced when she saw the water was almost gone. She'd been so careful the other days to preserve the water throughout the day. Today she was too distracted to do anything right.

Imara drank the rest of the water, but there were still a few stray drops at the bottom. She flicked the mouthpiece to send the last of the water up the straw. That way she could drink every last drop.

She sucked on the straw as she flicked when out of nowhere, a firm hand grabbed her arm, just above the elbow. Imara's skin bristled at the touch.

"Don't do that," Abe said in a low voice.

Imara took the water bottle from her mouth without a thought. When did he get over here? She thought he was still by the wall talking to his dad. Imara got ready to pull her arm out of his grip and yell at him for telling her what to do.

But then she saw his skin.

In an instant, every bit of her anger and frustration melted away. The wine-colored fear spikes growing off him were so long, they almost reached the walls on either side of the passage. They sharpened and pulsed with each of his heartbeats. And here she was, expecting him to be annoyed by the flicking sound.

Instead he felt fear. Real fear. A raven black rash of anxiety spotted each of the wine fear spikes. Imara blinked, trying to figure out why he was so afraid. All she did was flick the straw in her water bottle. Abe stood still and let out slow breaths, but Imara could feel from his hand that his heart was racing. She was taken with the overwhelming desire to comfort him. But from what, she didn't know.

Imara let her free hand fall to her side. Her mind was full of questions, but all she could do was muster out a quiet, "Okay."

Abe loosened his grip on her arm, but he didn't let go. Though it didn't hurt, Imara became aware of how tight he had been gripping her. Imara wished she had the guts to wrap her arms around him, but she couldn't bring herself to do it. After what she'd said about his dad, she didn't know how he would take it.

Abe's breaths rattled through his throat while he tried to calm himself. Imara turned toward him, and she caught another unexpected sight. Abe's were not the only fear spikes in the room.

Mr. Nazari leaned against a wall and cleaned under his fingernails. He seemed engrossed in the task and unaware of everyone around him. No matter how he looked on the outside, Imara knew it was all an act. Mr. Nazari's fear spikes were as long as Abe's, and they were also spotted with a raven black rash of anxiety. With those added to Mr. Nazari's rainstorm of cobalt blue sadness, his burnt orange greed prickles were barely visible.

Abe's face remained expressionless while the fear spikes started to shrink at last. Imara couldn't believe everyone else in the passageway continued on as if there wasn't some crazy, unexpected thing happening. But there was something unexpected happening. Unexpected and unexplained. Imara held her breath trying to understand what had triggered the fear.

Then another color came from nowhere. Abe breathed out a long, but silent sigh. He slid his thumb across Imara's skin, just above her elbow. A glint of periwinkle erupted from his skin. Protective worry, and all for Imara.

She felt it again. That tug on her heart to comfort him. Squeeze his hand or hold him tight or put her head on his shoulder. Something. Maybe even apologize for what she said about his dad. She promised herself she wouldn't, but it was a stupid promise, and she knew it. What she needed was to be honest with him. Tell him it hurt when he questioned her hila and admit that was why she insisted his dad was greedy. Surely he would understand.

But before Imara could open her mouth, Siluk jerked his head down the passageway. "I think the Judge is coming," he said.

Darius swayed on top of Siluk's shoulders. His arms swung out to balance himself, and then he grimaced. "What is that supposed to mean?"

"It means stop talking so loud, and also we should get out of here."

Abe let his hand fall away from Imara as he turned his full attention to Siluk. The corner of Imara's lip twitched at Siluk's horribly timed interruption. She wanted to know more about Abe's fear, not deal with one of Siluk's stupid lies. "How do you know the Judge is coming?" she asked.

Siluk glared, but kept his voice lowered. "I can smell it."

Imara rolled her eyes. "You just want us to stop taking down projectors and go find the lair."

"I don't care about the lair!"

Lie. She knew it was a lie, but it felt good to see his skin dull all the same. With the new colors and Abe's questioning, Imara was forced to consider there was more to her hila than she thought. At least interpreting lies was one thing she knew how to do right.

"How do you know what the Judge smells like?" Abe asked.

Darius finished getting down from Siluk's shoulders. His pain at being betrayed had hardened to a thick anger. He scowled and said, "Yeah, maybe you're working for the Judge. Is that why you know how he smells?"

Siluk whipped around and clenched his fists. "Seriously, Darius? You'd accuse me of that?"

Darius shrugged with a tilt of his head. His glare deepened as he clapped his hands against his pants to clean off the dust. "How can we trust anything you say? You're a liar." Siluk opened his mouth to protest, but Darius

229

interrupted him before he had the chance. "I know you can't smell people from that far away."

"Shut up!" Siluk said in a loud whisper. "He's going to hear us and know where we are."

"You can't smell someone from that far away!" Darius yelled it just to annoy Siluk even more.

Siluk's eyes widened, and he put his pointer finger over his lips. Thick blood red flames burned from every angle of his skin. "I don't smell the Judge, I smell the transporter. It smells like hot metal. I smelled it at the party after the Judge took you guys hostage." Siluk scanned the passage then took off his backpack. "I can use explosives to create a wall so the Judge can't get to us. I'm positive it will work."

Lie. Imara huffed and put her hands on her hips. The last thing she was about to do was let Siluk get away with new lies.

"I thought you wanted to catch the Judge anyway," Imara said. "Who cares if he's coming? If he has the transporter, that's even better."

Siluk tried to force Darius and Naki down the passage. Darius glared, but Naki looked at Imara, waiting to see what she said. Siluk made a fist and grunted. "We don't have a plan. I don't want the Judge sneaking up on us, do you? We were supposed to ambush him in the lair, not meet him out in the open like this. What if he has weapons?"

Darius glanced at Imara. When she rolled her eyes, Darius turned on Siluk with renewed anger. "Why are you distracting us?"

Siluk stared back with a baffled look. Darius continued. "It's your fault I couldn't find the projector in the ceiling.

You probably moved me away from it on purpose. You're working for the Judge."

Siluk pinched the bridge of his noise while a flurry of sepia desperation burst from his skin. "That doesn't make any sense. Why would the Judge write a note accusing me of lying if I was working for him? Let me blow up the wall to block the path. Then we can run from the Judge until we make a plan. The wall will keep us all safe."

Lie.

Siluk got to his knees and tore open his backpack. Imara loomed over him with a glare. She vaguely noticed how everyone stared at her, waiting to see how she would react. Siluk took two black blocks and some clay from his bag. He pressed the first block against the wall, turning it a few times until he was happy with the position. Then he peeled a bit of clay off the large chunk and used it to keep the block in place.

He turned to grab the second black block, but Imara put her foot on top of it to stop him.

"I know you're lying," she said.

Siluk flashed his teeth. "I don't have time for this." He shoved on Imara's thighs, pushing her back into the others. He placed the second block before anyone could stop him.

Imara's hands smarted when they hit the stone ground. She never expected Siluk to be so aggressive, and it scared her. "Don't let him light the explosives," Imara said as she stumbled back to her feet. "I don't know what he's planning, but he's been lying this whole time."

Everyone looked at Imara then back to Siluk. Darius frowned and tried to snatch Siluk's backpack. Siluk pulled his backpack away from Darius. He snarled at Imara and said, "I'm going to save us all from the Judge, you arrogant freak."

"Lie." Imara spat the word back. "The Judge isn't here, and he isn't coming."

Siluk grunted and pulled the lighter from his backpack. Darius seized Siluk's wrist and held on fast. Mr. Nazari stepped forward ready to assist Darius if needed. Darius ripped the lighter from Siluk with a glare, daring him to take the lighter back.

Siluk tried to pull his hand away from Darius. When he failed, he let out a guttural cry in exasperation. "This is why it's illegal to trust someone just because she's a truth seer. She's lying, not me. If I blow up this wall, we'll have a chance to get away from the Judge and make a plan!"

"I have to say, this is very amusing."

A shiver went down Imara's spine when she heard her own voice inside of her head. Imara rotated her body, hoping against all hope she wouldn't see him standing there. But no matter how slowly she turned, there he was in all of his dramatic glory.

The Judge.

He stood tall, dressed in the same clothes as the party. The only difference now was a gun in each of his hands. The two guns were different from each other and also unlike any gun Imara had ever seen. This made Imara shiver even harder. She had no idea what came out of guns like that.

The Judge tilted his head to the side and the voice had a sing song lilt to it. "See what happens when you lie? Nobody believes you even when you tell the truth."

Siluk ripped his hand from Darius, taking advantage of his distraction. Siluk snatched the lighter and lit the explosives before anyone realized what he was doing.

The Judge shook his head. "You'll never escape me."

The Judge pulled the trigger on the gun in his right hand just as the explosives started blowing up. A hissing sound filled the passage as thick seaweed green fog seeped from the gun. The air grew thick and dusty in Imara's mouth. But the seaweed green fog was the last thing on Imara's mind now. The stone wall cracked and Imara watched in horror as a rock disconnected from the ceiling above. It took less than a second to realize the rock was headed right for her. In her head, Imara screamed, telling herself to run. But her muscles felt as heavy as lead as she tried to move away.

A heavy hand pushed on her back and propelled her forward. She saw Naki hurtling through the passage just ahead of her. Imara rolled onto the path next to Naki who fell at almost the same time as her. Imara got one glance at the hand that pushed her to safety. One glance to see her savior before rocks crashed down and blocked her view.

Siluk.

He saved her and Naki. Now he and the others were on the other side of the rock pile with the illusion, the Judge, and those two guns.

Imara jumped to her feet. The stone wall had crumbled into a pile of rocks that piled all the way up to the ceiling. It made a perfect wall to block the path. Just like Siluk said it would. Imara pounded the rocks, desperate to find a weakness. She had to get back to them. She had to keep them safe from the Judge. She screamed out their names. "Siluk! Darius! Mr. Nazari!"

Nothing.

"Abe!" Her voice sounded so little compared to the turmoil inside of her. Her throat burned when she called out his name again. This time her voice caught on the word and she had to cough to release the choking in her throat.

Imara pounded the rocks harder, but with each pound they only settled more. Soon, nothing budged. Imara's heart was full of despair. Her curls flew back as she turned to Naki. "What was in that fog? Are they dead?"

Naki got to her feet and shook her head. When her right foot touched the ground, she gripped her side in pain. She leaned over and let out a single cough. After a moment, she took in a deep breath and said, "It's just fog. Like a fog machine, but from a gun. It's water, glycerin, and coloring." Naki leaned over further and coughed as she squeezed her side.

A scream from the other side of the wall made Imara's heart stop. She called out Abe's name before she realized it was Darius screaming, not Abe.

Finally Imara heard a voice from the other side of the rocks.

"Imara."

"Abe!" Imara slammed the rocks again, trying to do something. Anything.

"You have to go, Imara." Abe spoke fast, his breath short.

"I'm not leaving you," Imara said.

"There's nothing you can do from that side of the rocks. Go find the lair. We'll try to get the transporter and meet you there."

Imara shook her head, touching the rocks, trying to feel Abe's presence through them somehow. "But you don't have the map. How can you find the fork in the road? And what if we're wrong? What if the lair is somewhere else?"

"We'll be all right," he said. "You have to—No! No, please don't."

"Abe!" she screamed, but he didn't respond. Imara heard him grunt and he moved away from the rocks. Or someone moved him.

"Abe," she called one last time. Quieter now.

There was no response.

Imara whirled around, her eyes staring with fierce determination.

Naki's eyes rested on the wall of rocks. Charcoal balls of panic bounced away from her skin while she rubbed her side with a frown.

"Can you walk?" Imara asked.

Naki nodded, and without warning, tears streamed down her face. She sucked in a shaky breath and said, "He killed them. He killed them all and we're next."

Imara shook her head and scoffed. "Pull yourself together, Naki." Imara started down the passage without looking back.

"Where are you going?" Naki asked.

"We." Imara answered. "Where are *we* going? We're going to find the lair. There has to be something there that can help them."

TWENTY-TWO

GREEN FOG SEEPING FROM A GUN. ROCKS tumbling from explosives. Crazed terrorist coming at them.

Yet the only thing Abe noticed was Siluk pushing both Naki and Imara to safety. Abe's nose wrinkled as if filled with a foul stench. What was he saving Imara for?

Of course Abe wanted Imara safe. He would have done the same thing if he knew how the rocks were going to fall and where to push her and all of that. But it bothered Abe that Siluk was so careful to save her. Why Imara and not Darius? Why didn't Siluk save himself for that matter?

He was glad Imara was safe, but he was suddenly also glad Siluk was nowhere near her. In the split second Abe took to worry over Siluk's intentions, the air filled with a heavy green fog. It was stale and thick in his mouth. His vision obscured completely. By the time Abe lifted his collar over his nose and mouth, he realized the fog was safe to breathe.

Abe tripped over Siluk's backpack, and his body moved through the fog without aim. He took in deep breaths as he flailed his arms out, trying to get a sure footing. That's when he heard her voice.

Imara called out names. A relief eased the worry Abe didn't even know he had. Following the sound of her voice, he scooted his way toward the fresh rock pile. It wasn't until then that he noticed the order she had called out those names.

She said Siluk first? Why was she so concerned about Siluk all the sudden? And she didn't even say Abe's name. Abe tripped over a rock, which only heightened his frustration. Didn't she care about him? He knew she was still mad, but didn't she care at least a little? And now there was a ringing in his ear. He shook his head, trying to get rid of the sound.

"Abe!"

There it was. And yes. She said his name different than the others. There was more worry, more pain. He felt a little guilty for enjoying it so much.

Abe heard Darius scream, but the fog was too thick to see why. Besides, right now Abe only cared about one thing.

Imara.

He called to her, and she answered without hesitation. She was so close, he could almost feel her. He told her to go find the lair. She protested, but only because she didn't want to leave him. He hated himself for asking her to go without him, but they had little choice now. At least Naki was with her. They would be safer together.

Abe urged Imara to go on without them. She asked how they could get through the catacombs without the map. Abe tried not to think about that too much. His dad had a good memory of the catacombs. The map was better than memory, but at least they had something. He worried more about the illusions.

The fog wafted down the passage and started to clear. Abe could make out shadowy shapes in the ugly, green air. The Judge's arms were wrapped around Darius's stomach. Darius threw his arms back, trying to strike the Judge.

Abe pressed Imara on, telling her they'd be all right. Abe was grateful she couldn't see him now. She would know it was a lie.

Abe watched as the Judge raised one of his arms from Darius's stomach and raised a gun to his head. Abe stopped midsentence and said, "No! No please don't—"

Before he could finish, Abe was knocked to the floor. Siluk tried to get to Darius and in the attempt, tripped over Abe's feet. Abe jumped up and ran toward the Judge, ready to tackle him to the ground.

Abe shoved into the Judge's side. The Judge pushed Abe away and swung one of his guns across Abe's face. The gun smashed against Abe's cheek, swinging his jaw out. Abe dug his fingers into his temples when the ringing in his ears got louder. Abe took a step back and then another as he attempted to regain his footing.

Now Siluk lunged for the Judge, but the Judge flicked him back with one hand. Siluk fell, but he didn't land on the ground. Or rather, there wasn't ground to land on. Siluk landed in one of the spike pits.

He screamed in pain, and Darius jumped forward to drag him from the pit. The fog was almost cleared now. When Siluk got out of the pit, Abe saw a large gash in his pants from his hip, down to his knee. Siluk grimaced in pain. Blood dripped from the wound, but Abe sighed in relief. The spike had merely grazed him with a superficial cut. It could have been a lot worse.

Mr. Nazari leapt toward the Judge, and without a thought, Abe leapt right after him. He figured a two-person tackle would be better than one. The Judge fired the fog gun again. A sickening hiss filled the air, and all Abe could see was green, green, green. Abe landed hard on his stomach on top of his dad, but the Judge was nowhere to be found.

"Over here," Darius called out.

Abe held his arms out and took short steps toward Darius. If they were going to win any kind of fight with the Judge, it would be together, not alone. After several seconds of calling out and reaching and tripping, the four of them found each other. Mr. Nazari insisted they wait until the fog cleared again before they tried anything new. They stood, huddled with their backs together, arms out ready to fight.

"There," Mr. Nazari said when the fog began to thin.

They lunged for the Judge, but he stepped away with a surprising amount of ease. Abe fell to the ground while the others fell beside him. Even with that helmet over his face, Abe thought the Judge looked amused.

Abe got to his feet as soon as he could. He dusted off his clothes while he tried to think of another way to attack. Something about this fight seemed strange. If there were four of them and only one of the Judge, why was this so difficult?

Abe turned as he scanned the passage. The constant ringing in his ears made it difficult to think. Abe stared at the rock pile and wondered if they could throw some of the large rocks at the Judge. Just then, an arm wrapped around Abe from behind and tightened around his neck in a strangling hold.

Abe choked, and his breath shuddered as he struggled to take in any air he could.

"Stop!" Mr. Nazari screamed out, but the Judge only tightened his grip.

Abe felt blood pounding in his ear, but the shock of it had worn off. He wished the ringing in his ears would subside, but he could work through it. He jammed his elbow as hard as he could into the Judge's stomach. It was far less powerful than he intended. Abe gasped for air. He was running out of ideas.

Mr. Nazari dropped to his knees in front of the Judge. "Please, stop. He's my son. I'll do anything you ask. Anything. Just let him go. I have money. I have influence. Anything you want, it's yours."

The Judge loosened his grip the tiniest bit, which opened Abe's airway. Abe sucked in a large breath right as Darius hit something against the wall. Abe took the opportunity to elbow the Judge in the stomach again. Now that he had some air, this blow was more productive.

The Judge shook when Abe hit him and responded by pushing Abe away. The Judge ran to a specific spot on the path and Abe heard a voice in his head. "Tackle me now and you'll fall in a pit of spikes." The words were followed by a laugh that seemed more sinister than Abe's laughs ever had.

Abe clenched his fists, but a realization hit him. The Judge was toying with them. He dodged and evaded. He used the fog gun and pushed them. But he didn't knock them out.

He didn't kill them. He had another gun, but it could have been decorative for all he used it.

The Judge wasn't trying to win this fight. It seemed like his only goal was to show them he was in charge. That they couldn't beat him no matter how hard they tried. Or maybe he was only trying to distract them. Images of a horde of taggers attacking Imara entered Abe's mind.

Abed gritted his teeth and clenched his fists tighter. It was time to end this fight. Abe tackled the Judge from the side. He aimed so the Judge would fall on the path instead of the spike pit. The Judge fell just as Abe predicted, but the Judge kicked Abe's foot back. Abe teetered backward toward what he assumed was the spike pit. Just before falling in, his dad was there to catch him. Abe was pulled to safety while the Judge went after Siluk and Darius.

While Abe panted, his head reeled with confusion. Why did the Judge have such an advantage over them? It took eight taggers to defeat them before, and even then the taggers had to retreat. But the Judge was in complete control of this fight. They attempted to inflict pain by tackling, hitting, and punching, but nothing hit its mark the way it was meant. The Judge evaded without even trying. Every once in awhile, a sinister laugh taunted them with their lack of capture.

Four against one, and it wasn't even a fight. It was a slaughter. And yet, the Judge hadn't seriously injured them either. Abe remembered how confused they all were after the boiling water. What did the Judge want? He didn't hurt them, but he wouldn't let them go? Was he only trying to scare them? And why?

Abe watched Darius and Siluk push the Judge with every ounce of strength they had. The Judge pushed back, but still seemed in complete control. Still, Darius and Siluk pushed the Judge backward, probably aiming for the spike pit that must have been near. Abe held his breath as he watched, sure that this time success was inevitable.

But then a chime came from the Judge. He tapped his ring, pulled out the golden transporter, and pushed Siluk and Darius back as if they were no heavier than pillows. In an instant, the Judge was gone.

When the Judge disappeared, there was no resistance to the pressure Darius and Siluk had spent on pushing. They fell forward, Darius first and Siluk ready to topple over him. They were midair when Abe remembered the spike pit was near. He couldn't see how close, but he didn't want to take any chances. Abe took hold of Siluk, and his dad was there a second later. Even with his speed, Abe couldn't get to Darius in time.

Darius grunted as he fell. When he hit the bottom, an unearthly scream erupted from Darius, his eyes flashing with pain.

Siluk and Abe fell to their knees and held their hands out. Siluk flinched when Abe accidentally bumped into the gash on his thigh. But soon he focused solely on Darius. Mr. Nazari held Darius from behind, and together they pulled Darius from the pit.

Abe tried not to gasp when he saw the blood seeping from Darius's side and his leg. Abe ripped open his backpack and dug through his supplies, already knowing Darius needed more than he had. Abe got a pile of gauze and held it tight against the circle of blood on Darius's side. "Hold that," he said to Siluk.

It was far from ideal. The gauze was still wet from the boiling water, though now it was cold. Abe had no idea what kind of dirt or bacteria was in the water, but he knew it was far from clean. But he had to use something to stop the blood. Abe glared at his bag, trying to fish out the last bit of gauze.

Now to the leg wound, which worried Abe the most. The circle of blood grew every second, and Abe had to focus to keep from clenching his jaw too tight.

Abe pushed the gauze against Darius's leg. Darius flinched and groaned at his touch. "Sorry," Abe said. "But try to hold still."

Abe held the gauze tight against Darius's leg and stared off into space as he pressed all around the top of the wound. He slid his fingers across, covering every inch of the wound. After several agonizing seconds, he breathed a short sigh.

"I don't think it hit your femoral artery," Abe said.

"What does that mean?" Siluk asked.

"It means he's not going to die." At once, Abe wished he hadn't phrased it so bluntly, but it was too late now. He retrieved the ointment with pain killer and squeezed it under each of the gauze pads.

Abe found some tape from his backpack, but it dripped with water. Abe had no idea if it would work wet like this, but he didn't have much of an option other than to try it. He wrapped the tape around Darius leg, securing the gauze, but it didn't stick at all. Instead, Abe got a longer length of tape and tied it off around Darius's leg. He did the same thing around Darius's stomach.

Next, Abe ripped a strip of cloth from his extra shirt. He wiped the gash on Siluk's thigh with it, and then got a long length of gauze to cover the wound. Siluk tied tape around the gauze to keep it in place.

Abe helped Darius to his feet, but Darius winced and whimpered when he tried to put weight on his leg. Abe put Darius's arm over his shoulder to help him walk.

"Come on," Abe said, remembering the chime from the Judge's ring. "We have to get to the fork in the road. I think the Judge might be after Imara."

TWENTY-THREE

THE WEIGHT FROM DARIUS'S ARM PRESSED on Abe's shoulder with each step. It was easy to ignore when Abe's mind was so full of worry. The Judge left as soon as his hologram ring chimed. It had to be a signal of some kind, and all Abe could imagine was a sensor that Imara set off. Abe focused on walking as fast as possible while Darius limped next to him. Once they reached the end of the passage, Abe turned to his dad and said, "Which way?"

Mr. Nazari pointed, and Abe noticed a cuff link missing from his dad's shirt. He looked at it, then at his dad. His eyes grew wide, but he tried not to make a big deal about it. "You lost a cuff link," Abe said.

Mr. Nazari did a long blink and shrugged it off. "Ah well, at least I'm not dead. What's a flapping cuff?"

Abe held his breath knowing that he alone could see the pain in his dad's eyes. They could mourn the loss of the cuff link later. Now they needed to focus on finding the fork in the road. Abe swallowed over a lump in his throat, but didn't say a word. He lumbered forward in the direction his dad pointed.

Darius flinched, and at the same time Mr. Nazari said, "Stop!"

245

The tension in Abe's stomach only tightened. He turned and said, "What? We have to hurry."

Darius took a small hop on his good leg to get better balance. "There's a curvy-shaped pit up there, remember? How do you expect to get past it without Imara?"

Abe's nostrils flared. "We know basically where it is. Let's just try to avoid it."

Darius laughed. "Hey, if you want to march forward without a clue where you're going, be my guest. But don't drag me along with you. I'd prefer to live."

Siluk frowned. "Except don't do that because if you get hurt, none of us has medical training."

Abe huffed. "We can't stay here and wait for Imara to find us. What are we? Damsels in distress?"

"She found us last time," Siluk said with a shrug.

"The Judge is after her!"

"Abraxas, think about what you're saying." His dad's voice sounded as cold and calculating as his logic. "None of us wants to leave Imara and Naki to fight the Judge alone, but we can't get past this curvy pit without Imara. The shape is too abnormal. Unless we think of a safe way to maneuver the illusions without her, we're stuck."

Abe hit the side of his leg with his fist. He helped Darius wrap his arm around Siluk's shoulder so Abe could pace across the width of the corridor. Abe stared at the ground, desperate for a solution. When he thought of nothing he said, "You all stay here, and I'll go. I don't care if I get hurt."

Siluk laughed. "You really are reckless."

"Shut up," Abe said as he slammed his fist against the wall. A small cloud of dust lifted from the wall around Abe's fist. Abe watched as it swirled and floated to the ground. It landed on a pile of dirt, which Abe kicked with his toe. The dirt flew through the air from Abe's kick then it fell back again. Abe pointed his toe toward the dirt, ready to kick again, but his body froze, and he stopped mid kick.

Abe bent down and gathered a pile of dirt into his hand. He stood up, taking the dirt with him.

"What are you doing?" Siluk asked.

Abe gritted his teeth. "Just watch." Abe sprinkled the dirt out onto the path in front of them. He watched as it swirled and floated to the ground. He sprinkled more, farther down the path, watching carefully for any change. On the last sprinkle, part of the dust disappeared before it touched the ground.

He turned back to the others with a smile. "Did you see that?" he asked.

They nodded, and Abe gathered another pile of dirt. He sprinkled it again just a touch farther than before, and this time more of the dirt disappeared. Now they could see where the illusion began and where to step to avoid the pit.

Abe beckoned them as he sprinkled dirt with each step. It took longer than they were used to, but they made it through the corridor without harm. At the next intersection, Abe turned to his dad. "Which way?"

Mr. Nazari closed his eyes and scrunched up his face. "Give me a minute," he said.

Abe frowned. This was going to take much longer without Imara. Abe could only hope it would be fast enough.

Siluk adjusted Darius's arm over his shoulder, and Darius winced in pain. When Siluk adjusted again, Darius scowled and said, "Is the gaping hole in my leg too much of an inconvenience for you?"

"We have a problem," Mr. Nazari said.

Abe looked at his dad, afraid of what he was about to say. Mr. Nazari frowned. "There's only one way to get to the fork in the road from here. And Siluk blocked the path we need to get there."

Darius laughed. "Way to go, Siluk. Messing everything up as usual."

Abe squeezed his fists. He took deep breaths to calm his sudden desire to punch Siluk in the face.

"I'm sorry," Siluk said, not sounding sorry at all. "But maybe I can use my explosives to make a new path. If I blow it up, is there a wall that will open to a passage or chamber that can lead to the fork in the road? Maybe we can create a shortcut."

"Now you're willing to destroy the catacombs just like the taggers did?" Darius shouted.

"This is life or death, Darius. Would you rather die? It's just one more wall."

Mr. Nazari glanced down the passages in the intersection. He rubbed his chin, and a faint smile grew on his lips. Abe breathed in relief when he saw the smile. Mr. Nazari pointed to the left and said, "This way."

Abe grabbed another handful of dirt and threw it out in front of them so they could avoid any pits.

Darius clenched his jaw. "If you blow up more than one wall, I'm throwing you into a spike pit."

"Hey," Abe said with heat in his mouth. "You guys can fight. Just do it while we walk, all right?"

Darius huffed, and Siluk scowled, but they kept walking.

They went through two more passages, and Mr. Nazari pointed to a wall. "This one should get us closest. If it leads to the passage I think, it won't be hard to get to the fork in the road."

Siluk helped Darius to the ground then bent over his backpack to get out the explosives. This time he removed three black blocks and the same chunk of clay he used before.

Abe eyed the blocks as Siluk handled them. "How many of those do you have?"

"Why?" Siluk asked.

"Could you use them on the entrance of the catacombs? If we don't get the transporter, do you think you could get us out of here with explosives?"

Siluk sighed and kneaded the back of his neck with his fingers. He placed a block on the wall and sighed again.

"What? Is the rock pile at the entrance too thick? Or you don't have enough explosives? It won't work?"

"The explosives would work," Siluk said.

"What?" Mr. Nazari snapped. He was losing more control with each passing minute. "Why didn't you tell us before?"

Siluk used his thumb to spread a clump of clay around the edge of the black block. He frowned. "If I use explosives to get us out, it will crack the stone in the ground. We'd have plenty of time to get out, but the cracks would spread and eventually break. It would destroy the catacombs. The crypts, the shaft, everything."

Mr. Nazari pinched his nose, and took a deep breath. He said through his teeth, "We're stuck down here and you didn't think to tell us there was a way out? Who cares about the catacombs?"

"We still have a chance to get the transporter," Siluk said. He changed the subject by lighting the explosives. They stood back, and a few seconds later the wall had a gaping hole that led to another passage.

Mr. Nazari took a calming breath before he stepped through the hole. "Perfect," Mr. Nazari said when he saw the new passage.

Abe threw a pile of dirt before he stepped onto the passage. A sharp pain in his shoulder reminded him he'd been sleeping on stone the last few nights. He grimaced. Just the reminder he needed when he was trying to stay calm.

As Siluk helped Darius onto the new path, Abe glared at Siluk. "Why didn't you tell us you could use explosives?"

Siluk shrugged, unapologetic. "I didn't think Darius would approve."

At this, Darius exploded on Siluk. "Don't act like you did it for me. You were probably just scared you would get hurt when we tried to get out."

Siluk rolled his eyes, but didn't respond as they started down the new path.

This made Darius even angrier. "I've had enough, Siluk. I mean it. You keep acting like we're still best friends, but you betrayed me for no reason. Because you needed the money, and I didn't? Please. We both could have used that scholarship. You a little bit more than me, but not by much. I am sick and tired of your stupid half apologies."

Siluk glued his feet to the ground and stopped with a start. He turned to Darius and knitted his eyebrows together. "Fine, you want to know the truth?"

"Don't stop walking," Abe called back.

Siluk hissed through his teeth, but kept walking. "You're right, Darius. It wasn't about the money. At least not entirely. It was mostly about you."

"What is that supposed to mean?" Darius said through a clenched jaw.

Siluk said each word as pointed jabs. "You are jealous of everything and everybody. I knew I was going to win that scholarship. and you were going to lose. My essay was better and so were my grades. Plus I had excellent recommendations from all my professors. I was afraid that when I won, you would be jealous, and you would let it fester, and then all the sudden we wouldn't be friends anymore. I didn't want that to happen, so I made sure you never applied."

When Siluk stopped talking, the catacombs rang with an eerie silence. Darius's good leg clomped every other step. Abe almost glanced back to see Darius's reaction, but decided against it. This had nothing to do with him. He was only aware of the conversation because of pure circumstance. But the clomping got louder as the silence grew.

Finally Darius said in a low voice, "You still committed scholarship fraud for money."

Mr. Nazari's calm, but cold voice cut through the air. "That is true, Siluk, and don't think I've forgotten it. I should kick you out of the school for what you've done. I know you won't do it next year since Jabari is—"

At that Mr. Nazari stopped and shut his eyes tight. He balled his hand into a fist and held it over his mouth. The breaths coming out of his nose were short and hard. Abe stood watching his father. His thumb found itself at his chin, and Abe scratched mindlessly as he watched his father suffer in silence. Mr. Nazari never lost his cool in front of anyone. Sure, Abe had seen him cry lots of times, but that was when they were safe at home. But his dad had known Bello for years, and his death was still so fresh.

It took awhile, but Mr. Nazari lowered his fist and coughed a few times. "Let's go," he said in a low voice.

It took an entire passage before anyone spoke again. Mr. Nazari said, "What are we going to do when we get to the Judge? He might be after the girls, but if we don't have a plan, he'll beat us just as badly as he did earlier."

Darius shifted his weight before he spoke. "I think I might know something that could help us. It's about that gun the Judge had. Not the fog one."

Abe nodded as he walked. "Yeah, that gun was so weird. I've never seen anything like it. And why didn't he use it?"

"I actually think he did," Darius said.

"I didn't see him use it," Siluk said.

"You didn't see anything come out of it or you didn't see him use it? Because his finger was pulling the trigger the entire time."

Everyone looked to Darius in surprise, and he continued. "I noticed it at the beginning when the Judge had me around the stomach and held the gun to my head. I was trying to reach back and hit him or something, but my movements weren't as sharp or as fast as usual. And when he put the gun to my head, everything went all fuzzy in my mind. And didn't you guys notice the ringing in your ears?"

Abe nodded as he walked. "I did notice a ringing in my ears."

"Well I hit the gun and listened to what it was made of. I'm pretty sure the gun shape was meant to throw us off because the inside was nothing like a gun. It was filled with metal things, like tuning forks. I think they work like a dog whistle where you can't hear the noise, but it's bothersome to our physiology."

Mr. Nazari frowned. "That seems unlikely. Technology like that has been in development for years and still the only kind of noise that affects human physiology has to be heard by human ears."

Darius nodded. "There was a ringing in our ears, wasn't there? And besides that, I tested it. The tuning forks were made with a certain kind of metal, and the projectors have an opposite composition. I had a projector in my pocket and I hit it against the wall so the two sounds would cancel each other out. It was while the Judge was strangling you, Abe. As soon as I hit the wall, you elbowed the Judge and got away."

Abe narrowed his eyes in thought. "That's right. I tried to elbow the Judge before, but my blow was too weak. He loosened his grip on my neck and I elbowed him again. I thought it worked the second time because I had air, but now that I think about it, I probably had more air the first time because he only just started to strangle me."

"The Judge loosened his grip on you?" Mr. Nazari asked. "Why would he do that? Why didn't he kill you? Or any of us?"

Abe shook his head. "It's the same thing it's been this entire time. The Judge acts like he's going to kill us, but never actually hurts us. But he killed Headmaster Bello. Why not us? And what happened to the taggers that were down here?"

Siluk grunted and helped Darius readjust. Then he said, "It's pointless to try to understand a fanatic like the Judge. But knowing about the gun does help us. We have a fair chance at beating him if we can get rid of that gun. Then we can make him pay for what he did to Headmaster Bello."

Mr. Nazari showed instant relief at these words. Abe even saw a smile tugging at the corners of his dad's mouth. Mr. Nazari took a deep breath, and his chest heaved out. "That gun is the key. Without you, Darius, we wouldn't know. And without your explosives, Siluk, we would be stuck down here. If we ever get back, I'm giving you both an award."

Siluk laughed. "Nice. Give me an award right before you kick me out. Just what I need."

They turned a corner, and Abe was happy to see they wouldn't need any handfuls of dirt in this corridor. Imara had already destroyed the illusion that morning. Before them lay the checkerboard of foot pits. Abe felt a pang of guilt when he passed the large silver spike on the ground. It was the one Abe tossed even though he couldn't see it. Imara saved him even when he was being a complete idiot. A reckless idiot.

Mr. Nazari brushed his jacket and said, "You committed scholarship fraud, Siluk, but it was partially my fault it happened in the first place."

Abe's mouth dropped. He stopped walking for a full second to stare at his dad.

Mr. Nazari nodded. "Jabari begged me for years to create a scholarship fund for students with financial need. He had donors and an investment plan and everything. I thought it would take too much time or resources to get it set up, so I always refused. And I wasn't in love with the idea of setting up something that had no direct profit."

Mr. Nazari looked down and sighed. "I was too greedy to consider how beneficial it was to the students. And I should have expected Headmaster Bello to take matters into his own hands. He always liked the idea of a vigilante."

Abe's mouth continued to drop with each step he took. It wasn't like his dad to admit guilt. And in front of students, no less. Then again, these catacombs had taken them all past their breaking points.

Mr. Nazari rubbed his nose and did a quick sniff. "I shouldn't blame you, Siluk. You're not getting kicked out, and I'm going to implement Jabari's scholarship plan. I'm sure I still have his notes somewhere. I'll call it the *Bello Scholarship Fund* and all the money will go to students in financial need."

Abe smiled, and when they rounded a bend, his smile grew. They were getting closer to the fork in the road. This was the passage with two large pillars covered in spikes. At that thought, Abe frowned. If they were avoiding pillars and not pits, the dirt trick might not work.

Abe threw out a handful of dirt and it fell to the ground a little funny, but it didn't make the pillar stand out like it did the pits. "Stay here," Abe said. "I'm going to get that long spike and see if we can feel our way around the pillars with it."

He dashed back around the bend and zigzagged through the foot pits. He grabbed the silver spike and felt a rush of anticipation. They'd be back to Imara soon.

When Abe rounded the bend to everyone else, Darius and Siluk were arguing again.

Darius said, "Egypt has not *always* been the center of the world. Britain used to have colonies all over the world, remember? That's the main reason the global language is English."

"Okay, sorry," Siluk said. "But I do think it's fresh the catacombs are a record of another time when Egypt *was* the center of the world."

255

"You always lie! You act like you care about the catacombs, but I know you don't."

Abe passed them and held the spike out far in front of him and waved it around, trying to make contact with the pillar.

Siluk did a long, drawn-out sigh. "Fine. Maybe I don't care about the catacombs, but I know you do, and I do care about you. Did you really want me to say, 'I think it's fresh that you think it's fresh that the catacombs are fresh?' Even if it was technically a lie, what I said meant the same thing."

Abe swung the spike out and heard a bump as it clashed against the pillar. Abe did small taps against the pillar to figure out its exact location. He moved forward on tiptoes to get past it while the others followed behind. He took careful steps forward, swinging the spike to find the second pillar. "Is that what happened when you blew up the wall?" Abe asked.

"What?" Siluk said.

Abe took short steps and swung the spike in a methodical rhythm. He was so focused on the path it was hard to think of the words. "Imara said you were lying. Maybe you were, but not about what she thought."

"I was not lying!" Siluk said.

The spike finally tapped the second pillar, and Abe's steps grew longer. He stepped with confidence as he hit the pillar, walking around it. "You called her an arrogant freak," Abe said with no explanation.

Siluk scoffed. "Were you offended by that? I hurt your precious Imara and now you're mad?"

Abe's lip curled up while a bitter taste filled his mouth. He took a slow breath then said, "Was that the lie? You don't think she's arrogant?"

256

"*Pshh*, she is arrogant. Why would you assume that was a lie? I don't care about her."

"You saved her." Abe sounded too resentful. He knew it the minute he said it, but it was too late to take it back now.

Siluk heard the tone and hounded Abe for it. "Oh, you're jealous? You're mad that I saved her, and you didn't get the chance? Good to know. Next time I'll let her get crushed by a pile of rocks. Would that make you—"

Siluk went silent. Abe turned back and saw the color draining from Siluk's face. "Oh," he said.

"What?"

"Oh no." Siluk closed his eyes and hit his forehead with the palm of his hand. "I did lie." Siluk hit his head repeatedly with his palm and then huffed. "I said, 'I'm going to save us all from the Judge.' But I knew that wasn't going to happen. We were running out of time, and I didn't think I'd be able to save everyone. I was trying to make it sound like we had a chance so everyone would be hopeful. But technically it was a lie."

Abe clenched his jaw and went back to walking down the passageway. He had to clear his head of some steam before he spoke again. "Was that the only lie?"

Siluk was quiet for a moment before he spoke again. "No. I said, 'I'm positive it will work. I can keep us all safe.'"

Abe heard Siluk grind his teeth together. "I like to make everyone feel better. That's pretty much the only reason I lie. I told Darius the baba ganoush was as fresh as it was at the party, but it wasn't. It only tasted good because I made it smell good. I never think it's lying because I always do it for a good reason. But I guess doing the wrong thing for the right reason is still doing the wrong thing."

257

Darius scoffed. "I don't know what's worse. The fact that you don't think you're lying or the fact that you don't care."

Abe expected a quick retort, but it was quiet for a long time. When Siluk did speak again, he sounded remorseful. "I lied to you about the scholarship. Not directly, but what I did was deceitful. I should have told you I was afraid you'd be jealous and how I needed the scholarship. I'm sorry I lied to you."

Again the passageway was filled with silence, apart from Darius's good leg clomping along. When he did speak, his voice was heavy. Darius swallowed and said, "I knew you were going to win that scholarship. I tried to be okay with it, but it was hard. Honestly, when I got the message saying I couldn't apply, I was relieved. I didn't have the chance to be jealous that way. But I should have figured out how to get over my jealousy so you weren't afraid to lose our friendship. I'm sorry too."

Siluk sniffed, and Abe glanced back to see a small smile on Siluk's face. Siluk stopped and said, "So, are we good?"

Darius punched Siluk in the arm and nodded. Siluk smiled bigger and was about to go forward, but Darius said, "Bring it in, man."

Abe grinned as Darius wrapped his other arm around Siluk and thumped him on the back.

But then Abe tapped his foot. "Great, guys. This is really heartwarming and all. Okay, it is… it actually is fresh. But the Judge is after the girls! Can we please hurry? We're almost there."

TWENTY-FOUR

IMARA WATCHED THE MAP AS SHE TURNED
right at an intersection. Her feet faltered, and she tried not to
think about how the others didn't have a map anymore. She
had to find the Judge's lair now. Imara wasn't sure what she
would do when she got there, but she knew she would do
whatever she could. Find some evidence. Maybe destroy any
devices. She didn't know, but something. There had to be
something she could do.

Imara walked, but noticed the footsteps beside her
slowed then stopped. "Naki, hurry up," she said.

Imara turned back to see Naki staring at a blank wall in
the middle of the short passage. Imara frowned and said, "Do
you see something?"

Naki licked her lips and smacked her mouth open and
closed. She touched the wall. "I think this is where the boiling
water came from. Do you think there's a door here?"

"We don't have time to open random doors. We need to
get to the lair."

Naki rolled her eyes back as far as she could and put her
hand on one hip. "It's not a random door. The boiling water
came through here. What if there's a switch? We can turn it

off before the Judge tries to send boiling water after us again."

Imara made sure to drag out each sound as she said, "Fine."

Imara stared at the wall, searching for anything strange. She bit her thumbnail and tapped her toe. She tugged the hair on the back of her neck. She touched the stone, but shook her head in frustration.

"There's no door?"

"There is a door," Imara said. "The illusion is in the color. It's hard to see past."

Imara stepped away from the wall and put her hand over her forehead, trying to remember the lesson on color illusions from two summers ago. There were holographic cubes floating in the air. Professor Santini told her to look at the cube, look at the color, then look deeper.

Imara remembered how frustrating it was to figure out the puzzle. Professor Santini said to look deeper, so Imara always looked inside the cubes. But the cubes were empty. It took her three weeks to realize she wasn't supposed to look inside the cubes, she was supposed to look at the color. More specifically, the depth of color. It was easy to see the color on the outside, but she had to look at the different hues on the inside.

Imara rubbed her eyebrow and stared at the wall. Natural stone had many colors, and the walls of the catacombs were no different. Imara ran her hand across the wall, carefully observing the sand, oatmeal, caramel, and umber hues. Her eyes followed after her fingers until she found a spot that just looked tan, with hardly any depth at all. It looked like stone, but when Imara looked deeper, she saw metal.

Imara tilted her head and leaned in close to the wall. She felt it for a moment with her fingers then used her thumbnail to lift a cover, which revealed a button. She pushed it, and with a click, the door moved to reveal a small chamber with a long tunnel at the end of it.

Naki smiled and said, "Nice."

Imara did a half smile when she saw the pride glowing from Naki's skin. It was tangerine, like pride always was, but Imara raised an eyebrow when she noticed something else.

"Would you stop staring at my skin, Imara. It weirds me out."

"Sorry," Imara said. But then she grabbed Naki's hand and pulled her arm closer. "I know you hate it, but—" Imara looked closer at the tangerine glow, and she saw another color underneath it. Tiny canary yellow bubbles fizzed and popped beneath the glowing pride.

Naki pulled her arm back and scolded Imara. "Stop that."

"It's a strato feeling," Imara said as excitement surged through her.

"Strato? Is that even English?"

"I don't know," Imara said with a shrug. "That's what Professor Santini calls them. It's when a feeling has two layers. I usually only see it with fear and anxiety."

Naki tried to hide her smile as she pushed past Imara, but the glowing tangerine pride grew as she entered the chamber. Naki licked her lips and bent over a mechanical panel coming out from the wall. The tunnel sat just beyond the panel, and it seemed to go on forever.

"This is definitely where the water came from," Naki said. "I bet if we break this lever, the Judge won't be able to send the boiling water after us again. How can we break it?"

Imara picked a heavy rock from the ground. "Try this."

Naki took the rock and slammed it against the lever. It pushed the lever up then broke the lever away from the panel. The handle was broken off now and left a rugged circle that was flush with the control panel. Naki's eyes went wide, and wine-colored spikes of fear soon drowned out every other feeling. "That turned it on! The boiling water is coming, and now the lever is broken!"

Charcoal balls of panic bounced away from Naki's skin. She squeezed her fists and backed away from the mechanical panel. "Imara! How could you let me do that? You should have told me to break it the other direction so I didn't turn it on."

Imara gritted her teeth and scrunched up her nose. "This is your fault, Naki, not mine. You never take responsibility for anything." Imara let out a small scream of frustration as she left the room and went back out into the passage. She took hold of the first spike she saw and pulled to break it away from the wall.

"Hurry!" Naki said, her voice rising by the minute. "The water is coming. Do you know how to fix it?"

Imara got back to the mechanical panel and saw where the lever had broken off. Imara held the spike tight in her hand and aimed for the rugged circle. When the spike made contact, Imara pushed into the circle to pull the lever down. "I need your help," she said to Naki.

Naki wrapped her hands around Imara's and added her strength to pulling the lever down. Naki began licking her lips, and Imara tried to ignore the fluttering pulse in Naki's hands.

"IMARA!" Naki called out again. Imara felt the air grow hot, and her mouth became sticky. Imara heard water splashing against her shoes.

At last, the lever crawled downward. Naki grunted and pulled harder. Imara released every last bit of strength she had. Millimeter by millimeter, they pulled the lever to the *off* position. Naki let out a great sigh and backed up against the wall behind her. She wiped the sweat from her forehead and flicked her hand to remove the sweat.

Imara brushed the curls off her forehead and said, "Let's go."

Imara shut the door to the chamber before they started down the passage. She shook her head. "I can't believe you turned that lever on before you broke it."

"Well, I turned it back off again, didn't I?"

Imara laughed. "Oh, you take responsibility for that? I'm the one who figured out how to do it."

"Oh shush, I helped. What difference does it make now that we're safe?" Naki changed the subject. "What feeling did you see? You said it was mixed or something."

"Layered," Imara said with a smile. Her heart skipped a beat as she remembered. "It was pride mixed with excitement. I've never seen excitement before. It looked like canary yellow fizzy bubbles. They were tiny and popping and beautiful. That's the third new emotion I've seen since this morning."

Imara bounced as she walked, feeling a warmth in her chest.

Naki walked without a word, but Imara saw it again. The glowing tangerine pride with canary yellow bubbles of excitement layered underneath.

"What were the other new emotions?"

Imara grinned, and the warmth grew through her chest, down her arms and into her fingertips. "Sympathy, protective worry, and excitement. All positive emotions."

Just then, they got to the fork in the road. They rounded the bend and stopped at the tall spikes. Imara held her flashlight out to see if a path continued beyond the spikes. It looked dark, but Imara couldn't see a wall behind the spikes. She held her hologram closer, and the air got thicker. "Come taste this, Naki."

Naki bent down, and Imara guided her head so she didn't hit a spike. After a few moments of tasting, Naki said, "It's fog like from the fog gun."

"That's what I thought," Imara said. She sighed. "You'll have to stay here. I can't help you through the spikes with the fog. They're too close together, and I can't see them unless I'm right up close."

"Are you sure you want to go in there alone? What if the Judge is in there?"

"I'll be fine," Imara said with a voice braver than she felt. "The Judge is back in that corridor with the others, not in here."

Imara lifted her foot to walk, but Naki stopped her. "Imara," she said with a timid voice.

Imara turned back and bit her lip, afraid of what Naki would say.

Naki frowned, but continued. "Siluk was right that the Judge was coming. He was right that the explosives would keep us safe."

Imara tucked her head to her chest and said, "I know."

"You said he was lying. And he said you were lying. I believed you, but he was telling the truth."

Imara sighed and kicked a small stone in front of her. "I thought he was lying."

"Can't you see when someone is lying?" Naki asked, the tone of accusation clear.

"Yes, and he was lying." Imara shook her head and frowned. "I thought I knew what the lies were."

Naki lowered her eyebrows, and blood red flames of anger shot out from her skin. "You say truth is truth. You should have known what the lies were. We all trusted you when we should have trusted him."

"I know," Imara said. She buried her face in her hands then smacked a wall with her palm. She choked on her words as she tried to get them out. "Apparently my interpretation is subjective." Imara covered her eyes again and ducked her head down. "Some of his words were lies and some were truth. But I saw only lies."

TWENTY-FIVE

IMARA TIPTOED PAST THE SPIKES, TRYING TO forget her conversation with Naki. The guilt was crushing, but she had more important things to worry about at the moment. Imara sniffed and screwed her face up in concentration. She adjusted her hologram screen so the flashlight was at eye level. The fog got thicker with each step, and she had to both see and feel her way around the spikes. It seemed like ages before the fog started to clear. Just as the air thinned, she reached a door.

Imara examined the colors in the door. It had the same illusion as the door to the water tunnel. She recognized it faster, and soon she found the button to open it.

When she stepped through, she saw the evil lair was nothing more than an office. A large wooden desk with filigrees and golden knobs sat in the middle of the room. Next to the desk was a nook with a small brown table. Above the nook, a strange golden spigot came out from the ceiling. It was long and flat and hung over a drain in the floor. On the other side of the room, a worktable sat in front of a black bookshelf. Books, binders, and loose papers filled the bookshelf to the brim. Imara stared in wonder. She'd never seen so much paper in her life. She forced her eyes away to

266

look at the worktable. The top was covered with drawers, knobs, and tools. It was messy, but an organized messy.

Imara lifted a set of papers, which looked like blueprints for the strange gun the Judge had. She saw metal shaped like tuning forks that went inside the gun. Imara narrowed her eyes as she stared, but couldn't understand what the gun was supposed to do. Though the design looked familiar somehow.

Imara noticed another set of blueprints with plans for locator buttons. These plans she did understand. As she read, a loud click came from the door, and Imara almost jumped out of her shoes. With a gasp, Imara ducked behind the desk. Her heart raced as she searched for something to fight with. Imara heard a strange rustling of cloth when her eyes fell on a long broom. Imara grabbed the broom like a cricket bat and squeezed it tight.

Imara's shoulders tensed as she tried to make her breaths silent. It was difficult when they came out so fast. A line of sweat beaded her hairline. She didn't think the one self-defense class she took when she was sixteen would be enough to fight the Judge. But she tried to remember everything she could anyway.

Imara shivered, but then a familiar pair of shoes and a neat pair of gray slacks appeared before Imara's eyes. Imara's head flew up, and relief swept over her body.

"Professor Santini!" she said as she swung her arms around her beloved professor's shoulders. "You wouldn't believe what I've been through the last few days. I thought you were the Judge. I was ready to fight you with a broom." Imara laughed at the lunacy now that the tension had passed.

Imara turned on her toe to look at the door. In an instant, Imara's eyes turned to slits, and her voice lowered. "How did you get in here?"

Professor Santini smiled. "The same way you did. I can see the spikes and walk past them without getting hurt."

Professor Santini reached out to brush dirt from Imara's shoulder, but Imara took a step back. "No, I mean the catacombs. The entrance is blocked. And why aren't you at the school?"

"I have been at the school. I was busy getting things ready. But you've been down here a long time. Longer than I expected."

Imara reached back to grip the desk behind her. She swallowed and let her eyes wander around the room while her head reeled. She searched for any kind of explanation, and unfortunately, she found one.

Sitting on the little table in the nook was the golden transporter with all of its little knobs and levers. It wasn't there when Imara first came in the room. Without a thought, Imara moved forward to grab it. Professor Santini pressed a button on the desk and a rush of water fell from the strange golden spigot. The waterfall fell in front of the table, its characteristic golden sparkles glinting brightly.

A drop of the water fell onto Imara's hand and she stepped back in terror. Ignoring her recent revelation, she turned to Professor Santini. Imara's eyes filled with tears as she reached her hand out. "A drop of it fell on me. What do I do?"

With great tenderness, Professor Santini took Imara's hand and rubbed over the wet spot. When it was dry, she squeezed Imara's shoulder. "It's okay," she said. "One drop won't take away your hila. You have to go under the eraserfall for any real damage. You're in no danger here, Imara. I promise."

Imara nodded, trying to purse her quivering lips. Imara's heart wrenched when she saw a pile of black clothes by the door, a black helmet sitting on top. Imara clenched her fists and tears slid down her cheek. Her breathing was labored as she forced the words out. "It's you?" she asked.

Professor Santini cocked up an eyebrow. "Not exactly the reaction I expected, but yes."

Imara shook her head, refusing to believe the truth. "But the Judge is a telepath."

Professor Santini laughed. "There's no such thing as telepaths. Everyone knows that." She chuckled again as she retrieved the helmet from the pile of clothes. "And they call me a fanatic."

Professor Santini handed the helmet to Imara. "A former student helped me create it. It hacks into everyone's hologram rings within twenty-five feet and uses recordings of their voice to speak into their headphones. I just talk into this microphone here. Takara said everyone would assume I was a telepath, but I didn't believe it. I guess she was right."

Professor Santini stood poised and relaxed while Imara's entire world was crashing down. She couldn't embrace an ounce of calm. Imara shuddered. "But what about your brother?"

Professor Santini narrowed her eyes and frowned. "Who?"

"Marco," Imara said, wondering if Mr. Nazari had lied.

Professor Santini's face contorted, and she flashed her teeth. "HE IS NOT MY BROTHER!"

269

Imara took a step back in fear. Though she had seen Professor Santini angry, she had never once raised her voice to Imara.

Professor Santini took a calming breath and held her arms out like a peace offering. "I'm sorry," she said.

Professor Santini's eyes turned to the ground while drips of cobalt blue sadness pelted off her skin. Then came a flash of blood red anger flames as she said, "I got Marco the job here in Egypt. I paid for him to change his name. He promised he was a changed man. He promised he wouldn't do it again. And since he was family, I did everything I could to help him. And how did he repay me? BY MURDERING SEVEN PEOPLE!"

Imara took another step back and bumped into the desk. Every muscle in her body seemed full of electricity, tingling with this new reality. "Why?" she asked.

"Why what, Imara? Be specific. How can I answer your question if I don't know what you're asking?"

Imara looked down and leaned on the desk, trying to quiet her racing heart. She had so many questions she didn't know where to start. She decided on the most important one. "Why are you doing this?"

"What? The boiling water? The catacombs? I had to get you to come here so I could talk to you alone. I thought it would be easy once I got you into the catacombs, but the others never leave your side. The one time you were alone, I was in a meeting. By the time I got away, it was too late. And then my taggers were supposed to capture the others, but that didn't go as planned. Luckily for me, Siluk separated you with that pile of rocks. Then I just had to wait until you found my workshop."

Imara shook her head. It didn't make any sense. None of it made any sense. "Why did you want to talk to me?"

Professor Santini smiled. It was the same smile that had always brought Imara comfort and praise. Now it made her feel queasy. Professor Santini said, "I want to recruit you, of course. Truth seers are rare. I need all the ones I can get. But don't worry, I'll pay you. I have a business plan. It will be similar to what you would have done with the police in Kenya. But you'll be doing it here in Alexandria."

Imara watched a grass green thread of desire flip through the air around Professor Santini. Of course Imara had seen the threads from Professor Santini before. But they flew through the air, seemingly unattached to any specific thing. Thousands of threads always surrounded Professor Santini, but Imara just assumed she wanted her family or more students or food even. Her classes with Professor Santini were so small, she never noticed that the threads of desire were meant for people. Not specific people, just all people. The lust for power so strong, and somehow Imara had never noticed. Once again, her interpretation allowed her to see only what she wanted to see.

Imara frowned. "I don't want to tag people."

"Think of the good it will do, Imara. We'll be able to protect people from the evils around them. Finally everyone will see what we see. I know you want to work in Kenya, but we can start in Egypt and go to Kenya next. I promise."

"I don't want to do that." Imara's throat was sore from the lump growing inside it. She tried to swallow the lump, but with each second it grew harder and more sore.

"Think of what we can accomplish together. You have a gift, Imara. I've always said that. Think if we worked together.

271

Two truth seers committed to bringing truth to the entire world. Defeating darkness by bringing it to light."

Imara frowned deeper. She never expected her respect for Professor Santini to make her so conflicted. But she realized, more than a little surprised, respect wasn't enough. "I don't think tagging is the answer," Imara said.

Professor Santini tilted her head in a sweet, but patronizing look. "It is the answer. I've lived longer than you. I know the true power tagging has."

"It is powerful, but it's also damaging."

Professor Santini wore a sweet smile and spoke in her most soothing voice. "No, I don't want to hurt anyone. I've never wanted that. I only want to protect people. Sadly, almost everyone deserves to be tagged for something, but for now, we'll only tag people who have committed the worst crimes."

"Professor." Imara started then stopped, unable to explain the thousands of thoughts racing through her head.

"You have to help me, Imara. You're the only one who has never let me down."

Imara narrowed her eyes, and her nose stung from a wave of fresh tears. "Just because someone lets you down doesn't mean they're irredeemable. Everybody makes mistakes."

Professor Santini chuckled. "That's easy for you to say; you can see if someone's intentions are good or bad. All I want is to give everyone that same chance."

Imara twisted her mouth into a knot and felt a deep crease form between her eyebrows. "Tagging defines people by mistakes instead of strengths. It takes away their ability to change. If you only see the worst in people, they become the worst."

"Your logic is flawed, Imara. Maybe I see the worst in people, but that's because people are the worst. The truth hurts; that doesn't make it untrue."

Imara let her head drop as she closed her eyes. She took in a painful breath. Her mind and heart fought, but when she raised her head and spoke, she was resolved. "What if I refuse to help you?"

Professor Santini looked Imara in the eye with a sad smile. "I was afraid you'd say that." She sighed, but looked as calm as ever. "I know my ideas seem radical, but once I start tagging, everyone will understand why I'm right. You'll agree with me too one day, but I won't force you now. I'll wait for you to join me when you're ready."

Professor Santini put a ruby red crystal into Imara's hand.

"That's a transporter crystal," Professor Santini said. "It will transport you anywhere in the world. It's similar to my golden transporter, but you can only use it once."

Professor Santini laughed and said, "No." She pointed to Imara's skin then drew her finger away from it. "I can see that. No, you can't transport behind the eraserfall to get my transporter. This room is protected. You can transport out of the room, but not into it."

Professor Santini put her hands on Imara's shoulders. "You can't stop me. But you can go home. Take Naki and go home to your parents. Take Abraxas too if you want. I saw how you were looking at him during the party."

Imara frowned, turning the red crystal over in her hands. "What about the rest of my friends?"

Professor Santini smirked. "They aren't really your friends. You know that. You are useful to them right now because of your hila. You think they'll care about you when you get out of here?"

Imara's stomach tightened and twisted as a single tear dropped from her eye. She sniffed and pursed her lips. "I don't want them to die."

Professor Santini looked into Imara's eyes with careful study. In her most soothing voice she said, "Protecting people is your greatest strength, but it's holding you back. Someday you'll realize not everyone is worth protecting."

Imara looked down, and two more tears escaped her eyes. She clenched her empty fist until deep crevices formed in her palm from her fingernails. She straightened her back and said, "I'm not leaving here without them."

Professor Santini sighed and brushed a stray curl from Imara's forehead. "Fine then. The crystal will transport all of you. They just have to touch you when you use it."

Imara looked over the transporter crystal. It was ruby red and almost transparent with light glinting off each side. On one edge, a dark square lay under the surface. On closer inspection, Imara saw the dark square was a microchip embedded within the crystal. Imara ran her finger over the smooth surface of the crystal and asked, "How does it work?"

Professor Santini pointed to the microchip. "Hold this part in the palm of your hand next to your ring. It hacks into your location history and takes you to the coordinates."

Imara's face screwed up in confusion. "But there's no service down here."

Professor Santini raised an eyebrow. "Do you think I'd ever cut off service if I didn't have a way around it? Your hologram ring still records your location down here as well as physiometrics. All you have to do is squeeze the crystal with the microchip against your ring then think of a specific location as you squeeze. It helps if you have a strong emotional connection to the place you are thinking of because the crystal uses your heart rate, skin temperature, and brain activity to match you to the location. Make sure everyone touches you when you use it."

Imara glanced up at the eraserfall and said, "When you used the transporter before, you had to push buttons. I don't understand how this crystal can work without buttons."

Professor Santini smiled. "You're always asking questions, Imara. That serves you well. I can put coordinates in my golden transporter using the buttons and levers. But my transporter also works the same as the crystal. The microchip is on the side."

Imara eyed the ruby red crystal and slid her thumb across it. "How do I know you won't try to stop me from saving the others?"

"Why would I do that?"

Imara took a deep breath and bit her lip. She spoke in the quietest voice she could manage. "I know what you did to Headmaster Bello."

"I didn't do anything to him!" Professor Santini said, flashing her teeth again. She looked down, and Imara was surprised to see genuine sadness pelting off Professor Santini's skin. "He wouldn't listen. He wasn't supposed to be so stubborn."

"He's dead."

"That isn't my fault," Professor Santini insisted. "I would have given him everything he needed if he had listened to me. We needed him, and he wouldn't listen." Professor Santini squeezed her eyes shut as she swallowed hard. When she looked up again it was with a determined expression. "It's not my fault he chose to die."

"You withheld water. You let him die a painful death because he didn't agree with you. How is that not your fault?"

Professor Santini's nose twitched. "No more questions! You don't understand the importance of my work. People always resist change, but once I show them how much better everything is, they will stop resisting. Don't you understand, Imara? This is for the good of the world. So people can see what we see."

Imara considered her words for several seconds before she spoke. "What are you going to do? Why do you need my help?"

Professor Santini smiled. "First, I'm going to fill these catacombs with boiling water. The water is heated with microbots, so once it's filled, the catacombs will be inaccessible for fifteen years. That should be just enough time for the microbots to destroy all the evidence incriminating me." Professor Santini's mouth screwed into a knot. "That is, if the microbots work the way Takara says they will. She's not the most trustworthy person, but she does know technology."

Imara gulped, feeling more powerless than ever.

Professor Santini continued. "Then, tomorrow I'm breaking into the prisons and tagging as many people as I can. That's why I need your help. I'll give you your own tagging device and we can do it together. Just read the prison records, and look at their intentions."

Imara nodded, staring at the crystal. "And if I go home, there's nothing I can do to stop you from tagging?"

"Of course not. This is my life's work. But I won't force you to help me until you're ready."

Imara turned the crystal over in her hands while she watched the light glint off it.

"I know you are conflicted, but I promise this is the best way. We can tag twice as many people if you help. What do you say?"

Imara stared hard at the crystal in her hand. It was her ticket home. She could transport out and leave all this tagging nonsense behind. She could start her job and help people like she always dreamed. She could save Naki and Abe and everyone else even if she couldn't stop tagging. And she could continue to improve her hila. She could teach herself to see both good and bad in people.

Everything she ever wanted.

Except who would stop Professor Santini? Who would keep the prisoners names' safe? The responsibility didn't have to fall to Imara. Surely there was someone else who could stop Professor Santini. The police or the prisoners' family members or people like Abe. Why did it have to fall to Imara when she didn't even want to join this fight in the first place? And how could she do it when everything she ever wanted was attainable with the crystal in her hand? A few days ago, the decision would have been easy to make.

Anxiety jittered through Imara. Her fingers twitched over the crystal while her mind raced. Professor Santini needed a way out of the catacombs and she needed a way to tag people. Imara knew the transporter did both of those things. Imara frowned as a strange calm took hold of her. With a resolute stare, she dropped the crystal to the ground and said, "Tagging is dangerous and stupid."

Professor Santini squinted down at the crystal, and Imara leapt toward the eraserfall.

"Imara, NO!" Professor Santini yelled.

TWENTY-SIX

ICE COLD WATER RUSHED OVER IMARA, making every vein tingle. The water cut like knives on her skin, prickling and burning. She wrapped her fingers around the golden transporter, careful to position her ring over the microchip. She closed her eyes and imagined the passage outside, just beyond the spikes. She thought as hard as she could, and then she felt her stomach tighten.

Everything went black, and in the next moment, her feet hit solid ground. Her stomach throbbed as if she had been punched by a thousand fists. It took all her strength to keep from collapsing on the spot. Imara knew she would have to choose a location with a stronger emotional connection next time she used the transporter. Her body doubled over in pain, but she heard a voice that gave her the strength to stand.

"Imara!" Abe said. "You got the transporter!"

Imara held a fist against her stomach to ease some of the pain. "Good, you're all here. We need to get out of here before she comes out. Everyone touch me and I'll transport us somewhere else."

They all seemed to sense the panic in her voice and reached out while she checked that the transporter was still in position. Abe wrapped his arm around her waist and narrowed his eyes. "Why are you all wet?"

Imara's heart jumped until she remembered the water couldn't hurt them unless they went under the eraserfall. "It's a long story," she said. "Is everyone touching me?"

After hearing a yes from everyone, Imara said, "Hold on tight." She squeezed her eyes shut and thought hard about the room in the catacombs where she had the strongest emotional connection.

Her feet hit the ground, and her stomach relaxed with the strength of her emotional connection. Imara lifted her eyelids slowly. She breathed in relief when she was met with exactly the sight she expected. Everyone huddled around her in front of the stone couches where Abe had kissed her. She counted everyone one last time and breathed another sigh of relief knowing they were all safe and sound.

Naki took her hand away from Imara and licked one of the fingers that had been wrapped around Imara's arm. It wouldn't be long before Naki would taste the water and know what Imara had done.

Siluk, Darius, and Mr. Nazari all took a step back when they saw they were transported. The moment they stepped away, Imara could see the ground. Except now it looked like an empty nothingness. The term *pit of doom* seemed more appropriate than ever. Imara sucked in a desperate breath as anxiety pulsed through her. Her arms swung out, reaching for anything to grab. She was sure her heart would break through her chest with how fast it was beating.

"What happened?" Abe asked. He pulled her closer, and she grabbed him tight around the shoulders and hid her face in his chest so she couldn't see the deep pit beneath her.

"What's wrong?" Abe asked. She felt his fingers itching at her sides as if trying to decide whether to comfort or search for an injury.

"She's afraid of heights." The agony in Naki's voice was enough to bring a tear to even the coldest eye.

"So what?" Abe said. "She can't see the illusion. She sees—"

Abe's voice trailed off, and Naki smacked her lips before she spoke again. "Eraserfall," she whispered.

"What?" Abe asked horrified.

Imara kept her head down, and her eyes closed, trying to breathe through the shivers crawling through her skin. She gripped Abe's shirt tight in her fingers and said, "She put the transporter behind an eraserfall. It was the only way I could get to it."

Abe's heart thumped as he stuttered. "You sacrificed your hila to get the transporter?"

Imara looked up into his bright eyes. "You said we needed it."

Abe's mouth dropped, and he let out a breath of air as if he'd been sucker punched in the stomach.

"Let's get out of this room," Naki said. "We can talk in the crypt room."

Imara shut her eyes tight before she nodded.

"I'll help you," Abe said as he tightened his grip around her waist. He led her out of the pit of doom and into the crypt room. Imara wouldn't open her eyes until Abe assured her she was far from the never-ending pit.

The first thing Imara saw when she opened her eyes was Mr. Nazari stepping forward with a cautious expression. "I'm so sorry about your hila, Imara. I can't believe you would sacrifice like that for us. And I don't mean to be insensitive. But you said, 'she?'"

Imara sniffed, but managed a short nod.

"You saw the Judge?"

Imara swallowed and looked down at the ground. "Yes."

"So it *was* a woman," Naki said, but without the tangerine glow of pride Imara was used to seeing.

"What did she look like?" Siluk asked. "Did she do weird telepath stuff to your head?"

"She's not a telepath," Imara said. She swallowed over and over and felt tears forming in her eyes. It was hard enough to see it, but now to have to explain it. The tears started flowing and she rubbed her nose with the back of her hand. She gulped in fresh air, but nothing seemed to help. Everyone stared at her, waiting expectantly for information. All she could manage was, "Her helmet hacks into rings and uses our voices to speak into our headphones."

"Well, what did she look like?" Mr. Nazari asked while he fidgeted with his jacket. "Do you remember seeing her at the party?"

Imara buried her head in her hands as more tears fell. She managed to swallow a sob before it came out, but her shoulders shook from the effort. She could feel everyone's eyes on her. She glanced through her fingers and noticed how empty the world seemed without colors surrounding these people she knew.

Imara swallowed another sob, trying to focus. No more hila. She knew that was the price when she jumped through the eraserfall, but this was a world she didn't recognize. The absence of colors was heavy and desolate.

Imara swallowed and wiped her nose with the back of her hand. She opened her eyes and tried to ignore how much it hurt. She knew this life was better than the alternative. Imara stood up, ready now to fight. She brushed away the tears on her cheeks and said, "The Judge is Professor Santini. She knows how to get out of here so we need to stop her before she can leave."

Naki clapped her hand over her mouth as a gasp escaped.

"What?" Darius said confused. "But what about her brother? She's obsessed with her family."

Imara dug her fingers into the side of her leg, trying desperately to steady her breath. "She hates him, I guess. She doesn't acknowledge him as family anymore. Come on. I know where she's going next."

Imara left the crypt room, grateful the illusion outside of it was already destroyed.

Mr. Nazari walked with everyone, but his spirit seemed to hang back. "Imara, are you sure it was Carlotta? I want to believe you, but it seems impossible."

Imara tried not to laugh at the horrible irony of it all. "I'm sure it was her. She was trying to recruit me. That's what this entire thing was about. She took hostages because she knew I would go after Naki. That's why she acted dangerous, but never hurt us. She just wanted to talk to me."

As she said the words, the guilt hit her like a ton of bricks. It had been creeping on since the moment she realized who Professor Santini really was, but now her shoulders crushed from the weight of it. They were all down here because of her. Darius limping. Abe worrying. An angry gash on Siluk's thigh from his hip to his knee. Naki getting kidnapped. It was all because of her. Professor Santini must have thought bringing Imara down here would prepare her for tagging. Strangely it had done just the opposite.

"How did she know where you were?" Siluk asked.

"I don't know for sure, but I saw plans in the lair for locator buttons. They each emit a unique signal. She must have put them on us at some point."

When they got to the shaft, Mr. Nazari grabbed his shirt cuff to adjust the cuff link and grimaced for a split second when he touched only shirt and no cuff link.

"You lost your cuff link," Imara said without thinking when she noticed its absence.

Mr. Nazari looked startled and said, "It's fine."

Imara felt a jolt to her gut. Would the guilt ever pass? She swallowed, but failed to hide her frown. When Mr. Nazari met her eyes, he saw that Imara knew, no matter what he said, that his missing cuff link was not fine.

He grimaced again, a little longer this time and said, "Maybe you should stay here while the rest of us look for her."

Imara felt a sting in her heart. She didn't know if Mr. Nazari was being kind so she wouldn't have to fight someone so important to her or if he questioned her ability to do so. She tried not to take it personally, which was easier said than done. With heavy steps, Imara climbed the short flight of stairs to the shaft.

Siluk turned to Mr. Nazari with a serious face. "We need Imara. It took way too long to get through the catacombs without her."

"I don't have my hila!" Imara snapped back louder than she expected. Her self control was one wrong glance away from flying apart. No more colors. No more truth seer. She didn't need anyone rubbing it in.

Imara was grateful for the fuming glare Abe shot to Siluk, even more so when Siluk wilted with guilt. Abe pulled Imara closer to him, and she wished more than ever that there had been some other way. Any other way. Why did it have to be an eraserfall?

Here was Abe, comforting her and glaring at Siluk for her and all she could think about were those grass green threads of desire floating over to Naki. Imara wanted nothing more than to give in to Abe's comfort. But how could she do that when the desire for Naki twisted so tight around her arms last time Imara saw him? And now she would never know if the desire grew or died down.

"I'm so sorry," Siluk said, breaking Imara from her thoughts.

Mr. Nazari stared at Siluk through the side of his eyes, but then confirmed Imara's worst fear. "You all know how close Imara is to Professor Santini. She didn't want to hurt the Judge before. How can we expect her to now?"

Imara rushed to her own defense, desperate to show how against tagging she was. "She has no guilt for killing Headmaster Bello. She would have killed you guys too if I did what she wanted. She's going to infiltrate the prisons tomorrow. We have to catch her before she can get out of here, but then we'll let the police deal with her. I still have no intention of killing anyone."

Mr. Nazari conceded, and even that felt like a defeat. She didn't know if he believed in her or if he simply thought he couldn't win the argument.

They reached the shaft, and Imara grabbed the rope to go down. As she lowered herself down through the shaft, Darius shouted after her. "You know that gun the Judge had?"

"The one that fog came out of?" Imara asked.

Darius started down the rope once she got to the bottom. "No, the other one," he said. "It plays a sound that makes your brain fuzzy and your movements weak. We need to get that gun away from the Judge if we want to catch her."

He let go of the rope and hobbled to the wall. As he watched the rope swing, he seemed to have a thought. "Hey, let's take this rope to tie her up."

"We can't take the rope. How would we get back up again?" Imara asked.

Abe slid down next. "Can't we use the transporter?"

A frown appeared on Imara's face. "Well, we can I guess, but I'd rather not. You have to know the exact coordinates to use it and I don't know any coordinates down here."

Siluk gave her a sideways glance. "You transported out of the lair. And up to the room where we slept."

Imara twisted up her mouth and huffed. "I know. You can also use it by thinking of a location and it takes you there. But you have to have a strong emotional connection to the location. It hurt me when I transported outside the lair. I'd rather not use it again unless we're desperate."

"Does it still hurt?" The concern in Abe's eyes was almost enough to make Imara's heart flutter. Instead, all she could think about was that stupid desire.

"It's fine," Imara said as she pulled up the map on her ring. After Siluk put a length of rope into his backpack, Imara started walking. She was confident she could get through the catacombs despite the illusions. She had notes on her map

285

specifying which illusions were on which paths. And she had her memory to rely on. It only took three seconds before her foot brushed the edge of a foot pit.

Abe was by her side in an instant, already chiding her. "Hey now. I thought I was the reckless one."

Imara huffed. "Well now you know how scary it is for others when you do stupid stuff." Imara glowered at the ground. "At least I assume you were scared. I guess I don't know."

Abe was bent over, but he stood upright and held onto her hand. Comforting her. That only made her frown more. It was hard enough for Imara to trust people with her hila. How was she ever going to trust anyone without it?

Abe threw the dirt from his other hand, and some of it disappeared when it landed on the invisible foot pit. Imara sighed in relief when she saw his trick. At least they had a way to stay safe through the catacombs. With the map, her memory, and the dirt trick, they could move almost as fast as when she had her hila.

She marched straight to the spot where she knew the Judge would be. She told everyone about the control panel for the boiling water and how Naki had broken the lever. They devised a plan to surround Professor Santini and catch her by surprise, hoping to get the noise gun in the confusion. Imara had to walk slower than she liked so Darius could keep up on his injured leg.

They reached an intersection, and Imara put a finger to her lips reminding everyone to walk with silent footsteps. A few seconds later, Imara saw Professor Santini leaning over the water control panel. Her face was hidden under the helmet, but Imara imagined Professor Santini was glaring at the broken lever.

It was strange Professor Santini had taken the time to put her full costume on again. Did she think Imara wouldn't tell everyone who she really was?

Imara swallowed hard and licked her lips, preparing for her part. Distract Professor Santini while Abe and Siluk went for the gun. Naki would hold Darius up, and Mr. Nazari would join the conversation if Imara needed help. Maybe it was silly, but Imara hoped she could get Professor Santini to start monologuing. Just like an evil villain.

Imara took one last breath to steady herself. "We're here to stop you, Professor. We have the transporter from your lair... or uh, workshop."

Imara tumbled over the words and mentally slapped her palm against her forehead. She got so used to calling it a lair she didn't even think. But Professor Santini called it a workshop and would probably smirk at Imara calling it a lair. Imara was already losing ground, and Professor Santini didn't have to speak a single word.

At least Professor Santini was facing her now. Imara took several steps down the passage so Professor Santini had to turn even further away from the other side of the passage to talk. Imara tried to ignore Abe and Siluk creeping up behind Professor Santini and toward the gun. If Professor Santini saw Imara's worry for them, it would be disastrous.

Imara shook her head, trying to erase her fluster from saying *lair*. She spoke again, louder, and she hoped, maybe a little braver. "The lever is broken. You can't use the boiling water. We're taking you to the police."

Professor Santini turned as soon as Abe and Siluk jumped toward her. She didn't bother to raise the noise gun as she pulled the trigger. Professor Santini pushed them away as easily as if they were cardboard cutouts and not solid people. She jogged away with far less effort than they spent chasing after her.

In her head, Imara heard a voice. "I can activate the boiling water with my ring. You cannot stop me."

TWENTY-SEVEN

"EVERYONE FOLLOW ME," IMARA SAID through gritted teeth. "We have to try again."

"Agreed, but with a new plan," Darius said. "We need a better way of distracting her."

Mr. Nazari nodded. "We could throw rocks at her."

"We could all throw rocks from different angles so she doesn't know where to look," Abe said. "And we should cover our ears to block the noise from the gun."

"Maybe I can distract her with a smell too," Siluk said. "If I make it smell bad enough she might gag, and we can use that moment to attack."

"To capture, not attack," Imara said. She wanted to make sure nobody got hurt, including Professor Santini.

Naki said, "I'll help Darius walk so the rest of you can get the gun."

They started after Professor Santini again. As they walked, they pulled out their extra shirts and ripped them into long strips. They covered their ears with two strips each, wrapped around like a headband. They hoped it would be enough to block some of the noise from the gun. With the remaining fabric, they stuffed their noses so Siluk's smell wouldn't distract them.

Abe started talking strategy with words like perimeter, diversion, and angles of attack. Imara nodded with everyone else, hoping she understood everything. When they got closer, everyone walked on the balls of their feet and crept through a tunnel. They heard Professor Santini through a tunnel and down a passage. Imara grabbed a rock for each hand and tugged the strip of cloth around her head to make sure it covered her ears.

Abe peeked around the end of the passageway. He started waving hand signals. They made no sense to Imara, but she didn't think now was a good time to point that out. Abe nodded and jumped around the corner. He threw dirt onto the path so they could make out the line of spike pits.

Abe, Siluk, Mr. Nazari, and Imara scattered before throwing their rocks. Professor Santini dodged them, but with the rocks coming from so many directions, she couldn't run away.

Imara bent down to grab another rock when Professor Santini snatched the cloth away from Mr. Nazari's ears. He reached for the noise gun, but Professor Santini batted him away like a fly. Nothing more than a minor nuisance.

Darius had joined the fight, much to Naki's dismay. Abe snapped his fingers, which was Siluk's signal. Imara jumped in between Professor Santini and Siluk to hide him from view. They wanted his smell to come as a shock. Professor Santini reached for the cloth over Imara's ears, but she ducked away just in time.

Siluk pulled out his bottles, and Imara hoped the smell would still be potent through Professor Santini's helmet. Siluk said if she could breathe through the helmet, she could smell through it, but now was the moment of truth. Imara held her breath while Siluk sprayed. As he spritzed from his bottles, a thought entered Imara's mind. Why didn't the noise gun work on Professor Santini? Maybe it had something to do with the helmet. If Imara could remove the helmet, maybe they could capture Professor Santini.

That thought was interrupted by the smell from Siluk's sprays. Even with her nose plugged, Imara could smell the awful air. It was the same as Headmaster Bello's dead body, but more potent. Professor Santini doubled over and held her stomach while she gagged.

Abe and Siluk went for the noise gun. Imara sidestepped around Professor Santini while Abe and Siluk took turns reaching for the gun. Even with the distraction of the smell, Professor Santini still kept one step ahead of them.

But the distraction of the smell along with the distraction of Abe and Siluk was just enough for Imara to get behind Professor Santini. Imara tore the helmet from her head. A shower of wavy brown hair fell from the helmet as Imara lifted it. Professor Santini screamed and threw the noise gun to the ground in a fit of rage. Imara tore a wad of wires from the helmet just as Professor Santini turned to see. Hopefully those wires would render the helmet unusable. Professor Santini scowled and crunched the noise gun underneath her big black boots.

Professor Santini said, "Of course you figured it out, Imara. I'd be impressed except you just broke my favorite toy."

Imara gritted her teeth. "We're taking you to the police, Professor. There are too many of us to fight now."

Siluk reached for Professor Santini's arm, but before he could get to it, Professor Santini pulled yet another gun from her waistband. But this was a real gun.

Imara couldn't stop a tiny gasp from escaping her lips when the silver gleam of flashlights hit the gun. Professor Santini cocked the gun and put her finger on the trigger.

In a flash, it all seemed so real. No more costume helmet. No more cartoon noise gun. There was no more fighting, but not really hurting. This was real now. Real gun. Real danger.

Imara shivered as Professor Santini spoke in a cool voice. "I'm not going to the police."

A collective shudder passed through the room as Professor Santini turned and pointed the gun at Imara's heart. Imara narrowed her eyes, braver now. She was worried when the gun pointed at the others, but everything was fake again. She knew no matter how radical and crazy Professor Santini was she would never kill Imara.

Imara narrowed her eyes. "It's over. We have the transporter. Just come with us, and nobody will get hurt."

To her surprise, Professor Santini laughed. She stood firm without saying a word in response.

Imara leaned forward, and Professor Santini shouted, "STAY BACK! I will shoot if I have to. I am an excellent shot, and I'll kill anyone who takes another step forward."

Professor Santini moved the gun away from Imara, and Imara took the moment to attack. Imara lunged for Professor Santini, reaching out for the gun. Imara felt the cool metal in her fingers when she heard the hissing of the fog gun and then a shot from the real gun. Just when she thought she had it, the gun was ripped from her hands. Imara reached out instead for Professor Santini and tackled her to the ground.

Another gun shot went off, and Imara gasped. Professor Santini screamed, thinking she had hit Imara, but Imara continued using her hands to search for the gun.

The air filled with seaweed green fog, and Imara could do nothing but hope her friends were okay. She tried to ignore the grunts and screams around her as she searched through pockets and folds and fingers for the gun.

Another gunshot rang out followed immediately by a gut-wrenching scream from Abe. Imara felt her stomach drop, and her fingers seized with horror. Abe had been shot, and Professor Santini still had the gun. Imara lunged again with even more ferocity.

She felt arms fighting against her, but Imara fought back with all her strength. There were more grunts and curses, but Imara focused on one thing. She seized two wrists and put her full weight down on top of a body.

The seaweed green fog started to clear. Imara glared through the haze. She sat on top of Professor Santini's back, holding both of her wrists behind her. Imara looked out as the shadowy shapes took form. Siluk was on the ground, unconscious. Darius gripped his leg, which had fresh blood on the gauze. But Darius was oblivious to the blood as he hovered over Siluk, trying to wake him. Naki cowered behind Mr. Nazari. Mr. Nazari sported a welt across his chin and a swelling hit on his eye.

And Abe. He held the shirt out from his stomach to cover his arm. Blood seeped through the teal fabric spreading out from a wound near his elbow. Imara's eyes widened, and Abe reacted even with his eyes still on his arm.

"It's fine," Abe said. He looked at his dad then looked back at his backpack. "Can you get me some gauze? I think there's a little left."

Imara held her breath, and her eyes grew wider by the minute. Abe looked back at her. "Really, it's fine. I already checked, and I promise it looks worse than it is. It could have been a lot worse."

"I can't find any gauze," Mr. Nazari said with a shaky voice.

Abe shook his head. "Screw it," he said. He threw the backpack down and tore off his shirt. His dad helped tie it over the wound in Abe's arm. Abe huffed. "It was way too hot for that stupid shirt anyway."

Imara stifled a laugh, but didn't hide her smile. She couldn't believe he managed to find humor at a time like this. Imara brought her attention back to Siluk, whose eyelashes fluttered open.

"Finally," Darius said with a breath of relief.

Siluk grabbed the back of his head as he sat up and opened and closed his eyes several times.

Darius rubbed his forehead and allowed himself to smile. "Only one of us is allowed to be seriously injured at a time, and my leg has a gaping hole in it. So no more injuries until I'm healed."

Siluk laughed and got to his feet with only a little stumbling. Naki stepped out from behind Mr. Nazari. When she stepped, her foot crunched down on something metallic.

Imara's eyes flew to the sound. As Naki lifted her foot, she saw a golden mess of levers and knobs. A bullet hole in the center.

"What have you done to my transporter?" Professor Santini said in a contemptuous tone.

Imara helped Professor Santini to her feet, but kept hold of her wrists. Imara spoke in a soothing voice, which was a sharp contrast to Professor Santini's harsh one. "The bullet destroyed it, so whose fault is that?"

Professor Santini tried to look angry, but a proud smile escaped her. Imara knew Professor Santini was thinking her little protégé was acting just as she would have done.

Siluk came over with the rope from the shaft. He wrapped it around Professor Santini's arms a few times then plucked the gun from the floor. He held it to Professor Santini's head and said, "Let's go."

"Is that really necessary?" Imara asked, looking at the gun.

"Yes."

Imara shook her head, but didn't protest. She held onto Professor Santini's elbow as they started down the passageway.

With a whimper Naki said, "How will we get out of here without the transporter?"

Imara spoke without hesitation. "Professor Santini will open the door for us. The one I couldn't figure out at the entrance."

"What if she won't?" Naki asked.

"She will."

Professor Santini held her nose in the air. "Someday you will all understand the beauty of tagging. You'll wish you joined me when you had the chance."

Mr. Nazari clenched his jaw as he helped Darius walk. "You're going to jail, Carlotta. You took hostages and set the lockdown on my school. And besides that, tagging is evil. How did you think this would end?"

Professor Santini was undeterred by his words. She looked to the side, and her soothing voice was back as if it had never left. "Imara, are you sure you won't join me?"

Imara's heart wrenched. She wished more than ever that the Judge was anyone else in the whole world. She tightened her grip on Professor Santini's elbow. "I told you what I think about tagging. Why are you still trying to recruit me?"

Ahead of Imara, Naki held her hand out to Abe. He examined it, but Imara couldn't hear anything they said. "What happened?"

It came out of Imara's mouth before her brain even processed it. She wished her question came from pure concern and wasn't filled with jealousy. Abe rubbed Naki's hand and said, "It's just a bruise. She'll be fine."

They kept walking, but Professor Santini gave Imara a knowing glance. Imara squirmed under her stare. Professor Santini smirked and asked, "Do you want to know what I just saw?"

"No."

Professor Santini snorted and said, "I'll tell you if you join me. I'll save them both from these catacombs. Or just one if you'd rather." She snickered, and Imara felt her throat getting tight. At least Siluk had the decency to keep his mouth shut while he held the gun to Professor Santini's head.

"Just keep walking," Imara said in tiny voice. She missed her hila more with every minute that passed.

Professor Santini looked at Imara with loving concern. "Please, Imara. Even without your hila you are wickedly talented. I can train you to do incredible things."

Imara scoffed. "You're going to jail."

Professor Santini cocked one eyebrow up. "Am I?"

Imara glared at the ground. "Of course you are. Nothing you say will change my mind."

Professor Santini whispered, "I don't need you to change your mind. I have this."

Imara turned and the rope fell away from Professor Santini's arms. She pulled the ruby red transporter crystal from her pocket with a cool half smile on her lips. Imara felt a jolt somewhere around her navel and wished she could kick herself. She had forgotten all about the transporter crystal. Why didn't she take it with her when she went through the eraserfall? But no, she had to be dramatic and drop it significantly and now Professor Santini had a way out.

"Don't," Imara shouted.

"What is that?" Siluk asked, already cocking the gun.

"It's a transporter crystal." Imara lunged for Professor Santini, but hit the ground when Professor Santini moved to the side. Siluk lunged after Professor Santini, and chaos had returned.

Imara knew she had to get the crystal back as soon as possible, but lunging at Professor Santini wouldn't be enough. Imara ran through everything she knew about her teacher. Professor Santini's brain was ruled by sight. If Imara could distract Professor Santini's sight, it might give her the chance she needed.

Imara let the others lunge for the crystal while she removed a jacket from her backpack. It was a jacket Professor Santini would recognize as Imara's. Imara sprinkled dust to find a spike pit, and then threw the jacket inside it. Professor Santini saw the jacket from the side of her eye. She turned and shouted Imara's name before she realized it was a ruse. By then, Imara snatched the crystal from her hand.

Professor Santini jumped toward Imara, and Imara did the first thing she could think of to keep the crystal safe. "Abe, catch!" Imara threw the crystal and hoped he was as good at catching as he was at bandaging.

The moment the crystal touched his fingers he said, "I'll transport us out of here right now. How does it work?"

Imara said, "It only transports once. We all have to touch you and you think of a location where you have a strong emotional connection."

Imara's body folded in half when Professor Santini grabbed her from behind. She pulled Imara away from the others and laughed. "You think I'd let you get away that easily? If you touch me when you use the transporter crystal I can hack it and send us to a room full of taggers who will take you prisoner. You can try to get everyone else to touch you, but I'm not letting go of Imara so you can't transport her with you. And let's be honest, you can try to keep the transporter crystal from me, but I'll steal it back eventually. As long as that crystal exists, you're all in my control."

Naki held onto Abe's shoulder, and Mr. Nazari stood on the other side of Abe, holding his arm. Abe glared. "Then I'll just use the crystal now when you're not touching me. Then you can't hack it or steal it back."

"You'd leave everyone else behind?"

Abe's face grew hot from anger. "They have a way out. You can open the door at the entrance to the catacombs."

Professor Santini whipped her head back. "I'll die before I open that door. If you use the crystal now, everyone else is stuck here forever."

For a moment, Imara stopped pushing against Professor Santini's arms. She felt Professor Santini's breathing and pulse and the combination of them frightened Imara. "Abe don't use it," Imara said. "She's telling the truth. We need the crystal."

Abe looked at Imara and shook his head. "No, we need to use it before she can steal it back and transport us to the other taggers. Just trust me."

Professor Santini let out a maniacal laugh. "Oh just trust you. Such an easy thing to do, isn't it? What a simple request. Shall I tell everyone what I see, Imara?"

Imara's face contorted, and her shoulders hunched over. "Please don't," she said.

Professor Santini clicked her tongue. "Oh, so sweet. She's trying to save you from embarrassment, Abraxas. Too bad for you, I don't like you, so I'll say exactly what I see. How can she trust you when you have so much desire? Maybe you like Imara, but you desire Naki."

Abe clenched his fists, and anger flashed through his eyes. "That's a lie. I don't desire Naki."

Professor Santini shrugged, unaffected by his denial. "You want something from her. You can't hide it. I can tell the desire has been growing for some time now. I know Imara saw it before she lost her hila. Didn't you, Imara?"

Imara looked down at the ground, more ashamed than anything. People had no idea how much she saw with her hila. Sometimes the things they thought they could hide were the things she wished the most she couldn't see. "Please stop," Imara said, begging. She almost wished Abe would use the crystal just so this conversation could end.

Professor Santini tightened her grip around Imara's waist. Her words taunting while she spoke through a hateful smirk. "I've never seen such strong desire. It twists and writhes around Naki like a snake."

"It's not romantic," Imara said, cutting her off.

Professor Santini laughed. "Not yet. But you know a desire that intense always turns romantic."

Imara frowned, unable to meet anyone's eye. "Not always," she said, trying to convince herself more than anyone else.

"HA!" Professor Santini laughed. "And I didn't notice any uncertainty in your voice at all. See? It's not a lie if you say it sarcastically."

Abe glared harder, but Imara avoided his gaze. His nose wrinkled as he said, "Don't listen to her, Imara. You have to trust me. We need to use the crystal so she can't get away."

"Yes, just trust him," Professor Santini said. "Look, he already has his father holding one arm and Naki is holding the other. That's all he needs. He's going to save himself and the people he really cares about. He'll move on and you'll be dead."

"I wouldn't let her die."

Imara could hear the eye roll as Professor Santini spoke, "Oh. What heroics. Yes, I'm sure we all believe that. Without that crystal, you'll never get out of here. Is stopping me really that important to you, Imara? Are you really that against tagging?"

Imara tried to remove her thoughts from the swirling emotions inside her head. She tried to look at them like a school assignment. Nothing more than theoretical. Objective not subjective. She wanted to trust Abe, but without her hila it was difficult. Then again, it was difficult even with her hila. Her seeing was never the problem. Her interpretation was. True, she had only known Abe for a few days, but he never gave her any reason to doubt him.

Except that stupid desire. But it wasn't romantic. Maybe there was a good reason for it after all. And maybe there was a good reason Abe insisted they use the crystal. Maybe he knew something she didn't. It wasn't about what Imara could see, it was about trusting someone who had earned it.

Seeing the good instead of the bad.

Imara lifted her head and met Abe's gaze. She let her eyes linger on his for half a second. He stared back at her with an intensity she had never known. Her pulse quickened, but her determination didn't waver.

"Use it," she said.

The next instant, Abe was gone.

TWENTY-EIGHT

ABE'S FEET TOUCHED THE GROUND. HE pushed Naki and Mr. Nazari backward to make sure they were away from the cliff pit's edge. His eyes shot open, and he saw he landed right where he intended. He sighed in relief and looked down at his hand. In his palm sat a handful of red dust and a microchip that sparked. He shook his hand and dropped them to the floor.

Naki was ready to hyperventilate when she turned to him with terror in her eyes. "You didn't transport us out of here?"

Abe's lip curled up in disgust. "Are you kidding me? You think I would leave everyone here to die? You think I would leave Imara?" Abe shook his head, angrier than he had ever known. "SHE'S YOUR SISTER!"

Naki took a step back and grabbed Mr. Nazari's arm. She looked down with a small whimper. "Imara is the brave one. Everybody knows that. Maybe I'm the fun one, but she's always been better than me." Naki burst into tears and began sobbing into Mr. Nazari's shoulder. "She should have left me to die down here when I was taken hostage. She lost her hila, and it's all my fault. And now she's going to die because of me too."

Abe rolled his eyes and started down the path. "She's not going to die. Siluk can get us out of here using explosives."

Through sobs, Naki said, "No, he can't. He would have told us this morning."

Mr. Nazari stared at Naki's head for a moment, clearly considering whether or not to pat it. Instead he scratched his eyebrow and said, "He *can* get us out with the explosives. He didn't tell us this morning because it will destroy the catacombs."

Naki didn't say anything, but her sobs quieted.

Mr. Nazari looked down the side of the cliff pit. "How did you transport here, Abraxas? What emotional connection did you have to this place?"

Abe adjusted the shirt over his arm wound then started down the path with confidence. "Imara fell in that pit our first day here. I was terrified she would get hurt. And I was guilty because it was my fault she fell in. I was being stupid."

Mr. Nazari's eyebrow rose for half a moment, which he hid right away. "Your strong emotional connection was to Imara?"

Abe huffed. "Yes, it was. Get over it."

"What are we going to do now?" Naki peeked out over Mr. Nazari's shoulder, but kept her fingers wrapped around it. Mr. Nazari stared at her through narrowed eyes.

Abe kept his eyes on the path ahead. "We're going to find the others. Hopefully we can catch Santini off guard and tie her up again. And then we're getting out of here."

"Good plan," Mr. Nazari said with a nod.

"Before we get there, you…" Abe turned on Naki with his eyebrows furrowed so deep they almost covered his eyes. "Are telling me what I want."

Before Naki had a chance to react, Abe grabbed his hair in frustration. "I had no idea she could see it! I would have told her yesterday if I knew."

Abe hit his palm to his forehead three times before he turned to Naki. "What happened?"

Naki bit her lip. She looked down at the ground and shut her mouth tight.

Abe huffed and targeted right where he knew it would hurt the most. "Imara came down here to save your life. You owe her."

Naki frowned and sniffed. Her voice cracked as she began to talk. "I don't understand how it's going to help. If she's holding on to it still, what difference will it make if you know what happened?"

Abe shook his head making no attempt to stay calm. "You obviously don't care about making it right, but I'm guessing all you had to do was apologize. It doesn't matter anyway. You don't have to make it right, I will."

Naki looked down, her frown diving deeper with each step.

"Naki, please. It's hurting her more every minute. This wound is the reason she sees the worst in people, I'm sure of it. Just tell me what happened. I'll do the rest."

Naki squeezed Mr. Nazari's arm, trying to anchor herself as she talked. She stomped her foot and said, "Fine. I'll tell you. It was my biggest mistake." Naki gulped, "And my greatest regret."

Naki sniffed and started crying. Not loud sobs like her usual. These were quiet tears that slid down her cheeks like steady rain drops. "It happened when I was fifteen and Imara was twelve. Her hila was just beginning to manifest. She could see truths and lies, but she couldn't see emotions yet. We got in a huge fight; I don't even remember what it was about."

Naki covered her face with hands. She struggled to keep control of her breaths. After a few moments she said, "Imara was mad so she broke my weather machine. I made it at hila school, and I needed it to practice while we were home in Kenya. I was heartbroken."

Naki squeezed her eyes shut and pursed her lips while three more tears escaped from her eyelids. "Imara felt bad as soon as she did it. I think she only meant to scare me and not actually break it. She tried to apologize; she offered to take it back to hila school so someone could fix it. But I was furious. So I said, 'I hate you.'" Naki's head dipped down. "I guess it was true."

TWENTY-NINE

AS SOON AS ABE, NAKI, AND MR. NAZARI disappeared from view, Professor Santini's pulse quickened and her arms dropped away from Imara's stomach. "He used it," she said in disbelief. Her voice lowered and panic laced every word. "You'll never get out of here without that crystal."

Siluk laughed. Imara had almost forgotten he was there. He said, "We have a way out. Abe knew that, which is why he used the crystal."

"What's your way out?" Professor Santini asked.

Siluk rolled his eyes. "Yeah, like I would tell you. I'm not an idiot."

Professor Santini snickered. "You don't have to tell me with your words. You already told me with your feelings."

Professor Santini tore Siluk's backpack off him and ran down the path. Imara ran after her while Siluk helped Darius hobble through the passage. Imara slowed down so Siluk and Darius could catch up. By the time they reached Professor Santini, it was too late.

Professor Santini dropped handfuls of black blocks from Siluk's backpack onto the ground. She hung the backpack over her shoulder and dropped the lighter onto the explosives. Siluk's eyes went wide and he turned around, dragging Darius with him. "Run! Everything's going to blow!"

Professor Santini's eyes widened at Siluk's reaction, and she joined the others as they ran down the path. The rumble of a huge explosion reverberated through the hall. Imara covered her head with her arms and hands while sparks and pebbles showered them. She turned a corner to safety and collapsed against the wall. She examined her arms. A few scorch marks dotted them, but it was nothing serious. She turned to Siluk. "It didn't do that last time you used the explosives."

"That's because I know how to place them. And that was five times more than I used the first time I did it." He snatched his backpack from Professor Santini's shoulder and said to her, "You could have killed us."

"I didn't realize the explosion would be so big."

Darius rolled onto his side and groaned while he gripped his leg. Blood oozed out from the gauze. Darius rocked back and forth on the ground while he squeezed his leg.

Siluk sifted through his backpack with a growing panic. "Do you have any more clothes, Imara? We have to stop the blood. And we need to be gentle moving Darius from now on. Abe said the cut was close to some artery."

Imara pulled the last piece of clothing from her backpack. "Just some pants," she said. "They won't absorb much, but you can tie them over his leg to put pressure on the wound."

Siluk started tying the pants over Darius's leg. Darius huffed and moaned, then he shrieked. Imara held his hand to help him through the pain. He squeezed so hard she was certain her pinky finger would break. If not break, bruise at least. But Imara didn't let go. She wished there was anything else she could do to help besides just offer comfort.

When Siluk was done covering the wound, he tried to help Darius to his feet. Darius moaned and swatted Siluk's hand away. "What's the use?" Darius said. "We have no way out. We're all doomed."

Siluk stared at Darius's leg, and his shoulders tensed. Siluk turned to Professor Santini with his nostrils flared and his lip curled. He took heaving breaths through his teeth, but the anxiety in his face only grew. He reached into his pocket and pulled out the gun.

Imara expected Professor Santini to run, but she stood firmly in place with hardly any reaction at all. Siluk's body shook with rage as he pointed the gun at Professor Santini. Sweat dripped down his forehead while his finger twitched on the trigger. "Give me one reason not to do it."

Professor Santini looked eerily calm with the gun pointed at her. "You stupid boy," she said. "It doesn't matter if you kill me. I'll be nothing but a martyr. My followers will continue the work without me."

Siluk scrunched his face up, ready to growl. But even with the anger on his face, his hand wavered with indecision.

"You're not a murderer," Imara said. She put her hand over Siluk's, and he offered no resistance when she pushed it down. With the gun pointed at the ground, he replaced the safety. Siluk closed his eyes and breathed in and out before he spoke. "I know, Imara, but she is. We're all dead because of her. Darius is going to bleed out. We'll starve to death. She deserves to die."

Imara took the rope from Siluk's backpack. She didn't know why Professor Santini didn't run, but she wasn't going to let her get away if she could help it. Imara glanced at Siluk while she untangled the rope. "Do you really think she'd let herself die of starvation when she knows how to get out of here? She'll open the door eventually. That's her only chance."

Siluk frowned for seven whole seconds before he nodded. "You're right," he said. "It's not over yet." He helped Imara tie the rope around Professor Santini's arms then held the gun to Professor Santini's head. "You try anything, I will shoot."

Professor Santini's nose wrinkled, and she gritted her teeth, but she didn't say anything.

Imara wrapped Darius's arm over her shoulder, and they started down the passage. It took longer than ever with Siluk hovering over Professor Santini. Imara had to bend down to get dirt every few steps, which always made Darius groan. They traveled through two passages and a long tunnel and then entered a winding corridor.

They rounded a bend, and Imara stopped with a start. "Abe! You're still here."

Before anyone else could speak, something thumped to the ground behind Imara. She looked back and saw the rope lying on the ground.

"You should really learn how to tie a rope if you take someone hostage again. I've untied it twice now."

Siluk's mouth dropped, and his fingers trembled while he went to cock the gun. Professor Santini tore it from his hand while he fumbled. She pointed it straight at Siluk.

Imara breathed, willing herself to stay calm. She knew Professor Santini would be more willing to shoot Siluk than anyone else in the group. Imara spoke in the most soothing voice she could manage. "Professor, don't do this. Tagging is wrong. You don't want more blood on your hands."

Professor Santini looked at Imara, offended by her words. "How can you say that? You need tagging more than ever. How else will you know intentions? I have to protect you from criminals. I have to protect everyone."

Imara shook her head. Professor Santini had spent so many years teaching Imara, maybe just this once Imara could teach her something. "Tagging hurts people. If you constantly tell someone he's evil it's going to take a psychological toll."

Professor Santini considered Imara's words for half a second then held her head high. "I am protecting people from those who would be villains."

Imara frowned. "You're not protecting people from villains; you're creating them!"

Professor Santini screamed out, "ENOUGH!" In an instant, she tapped her ring and pushed a few buttons on her hologram.

Imara tried to remain calm. "What do you expect to accomplish with no service?"

"As I told you before, I have ways around that. I just had to wait until we were close enough." Professor Santini's eyes narrowed, and she focused on her hologram.

While Professor Santini was distracted, Imara plucked the gun away and aimed it at Professor Santini's chest. Imara tried to convince herself she would pull the trigger if she had to. Not that she ever would, but if she didn't mean it, Professor Santini would know.

Professor Santini looked at the gun bored. "There are no bullets left anyway."

Imara looked at the gun then dropped it to the ground with a huff. "You're coming with us," Imara said. She hoped no one noticed the quiver in her voice.

Siluk took the gun and confirmed there were no bullets left.

"The boiling water," Naki said with a start. She licked her lips and smacked her mouth furiously.

Professor Santini shrugged. "I told you I could activate the water with my ring."

Naki turned to Imara. "The water will be down this corridor soon. We need to get up the shaft so we can escape it."

Imara grabbed Professor Santini's arm, and everyone started down the corridor. They went no more than three steps when Professor Santini pulled herself from Imara's grip. Once free, Professor Santini ran in the opposite direction.

Imara froze in terror. "What are you doing? You'll burn and drown in the water if you go that way."

Professor Santini turned back, the corners of her eyelids drooping down. "I told you I would die before I opened that door. I prefer drowning to starvation."

Imara eyes grew wide. "You have to come back. I won't let you die."

Professor Santini's eyes showed real concern this time. "I'm sorry, Imara. I would have saved you if I could. The rest of you deserve nothing, but Imara, I really am sorry."

Professor Santini turned and went around the bend before Imara could say a word.

"Professor!" Imara called out. She started after Professor Santini, but Abe held fast to her hand and wouldn't let her go more than a few steps.

Naki marched in front of Imara and grabbed her by the shoulders. "Imara, that water is coming. We have to hurry or we're dead."

Imara tried to push Naki away, but Naki stood firm and pointed back the other direction. The way Imara was supposed to run.

"I'm not a murderer," Imara said. "We can't leave her."

Naki threw her hands into the air with a small scream. "Imara, the water is coming! There's no time."

Imara stood still, staring at the bend where Professor Santini had disappeared. Naki turned to Abe. "Just throw her over your shoulder or something. We have to leave now." Naki looked at Siluk, Darius, and Mr. Nazari and said, "Go, we'll catch up."

Abe put his arm around Imara and turned her around. "Come on," he said. "If she dies, it's not your fault. There's nothing we can do. We can't let everyone else get hurt because of Santini."

Imara's thoughts turned away from Professor Santini to Abe and Naki. They waited for Imara to move. They would die trying to save Imara if she wouldn't go with them. She wanted to save Professor Santini, but she couldn't let Abe and Naki get hurt either. Imara nodded, and they all ran toward the shaft.

When they got there, Siluk was already tying the rope they used for Professor Santini to the other one still hanging in the shaft.

"Hurry!" Naki said.

Siluk helped Darius up the rope, and Mr. Nazari wasn't far behind. Naki glanced over her shoulder and smacked her lips every other second. "You're next, Imara," Naki said.

"No, I'll go up last."

Naki folded her arms in front of her. "If someone is going to get burned by the boiling water, it's me."

"No," Imara said with a glare.

Naki tightened her arms in front of her and glared back. "Would you let me take care of you for once? I'm your big sister. If you don't climb up that rope, I swear I will slap you so hard your cheek will set on fire.

"Naki," Imara started.

"Please go," Abe said.

Naki glanced back and said with a whimper, "Hurry."

Imara clambered up the rope once she realized Naki wouldn't change her mind. Imara heard water trickling as she climbed. At the top of the shaft, Mr. Nazari grabbed Imara's arms and helped her up onto the landing. Abe was already on his way up the rope. Water splashed around Naki's feet and she let out a scream. When she took hold of the rope, everyone worked together to pull her up to safety.

At the top, Abe said to Naki, "Take your shoes off."

Naki sat down and took them off while Abe dug through his backpack. Imara bit down on her lip when she saw the bottoms of Naki's feet. Tiny blisters bubbled up in clusters on each of Naki's heels.

"Here." Abe handed Naki a tub of ointment, which she slathered all over her feet. Imara helplessly tugged the hair on her neck until Naki sighed. Imara gulped, unable to take her eyes off Naki's feet.

"Oh calm down, Imara," Naki said with a smile. "It's fine."

Everyone kept saying that. *I'm fine. It's fine. We're fine.* But they weren't. They were still stuck with no way out, and their injuries were going to need more than ointment pretty soon. Especially Darius.

At Siluk's request, Abe checked Darius's leg again. The resulting frown Abe gave to the leg did nothing to calm Imara. "It's already getting infected," Abe said. "The water on the gauze wasn't clean, and the wound is deep. I can try to clean it, but he needs a doctor and soon."

Mr. Nazari peered down the shaft. "Do you think there's enough water to get up to this level?"

"There is," Naki said. "But it will take at least two hours to get up here so we have some time."

Siluk huffed. "Time for what? Imara couldn't figure out how to open the door even with her hila. How are we ever going to open it now?"

"I just realized something," Imara said with a start.

Everyone turned to her in surprise. Naki and Abe's eyes full of hope. Siluk and Darius's full of despair. And Mr. Nazari was hard to read as usual. She'd probably never know what was going on in his head now that her hila was gone.

Imara cleared her throat. "The door has a troxler puzzle. It has to be. Professor Santini knows I can't do troxler puzzles. That's why she was so scared. She knew I wouldn't be able to open it. Especially without my hila."

"Great," said Darius sarcastically. "Not only do we know we can't open the door, we also know *why* we can't open the door. So helpful."

Imara shook her head. "You don't understand. I think I *can* open the door."

Siluk frowned. "But you just said you can't do troxler puzzles."

"And you don't have your hila," Darius added.

314

"It doesn't matter. Truth seers can see past troxler puzzles. I never figured out how, but I know how they work. When you stare in a certain direction long enough, your brain ignores things. It's like your nose. You can always see your nose, but your brain ignores it."

Imara got down on her hands and knees and felt for the small opening in the rock pile with her hands. It was harder to find without her hila, but her memory helped. As she crawled in she said, "We constantly move our eyes around to keep the image fresh for our brain."

Imara sat in the tiny opening and looked at the stone, which she knew was a door. Just as she expected, the stone was the same everywhere she looked. She couldn't see the blurry square, which was no surprise with her hila gone. But that wasn't the important thing. Everywhere she looked, the stone was the same. Not just similar, but the exact same square over and over again. A small crevice was always in the top right corner. And an extra large tan spot sat in the middle. And over on the left side was a small crack. No matter where she looked, the same exact piece of stone followed.

Imara crawled back out of the opening with a smile. "It's definitely a troxler puzzle," she said. "There's some kind of sensor to track your eye movements. There has to be a hologram screen in there that follows your vision so you're always looking at the screen, but it looks like stone. And since you're always looking at the same thing, your brain ignores the things around it."

Darius's shoulder twitched and he grabbed his leg. "You sound excited, but that's not exciting at all. We're still stuck in here with no way out."

"We have a way out," Imara said. "The trick is the tiny opening. The sensor can only track one set of eyes at a time. If someone goes in there with me, the sensor will track the other person's eyes. I'll cover my eyes and peek through my fingers and be able to see what is hidden. It's a really small opening so it will be tricky to fit two people. Anyone willing to try?"

Naki had just finished putting her shoes back on, and she jumped to her feet. "I'll do it," she said.

Imara showed Naki how to feel her way into the opening then let Naki go in first. When Imara crawled in after, she jabbed Naki in the back with her knee.

"Sorry."

But as she tried to readjust, Naki elbowed her in the side. The whole process was more difficult given that Imara's eyes were covered with her hands. Imara moved into one more position, trying to squeeze into the small space, and she accidentally smashed Naki's face against the wall.

"Sorry," Imara said again.

Naki snickered in response. "It's pretty tight in here."

Imara smiled and readjusted once more to a better position for both of them. "Okay, try to keep your eyes in one spot, Naki. It will be easier for me to see that way."

Imara was about to peek through her fingers when Naki said, "I don't hate you." Naki sniffed and said, "Maybe it was true in that moment, but it wasn't a permanent emotion. I was mad. I spoke in anger, and the anger was real, it was true, but it was only true in that moment. It didn't last."

"What?" Imara said confused.

Imara heard Naki's head fall to her chest. "Oh, I should have prefaced. You remember when we were kids and you broke my weather machine?"

"Yes," Imara said quickly.

"And I was mad so I said—"

"Yes," Imara nodded with her hands over her eyes. "Yes, I remember."

Naki sniffed again. "I'm sorry," she said.

Imara opened her fingers the tiniest bit and peeked over at her sister. For the first time ever, Imara realized she was the one holding a grudge all this time, not Naki. If she had seen the best in Naki, they might still be close. Imara frowned and said, "It's okay. You're passionate. That's what makes you who you are. I should have realized it was a fleeting emotion. I chose to see the worst instead of the truth. I'm sorry, Naki."

"It's not your fault, Imara. I should have taken responsibility. I should have apologized or done something to make it right. I'm sorry for hurting you."

Suddenly Naki was hugging her. It was an unexpected surprise with her eyes covered, but a welcome one. Imara tucked her head onto Naki's shoulder and felt a warmth that had been missing for a long time.

Naki gave her one last squeeze before sitting up again. Imara said, "I'm sorry I said you never take responsibility. I wasn't trying to make you apologize."

Naki laughed, "Oh, I didn't say it because of that. I said it because of your boyfriend."

"Abe?" Imara asked.

"He kept asking me what happened between us. He could tell there was something. He said he needed to know and kept pestering me until I finally told him."

"Wait. Is that what he desired? Information? About me?"

"Yes." Naki bit her lip. "He felt really bad about that. Anyway, I finally told him after he used the transporter crystal. All day today, he kept saying, 'She has a wound and it's hurting her. You have to tell me so I can help her.' He was very adamant."

"He called it a wound?"

"Yes, why?"

"That's just an interesting word choice." Imara shook her head before she whispered, "And can you stop calling him my boyfriend?"

"Why?" Naki asked.

"Because I haven't talked to him about that, and I don't want him thinking I assume it when we haven't even talked about it."

"Everyone else assumes it," Naki said.

"Naki."

"Whatever," Naki said. "There are five twinkles in his eye every time he looks at you. And he was pissed that I let you go into the evil lair alone. Plus, he touches you every chance he gets. 'Oh Imara, what happened to your hand? Let me caress it, I mean put this ointment on it. Oh, do you need help going to the crypt room? I'll just wrap my arm around your waist. That's the only logical thing to do. Let me hold your hand while I throw this dirt around the path. It's the only proper way to distribute dirt.'"

"Naki, *shush!*"

Naki giggled. "Oh calm down. He can't hear us."

"How do you know?"

"We couldn't hear you once you crawled into the opening. And listen to this. Hey guys, can you hear us? Guys! We're talking about you. Are you listening?"

Imara's ears were met with silence.

Naki snickered again.

Imara nudged her. "All right, we need to focus and open this door. Everyone is waiting for us, remember? Hold your eyes in one spot."

Imara peeked through her fingers. She saw a square in the middle of the door that looked like the stone she remembered. Crevice in the top right corner, tan spot in the middle, crack on the left. But now she saw a thin strip of glowing hologram surrounding the square. In the strip above the stone it said, "Four lines." On the left strip, "Never lift." On the right strip, "Never backtrack." On the bottom strip was a square of nine dots.

Imara grinned. She wasn't expecting a puzzle. All the other doors had buttons. But since the door lock was a hologram, it made sense to have a puzzle opener. Luckily for Imara, she knew this puzzle well. Imara traced over the dots with an arrow shape that went outside the square of dots. Just like she had when she was thirteen years old.

As soon as Imara finished the puzzle, the door creaked and started sliding to the side. The sun shone through the growing opening.

"Imara you did it!"

Naki hugged her tight, and Imara smiled so wide her cheeks hurt. "Come on," Imara said. "Let's go get the others."

Imara crawled back through the small opening, and the first thing she noticed was Darius groaning. Abe stared at Darius's leg. He stood up and said, "It's better than before, but you still need a doctor."

Siluk saw Imara and Naki coming through the opening. He whipped his head toward them, the question in his eyes.

"You're all lucky my sister is a genius," Naki said.

"You opened it?" Abe asked.

Imara nodded, and Siluk sighed in relief.

"Let's go," Mr. Nazari said. "I'll call the police and a medical team to meet us at the school."

Imara stood to the side while Naki showed Mr. Nazari how to get through the opening. Imara glanced at Abe who stood by the shaft. She stepped toward him and hoped he couldn't tell how frightened she was about talking to him. All she could think about was their last conversation together. She said greed was his dad's defining quality.

How could she explain that everything was different now? She understood the world so much better than she did just those few hours ago. She understood how important it was to see the good and not only bad. When Abe wanted to use the transporter crystal, Imara told him to do it. Would he ever understand the amount of trust it took for her to do that? Would it be enough to make up for the things she said?

Darius hobbled to the entrance while Siluk helped him. He winced in pain, and his arm flew to the side. His knuckles knocked into the back of Imara's hand. Stinging pain shot through her arm as Darius's knuckles made contact with the cuts from Headmaster Bello's crypt. She clenched her fist as the pain grew. Darius winced again as he took another step forward. With his own agony so great, he was clearly unaware

320

of how much he had hurt Imara. Darius apologized through a heaving breath, and Imara tried to hide her anguish behind a smile.

She kept the smile until Darius passed. Her face immediately screwed up as the cuts smarted. When she reached the shaft, she gritted her teeth and shook her hand out.

Abe frowned. "We'll be at the school soon, and a doctor can look at those cuts." He lowered his eyebrows. "But you should really think about not sacrificing yourself for other people so much."

Imara's lips pressed together as she started to say, "But…"

Abe shook his head with a short laugh. "I know. You're never going to stop." He pulled and bounced a curl hanging over her forehead. "That's what I love about you."

Imara blinked twice while her heart leapt from its place. The widest grin spread across her face. Did he just say *love*? Imara glanced at the ground and clumsily took a step backward. To stay grounded, she rested her hand on the shaft. A blast of hot air blew out, and smoke billowed from around the circular structure. The fire wasn't far behind. She knew it was an illusion, but she jumped nonetheless.

She stumbled back and tripped over her feet. She tried to right herself, but her body leaned too far back to balance, and she toppled backward into Abe. He wrapped his arms around her from behind to keep her from falling. When she steadied her feet, he pulled her tighter and then even tighter. He buried his face in her hair, and it rustled with each of his breaths. So much was said in no words at all. The acceptance of a thousand apologies. The relief that this nightmare was over now. The hope of what the future might hold. All encased in Abe's arms holding her tight. With each heartbeat, the fear, anger, and distrust that plagued her for days was healed. More than anything, she felt safe.

Finally, his arms relaxed, and Imara turned back with the reddest ears she had ever worn. She bit her lip and said, "I forgot about that fire. Apparently you and I have a thing with tripping at exactly the wrong moment."

Abe chuckled. The olive in his brown eyes glistened as he stared at Imara with a passion that made her heart stop. Without a word, he tucked his hand into her lower back and pulled her right back into him. His other hand slipped into her hair as he bent down to kiss her. When their lips touched, a surge of heat swept through her body. Imara melted into his arms, which only made his kiss hungrier. With each second he pulled her tighter, but it was never close enough to satisfy him. The emotions swirled so high, she was certain she could transport to this spot for a hundred years to come if needed. Electricity pulsed through her veins. Fireworks sparked. It was every cliché and more, but better because it was hers. And his. Their lives forever intertwined in the memory of this moment.

Naki cleared her throat. "The rest of us are leaving, but if you two want to stay here kissing forever I guess that's your call."

Imara pulled away and lowered her head against Abe's chest. With Darius's injury, they really did need to hurry. Abe released her, but immediately wrapped his arm around her waist. Together, they left the catacombs and never looked back.

THIRTY

THE RIDE BACK TO THE SCHOOL WAS excruciating. On top of everything, Imara remembered Professor Santini gave them her bubble car to get to the catacombs. A frown on Imara's face burrowed deeper than ever. "Do you think there's any chance Professor Santini is alive?" she asked.

The looks she received in return were more sympathetic than she expected.

"No," Mr. Nazari finally said.

Imara sat up. "But maybe there's a room down there that could keep her safe from the water." Imara looked down at her feet. "Except, she told me the water will be boiling for fifteen years so the microbots can destroy any evidence." Imara tugged the hair on her neck. "But maybe she has food and water and supplies to last..." Imara trailed off, knowing how wild the speculation sounded.

No one said anything, and again Imara felt more sympathy than she expected. She knew Professor Santini had tried to kill them, but it was Professor Santini. Again, Mr. Nazari broke the silence. "I'm sorry, Imara. I know you were close."

Guilt crept into her stomach. "I tried to save her. I didn't want to kill her." She said it more to herself than anyone. She was insistent they wouldn't kill anyone, but in the end it did no good.

Abe looked into her eyes with the slightest frown. He scooped up her hand and held it tenderly. "You didn't kill her. She had the choice between prison and death. She chose death. There's nothing you could have done."

It helped that he cared, but it didn't change anything. Professor Santini was dead, and Imara didn't know how to feel. She was angry and disappointed in Professor Santini's choices. She was mystified that someone she loved so much could murder without guilt. But Imara was also heartbroken that her beloved teacher was gone forever. Imara would never again receive Professor Santini's wisdom or advice. It hurt worse knowing that might be a good thing.

"What happened to the other taggers?" Mr. Nazari asked. "Did the police arrest them after we were taken hostage?"

"Yeah," Abe said with an eye roll. "They arrested them and put them into a room all alone with no guard. Santini came and transported them out almost immediately."

"Well, that's great," Darius said while clutching his leg.

"Do you think the police will find them?" Naki asked. "Maybe they found them while we were in the catacombs."

Imara tried not to laugh. Given how reluctant the police were to search the catacombs, she doubted they would search for the taggers at all.

"If they're smart, the taggers will lie low for awhile," Siluk said. "But this isn't over yet. Professor Santini said the taggers would continue the work without her. She said she would be a martyr."

Naki grimaced, and Mr. Nazari rubbed his forehead. Mr. Nazari said, "I have a feeling Professor Santini left some issues at the school that I'll have to deal with. I'm sure she took me hostage to make sure she was in charge." He did a tiny shake of the head. "I was grateful to have someone I could trust watching over the school while I searched for the Judge. I never imagined they were the same person."

Again the bubble car filled with silence. Imara picked at the scratch in her leggings. Things were far from perfect, but at least it was over for now. They were all safe, and even Darius's leg would be all right once he got to a doctor.

When they arrived at Nazari Academy of Hila, the police and medical team were ready and waiting. At the sight of them, the cuts in Imara's hand tingled. The pain resurfaced now that help was here. Relief filled Darius's face, and Siluk relaxed for the first time all day.

The medical team pounced on Darius first. Abe and Siluk were next since their cuts were covered with wet and dirty cloths. The police took Imara, Naki, and Mr. Nazari away to ask all sorts of questions.

Imara finished her statement to the police with only two outbursts of tears. She thought that was pretty good considering the enormous pressure she'd been through the past few days. When they were done with their questions, she was allowed to move over to a medical team. Naki sat down beside her and checked the messages on her ring. They all had about a thousand of them.

"Mom and Dad are coming," Naki said.

Imara bit her lip. "They don't have to come. They shouldn't have to come all the way here for a few hours just to leave again."

Naki shrugged. "They're already on their way. They put alerts on our location so they would know when we had service again. They left as soon as we got out of the catacombs."

Though she acted guilty, Imara was relieved they were coming. After fearing for her life so many times, she desperately needed to tell them how much she loved them.

Naki jumped to her feet. "I'm going to the kitchen. I need food that hasn't been in a backpack for days. Come find me if I'm not back when they get here."

Imara was alone now with the doctor who was putting stitches in the back of her hand. She said to Imara, "I don't know who bandaged this, but they did a great job. No infection at all."

Imara smiled and felt a hint of pride. "He has medical training."

The doctor was about to respond, but Imara's ring buzzed and a ringing sounded in her ear.

"Oh, you can answer that," the doctor said. "I won't listen in, I promise. I'm sure you have tons of people wanting to talk to you."

Imara tapped her ring and saw Safiya's picture on the hologram. "I'll just call her back," Imara said with a frown.

"No, I insist. Please don't wait because of me."

Imara sighed, but clicked on Safiya's picture. She wanted to avoid this conversation forever, but it would have to happen at some point. Might as well be now.

Safiya dispensed with pleasantries and launched into the conversation. "I can't believe you're alive. Imara, we're so glad. What happened? All we know is a terrorist took your sister hostage. The Egyptian police were useless. They said you were dead, but you've been all over the news in Egypt. We just heard you were alive. Did you find your sister?"

"Yes, she's fine. We're all fine. Well, except for the Judge. The uh, the terrorist. We tried to capture her for the police, but she wouldn't come. She's dead now."

Safiya didn't notice the pang of guilt in Imara's voice. Safiya wore a proud smile and said, "We are astounded by your bravery and dedication. The Egyptian police said you sacrificed so much. Don't worry about missing the deadline for your paperwork. We can have you start next week instead."

Imara's lip quivered, but she successfully kept the tears from her eyes. She gulped before shoving the words out of her mouth. "Unfortunately, I have to withdraw my acceptance of your offer."

Safiya's eyebrow twitched. "You can have more than one week if you need time to recover. We are happy to work with you."

"No, it isn't that." Imara sighed. This wouldn't be the last time she had to explain, and that thought alone was enough to make her weary. Imara put her shoulders back and tried to sound brave. "The Judge had an eraserfall."

The doctor stopped working and looked up at Imara with widened eyes. Safiya's mouth dropped, and words failed her. She blinked, and her jaw tensed as she tried to think of something to say.

Imara sighed again, but it didn't help. She tried to smile. "Maybe I can learn to read body language cues and use that to help with interrogations someday."

Imara stared at her lap. She hoped she didn't sound as broken as she felt. "But I'll need time to learn. For now, I don't think I'll be helpful without my hila."

Imara waited until her eyes were dry before she looked back up. Safiya had her hand clapped over her mouth. Her throat contracted with a swallow before she lowered her hand. Her mouth opened and closed twice before she could form any words. Finally, "Oh, Imara. They said you sacrificed so much. I didn't realize." The words stopped, and Safiya gulped. "I'm so sorry."

Imara forced a lump down her throat and said, "Thank you."

Safiya gaped back at her. In their first conversation, Safiya was in complete control the entire time. She knew just what to say and when to say it. Imara never imagined seeing Safiya so flustered. Safiya's lips parted, obviously trying to think of something to say. Imara decided to save her the trouble. Imara said, "Thank you again for your consideration. I will let you know if I can help Kenya in the future."

"Of course. Please contact us at any time." The words came out as more of squeak. Imara nodded and ended the phone call so she wouldn't have to deal with the awkward silence.

The doctor wrapped gauze around Imara's hand when the phone call ended. She looked at Imara and swallowed. "My friend got an asterisk at the graduation party. From the Judge."

Imara stared at the doctor, unable to think of a response. She remembered the asterisk on Abe's name and how the police still had no idea how to fix it.

The doctor finished the gauze and sniffed. She gave Imara's hand a quick squeeze and said, "Thank you so much for your sacrifice."

The doctor left without another word, which relieved Imara. She appreciated the gratitude, but the pain was fresh and she didn't know how to respond. Imara scanned the room and saw her parents had arrived. Naki was already talking to them. Imara headed for them straightaway.

As she neared them, Imara heard Naki say to her parents, "You didn't have to come all the way to Alexandria. We were going to come home as soon as we finished here."

Imara's mom stared at Naki like she was looking at her for the first time. "You were trapped underground for almost a week! The Egyptian police told us you were dead. We weren't going to wait for anything."

Imara glanced over at Abe, who was deep in conversation with a police officer. He gave her a grin, which she matched in a heartbeat. A few steps later, Imara reached her family. "Imara!" both of her parents said at the same time. Her dad pulled her into a hug, and his body shook with a sob. "Oh, my baby girls," he said.

He pulled away and sniffed. Then he licked his thumb and got ready to clean some dirt off Imara's face.

"Dad!" Imara said, pushing him away. "That's gross."

He wiped away the dirt anyway and smiled.

Imara's mom grabbed onto Imara and held her tight. "We're so glad you're both safe. You never should have gone into those catacombs without the police. They were so dangerous."

Imara stared at the ground while she shrugged. "Yeah, that's why I didn't tell you I was going."

Imara's mom tried to look angry, but it didn't last. Her furrowed brow soon turned to a smile filled with relief. Her mom said, "No one else could get into the catacombs. They said there was a fire."

"It wasn't real," Imara said. "It was just an illusion."

Imara's dad smiled. His chest puffed out with pride. "Of course you figured that out. Our little truth seer."

The moment the words left his lips, his face fell. He shut his mouth, and Imara's mom scolded him with her eyes. She took a deep breath and spoke in a solemn tone. "Naki told us about the eraserfall."

Imara shrugged and tried to keep her lips from wearing a permanent frown. "It's okay," she said. "I'll figure something out."

Her dad squeezed her shoulder with tears in his eyes. "We know you will," he said. He looked like he wanted to say more, but couldn't. He nodded, and patted her shoulder, and then let his hand fall away.

Her mom filled the silence. "Naki said Professor Santini was the Judge. Did you know before you went down there?"

Imara twisted her mouth up in a knot. "I was entirely shocked. I still am to be honest."

Tears rolled down Imara's dad's cheeks. With a frown he said, "Naki said you started to see new emotions with your hila."

Imara nodded and the tears welled up faster than she could stop. Her dad took her in a big bear hug, and her mom hugged her from behind. They told her they loved her and held on tight. Imara felt so much support she didn't know what to do with it. For years she felt alone as a truth seer. She thought Professor Santini was the only one who understood her. But this whole time they were right here. Naki and her parents. She spent years pushing them away and didn't realize how much she missed them until this moment. She couldn't change the past, but she could make sure things were different in the future.

Her parents didn't let go until Imara was ready. When they did, Imara realized how easy it was to feel the emotion, even if she couldn't see it.

Imara's mom gave her a glowing smile. "Naki said you were amazing down there. Never lost your cool. Saved everyone from certain death. She said you were basically the leader of them all."

Imara laughed. "That was an exaggeration."

Just then, Abe joined them and Imara's ears went hot. "This is Abe. He's Mr. Nazari's son. He did a lot to help, especially because he has medical training."

Imara's dad nodded. "Were you a rescuer or a hostage?"

"He was a rescuer," Naki said matter-of-factly. "And he's Imara's new boyfriend."

Imara's eyes widened, and her ears positively burned. "Naki!" she said.

Abe smiled.

"What?" Naki shrugged. "You don't see him denying it."

"Would you just…" Imara stuttered. "Just. No more talking."

Naki shrugged then covered her mouth on one side to block it from Imara's view. In a loud whisper she said, "You guys will like him, don't worry."

Imara's dad grinned while he and Naki shared a knowing glance. At least her mom was trying to act normal, though she failed miserably.

"This conversation is over now," Imara said as she pulled Abe away by the arm. "I'll be back in a bit."

Her head spun as she walked away. Her hands shook as she dropped her hands away from Abe.

Abe looked back and said, "They seem nice."

Imara shook her head trying to get some of the heat out of her ears. "I'm so sorry about that."

"I didn't mind."

Imara was astounded by the utter lack of embarrassment in his grin. He said, "They say Darius is going to be okay. I think Siluk was more relieved than Darius was."

"Is Darius not mad at him anymore?" Imara asked.

"Oh yeah, they worked that out. Hugged and everything."

Imara let one corner of her lips rise in a smile. But just as her smile went up, Abe's fell. "Imara, I'm really sorry about your hila. I know you'd do anything to protect others, but it's not fair you had to lose that."

Imara tried to smile, but her heart felt ripped in two. It was hard enough seeing an empty world, but everyone had to keep bringing up. But how could she be ungrateful to Abe who was being so sweet about it? She tried to shrug it off. "Oh, I'll be all right," she said. "Now I'm mashimo like you. You'll have to show me the ropes."

Abe laughed. With a tease in his voice he said, "But maybe I'm a healer. Hey, maybe I can heal your hila." He stopped walking and looked to the side. "Wait a minute. Can a healer do that? Like a real one?"

"I was just looking that up." Imara started at Mr. Nazari's voice. She didn't realize he was standing so close. He had his ring hologram up and scrolled through an article.

His eyes narrowed as he read. "It says they brought someone who was wrongly accused to a healer to see if he could heal the eraserfall. It says the healer could see the wound!"

Mr. Nazari looked up with the most sincere smile Imara had ever seen him wear. He looked back to the article and the smile fell. "Oh, but he couldn't heal it."

Mr. Nazari's eyebrows lowered, creating a deep crease in between them. He continued reading. "It says usually if a healer can see the wound, then he can heal it. They speculate the only exception is with an eraserfall." He looked closer. "But some people say it is possible and the wound being visible proves it."

Mr. Nazari tapped his ring off and evened out his shirt sleeve with his jacket sleeve. He shrugged. "Maybe healers aren't good enough yet, but someday they will be."

"I doubt it," Imara said. She didn't mean to sound so full of despair, but she couldn't help it.

"Well, I believe it." Abe nodded without an ounce of disbelief in his voice or body language.

"Hmm," Mr. Nazari said, though Imara wasn't sure what that meant. He patted Abe on the shoulder and left the two of them alone.

Imara turned back to Abe, and her fingertips tingled when she looked at his russet brown and olive green eyes. So bright and full of hope. She tilted her head to the side and squished up her mouth. "I think you have more than enough hope for both of us. I'll just be sad for a few days if you don't mind. I think I've earned it."

"Fair enough." He nodded, but then his eyes narrowed. "Oh, you've got something in your eye."

He leaned forward and cradled her chin in his hand. He used his other hand to pick a goopy substance from the corner of her eye. "Hang on," he said. "There's some in this eye too."

He finished picking the goop out of her eyes then rubbed his thumb across her temple. "You have the most beautiful eyes."

He was going to continue, but a chirp from his ring indicated a notification. He glared at it. "You know, it was nice not getting any notifications for a few days."

Imara nodded, but his ring chirped again. And again. Then three more times in quick succession. He stared at his ring worried and said, "I better check this."

He frowned at the hologram when it popped up. "They're all from Edrice. She's my business partner."

He opened a message, and his frown grew deeper every second. He started breathing heavier and tapped his hologram ring off. "I have to go soon," he said. "There are some kids who are afraid of my employees and won't go with them. The slave cartel is closing in on them. They're about to catch the kids and my employees."

He turned to leave, but immediately turned back. "Hey," he said. "You want to come with me? It's really hard to get kids to trust us when they've been hurt so much, but you were amazing with that girl who pushed the hover cart during the party. I'll hire you right now if you're interested. I could use someone with your skills."

Imara squeezed her fists and bit her lip. "I can't help with that. I don't have my hila anymore."

"Eh, you don't need it." Abe said with a confidence Imara didn't feel. "You're resourceful, you have good instincts, and you're good with kids. What do you say, Imara? You want to give it a try?"

It's not over yet!

If you enjoyed this book, be sure to grab your copy of the second book in the trilogy. *Healer* is available now!

Author's Note

Thank you for reading *Truth Seer*! I treasure each of my readers. You make this whole writing thing worthwhile.

I learned so many amazing things while doing research for this book, including incredible facts about the eyes. I also loved the catacombs of Kom el Shoqafa. I planned to create completely fictional catacombs, but these ones had such a rich and fascinating history, I had to use them instead!

If anything felt unresolved or unexplained, remember there are still two more books in the series. Oh, and can someone please do me a favor and invent temperature-controlled underclothes? I need those immediately!

Author Bio

Kay L Moody is proud to be a female science fiction author. Her books feature cool science and technology, strong female leads, and a dash of romance. There's a strong focus on character development and societal conditions. She lives in the western United States with her husband and children. Visit her website to get free access to her exclusive short story, *Cloned*.

KayLMoody.com

Acknowledgements

First off, a huge thank you to Michelle and Kristy for being my beta readers. Your insight was invaluable and you truly helped shape *Truth Seer* into the best story it could be.

Thank you to Alyse for convincing me to publish in the first place. Without your insistence, I never would have made it this far. And of course you provided help on so many things along the way that they are far too great to count. You helped more than you know.

Thank you to my editors, book cover designer, and everyone who turned my manuscript into a real life book.

Thank you to my treasured readers. Without you, Imara and Abe would just be a dream in my head. Because of you, they live in the minds of many.

And most of all thank you to Mark. You believe in me more than I believe in myself. Thank you for everything you did to make this book a possibility. Thank you for encouraging me at any time I needed it. And especially, thank you for asking me out all those years ago even though you didn't know my name.

Kay L Moody